Livadia Palace, Yalta

"The Riviera of Hades"

—Winston Churchill

The Crimea, the area in southern Russia on the Black Sea where Yalta is located, was often referred to as the "Russian Riviera" because of its temperate climate and its reputation as a playground of the imperial families. But at one point during the Yalta Conference in February 1945, Winston Churchill, gazing out over the sea and the mountains from his villa, called it the "Riviera of Hades."

The Riviera of Hades

BLACK SEA ASSIGNMENT

Michael Woodthorpe

WILLIAM B. EERDMANS PUBLISHING COMPANY
GRAND RAPIDS, MICHIGAN / CAMBRIDGE, U.K.

Wm. B. Eerdmans Publishing Co.

255 Jefferson Ave. S.E., Grand Rapids, Michigan 49503 /
P.O. Box 163, Cambridge CB3 9PU U.K.

Printed in the United States of America

08 07 06 05 04 03   7 6 5 4 3 2 1

Library of Congress Cataloging-in-Publication Data

Woodthorpe, Michael.

The riviera of Hades : Black Sea assignment / Michael Woodthorpe.

p.   cm.

ISBN 0-8028-2118-9 (alk. paper)

1. Americans — Russia (Federation) — Fiction.   2. Hospital patients — Fiction.
3. Moscow (Russia) — Fiction.   4. Missing persons — Fiction.
5. Diplomats — Fiction.   I. TItle.

PS3623.O68R58   2003
813'.6 — dc21

2003054327

www.eerdmans.com

For Lavender

Acknowledgments

My thanks to Deborah Cox, Sue Hodges, and Sandra Brown for turning my dictation into words; to Michael Jennings and Reinder Van Til for turning my words into prose; and to Bill Eerdmans for turning my prose into this book. I owe them all a great debt of gratitude.

Significant Events in Russian History

1682-1917	Imperial Russia
1894	Nicholas II becomes emperor; his empress is the German-born princess Alexandra, whose close adviser is Gregory Rasputin.
1905	The first Russian revolution
October 30, 1905	The "October Manifesto": Emperor Nicholas II announces the formation of a Duma; the Romanov empire becomes a constitutional monarchy.
Summer 1914	Russian forces enter World War I.
December 1916	Assassination of Rasputin
March 1917	Women's Bread Riots; collapse of the Romanov autocracy
November 9, 1917	The Great October Revolution is complete: Soviet rule is established in Petrograd under the designation Council of People's Commissars.
March 1918	Treaty of Brest-Litovsk, Russia's peace with Germany
November 1920	Evacuation of many czarist refugees, including the Dowager Empress and the Czar's sister, from the Crimea to Allied-occupied Constantinople on British destroyers
December 30, 1922	The Union of Soviet Socialist Republics comes into being, with Joseph Stalin as General Secretary of the Party.
January 1924	Death of Vladimir Lenin

December 27, 1927	15th All-Union Congress of the Communist Party condemns all "deviation from the general Party line," as interpreted by Stalin. Dictatorship of Stalin begins.
January 1929	Trotsky expelled by Stalin from the Soviet Union
November 1932	Franklin D. Roosevelt elected President of the United States
1933	The U.S. formally recognizes the Soviet Union.
1934	The U.S.S.R. joins the League of Nations.
1936-1938	Stalin's Great Purge, the "Terror Trials," in which Old Guard Bolshevik leaders are convicted of counter-revolutionary conspiracy, association with Trotsky, and alliances with Soviet enemies; most are executed. An estimated eight million people are arrested by the secret police and exiled. Lavrentii Beria takes control of the NKVD.
September 1938	Germany annexes the Sudetenland.
September 3, 1939	Great Britain and France declare war on Germany after Hitler invades Poland.
1940	The exiled Trotsky is murdered in Mexico, almost certainly on Stalin's orders.
May 1940	Winston Churchill becomes Prime Minister of Great Britain.
June 1941	Germany attacks Russia, and Churchill welcomes Russia as an ally.
August 1941	Roosevelt and Churchill formulate the Atlantic Charter, setting the stage for the United Nations.
December 7, 1941	The Japanese attack Pearl Harbor, and the United States enters the war.
July 1942	Second great German offensive on the southern half of the Russian front — Voronezh to the Black Sea — and the capture of Sevastopol
December 1943	The first conference of the "Big Three" (Stalin, Roosevelt, and Churchill) in Tehran
June 6, 1944	D-Day: British, American, and Canadian forces land on Normandy.
February 1945	Second conference of the "Big Three," in Yalta
April 12, 1945	Death of President Franklin D. Roosevelt

May 8, 1945	The Third Reich surrenders unconditionally in Berlin after the Red Army takes Berlin, Dresden, and Prague.
July-August 1945	The "Big Three" meet in Potsdam. President Harry Truman replaces Roosevelt; Clement Atlee, Churchill's opponent in the contemporaneous British election, comes to Potsdam as an "observer."
July 26, 1945	Churchill is defeated for Prime Minister by Atlee, who returns to Potsdam as head of the British delegation.
September 2, 1945	Japan surrenders aboard the battleship *Missouri*.
February 5, 1946	Churchill emphasizes the danger to the democratic world of Communist expansion in his famous "Iron Curtain" speech at Westminster College in Fulton, Missouri.
March 5, 1953	Death of Joseph Stalin. The triumvirate of Malenkov, Beria, and Molotov set to succeed Stalin.
Summer 1953	Nikita Khrushchev appointed First Party Secretary; Malenkov resigns as Party Secretary but remains as Prime Minister; Beria (and a number of his followers) arrested for treason and conspiracy, and secretly executed.
February 1956	Khrushchev denounces Stalin and begins the campaign of "de-Stalinization."

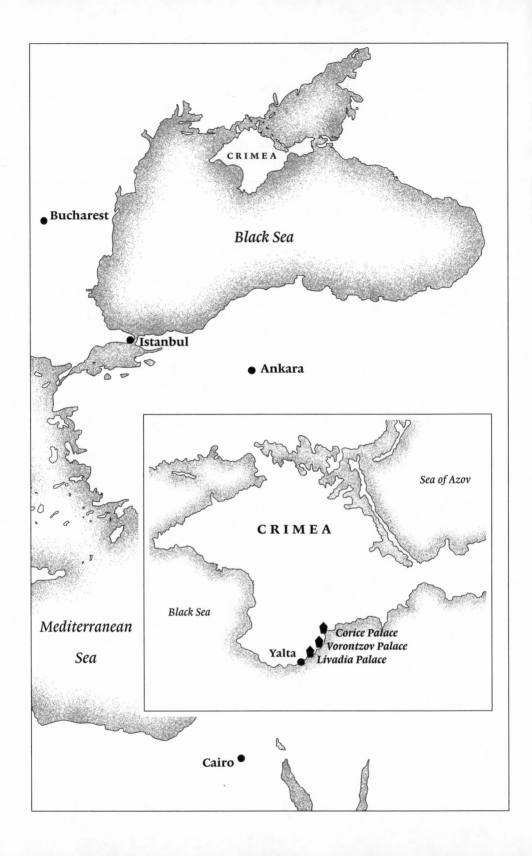

The Riviera of Hades

The Yalta conference was convened in the Crimea on the Black Sea in southern Russia. Livadia, the summer palace of the last czar of the then imperial country, was designated as the headquarters of the U.S. delegation — for the convenience of the paralyzed U.S. President, Franklin D. Roosevelt — and most of the meetings were held there. It overlooked perhaps the most beautiful harbor on a glorious coastline.

The three wartime leaders of the Allied nations, Winston Churchill, Franklin D. Roosevelt and Joseph Stalin, of the Union of Soviet Socialist Republics, were meeting together for the last time before the anticipated end of hostilities. If the gathering papered over the cracks in the grand alliance, and its communiqué was greeted in the free world as a triumph of diplomacy, it can also be said to have begun the Cold War and the enslavement of millions, as the Soviet regime blanketed the whole of Eastern Europe and much of Central Europe.

A majority of the conference delegates had already met on the island of Malta for previous discussions, and during the night of February 2 and morning of February 3, 1945, twenty Sky Masters, U.S. cargo planes converted for passenger use, and five Yorks, the civilian equivalents of the British Lancaster bombers, took off from Luqa airfield on Malta. They left at ten-minute intervals and flew at a set speed on a preordained course of three and a half miles due east, then made a ninety-degree turn to avoid Crete, which was still occupied by the Germans. They then skirted the Greek coast, flew over Turkey and across the Black Sea, made another ninety-degree turn at the radio transmitter of the Soviet airport near Saki to indicate that they were friendly aircraft, and then touched down on concrete blocks where the Russians had constructed a midwinter airstrip. The surface was icy, and it was only with difficulty that the great planes managed to come to a stop before reaching the end of the runway.

President Roosevelt's plane, dubbed the *Sacred Cow*, had taken off from Malta at 6:30 a.m. on February 3rd, and landed on the Russian airstrip at 12:10 p.m. local time. Having preceded Churchill's plane — also a Sky Master, which had been given to him by the U.S. Army — Roosevelt awaited the arrival of the British Prime Minister. On landing, Churchill went directly across to the *Sacred Cow*, from which Roosevelt was slowly descending on an elevator constructed specially for him. He was lifted off the elevator by the Foreign Commissar Vyacheslav Molotov, and his deputy, Lavrentii Beria, who had emerged in control of the NKVD after

2

the "Terror Trials" held in the 1930s, when Stalin had wiped out all his old comrades from the revolution of 1917 and indeed almost all of those who had brought the Soviets to power.

Molotov explained that Stalin himself was traveling down by train and would be arriving the following day. Stalin, it was later revealed, was terrified of flying; his one experience on the way to an earlier conference at Tehran had been enough for him. He had sat gripping the handles of his seat, his knuckles showing white, clearly feeling in minor measure the terror he had inspired among the tens of millions of his fellow countrymen during the bloodthirsty years of his power.

Following the playing of the three national anthems, Roosevelt in his Jeep, with Churchill walking by his side, reviewed the honor guard; they were then invited to a tent where the Russians had arranged an overwhelming display of food and drink for their reception. Roosevelt chose to set out immediately for Livadia Palace, a twisting and bumpy six-hour drive from the airstrip, to join the other members of the U.S. delegation. But Churchill, always a hearty eater and drinker, entered the tent to find glasses of hot tea with lemon and sugar; bottles of vodka, brandy, and champagne; caviar, smoked sturgeon, and salmon; various breads, butter, cheese, and hard- and soft-boiled eggs. He made short work of what he chose for his breakfast and then, with his daughter Sarah, a member of the British Women's Auxiliary Airforce, who had accompanied him to the conference, was driven to the British headquarters at Vorontzov Palace. Though it was perhaps the most interesting and ornate palace of those chosen to house the various conferees, it did not entirely satisfy Churchill. His initial breakfast did not deter him from stopping for lunch, with similar refreshments partway through his journey to Vorontzov Palace. Meanwhile Roosevelt, accompanied by his own daughter, Anna Boettiger, was eager to reach the safety and rest of his own headquarters.

The road they followed was initially flat and snow-covered, although it bore all the traces of the savage fighting that had devastated the Soviet land as the Germans and the Russians took and retook the Crimean peninsula: utterly destroyed villas, shattered tanks, ruined guns, and burnt-out German transport trains from the 1942 campaign littered the countryside. Even so, as Stalin later explained to Roosevelt, this was nothing compared to the destruction the Germans had wreaked in the Ukraine. The road led upward and past mountaintops to the eastern side of the peninsula, where they emerged from a cloud and were suddenly warmed by the sun. As they descended into Yalta itself, they were able to get a glimpse of the Black Sea, which shone green in the sunlight. Roosevelt was greeted at Livadia Palace by Kathleen Harriman, the U.S. ambassador's daughter, who had come down ten days earlier with a small party from the U.S. embassy in Moscow to cooperate with the Russians in arranging for the President's stay in their country. After dinner and a bath, Roosevelt quickly retired to bed.

CHAPTER ONE

MOSCOW, 1960

On a Moscow winter evening in 1960, shortly after the first of the year, my father's failure to return home from the U.S. embassy marked the beginning of my involvement in the sinister backdrop to the conference that had ended a decade and a half earlier. Father had been among the seven hundred or so delegates to the Yalta conference, but he could pre-date his involvement with some of those at the conference, at least indirectly, to many years earlier. He had not, in fact, flown to Yalta from Malta with most of the other Americans, because he was at that time assigned to the U.S. embassy in Moscow. Instead, like Stalin, he traveled by train to attend the conference. All I knew about Yalta that evening, fifteen years later in Moscow, was what I had learned in school: the general political considerations governing the conference, discussions about Roosevelt's health at the time, and to some extent minor details of the environment in which they worked. But everything else that I eventually learned about it came from Father's lips. In 1960, with Father once again in Moscow as a member of the State Department, I had come from Washington to join him and my mother during the New Year holiday of my last year in high school. I had brought with me my close school friend, Kate Harris, and together we explored the small part of Moscow we were allowed to move in freely. We introduced Kate to various Russian foods, played records of the Bolshoi Opera, ballet music, and the Red Army Chorus, and we were doing our best to entertain her with the limited facilities available in our official residence.

We spent that day anticipating the activities of the evening: Father had planned to take all of us to an English film comedy showing in Moscow despite Soviet censorship. We would certainly understand the dialogue, and there would be no problem disregarding the Russian subtitles.

In fact, Father, who was fluent in Russian, was looking forward to seeing how the Russian translators dealt with some of the idiomatic British expressions that even we might have difficulty understanding. Mother had prepared an early supper, and we waited patiently for the sound of Father's return. But we waited in vain, at first with a degree of curiosity at his late arrival, and then with growing anxiety and, frankly, fear.

Mother phoned the embassy, only to be told that Father had left at his usual time, and they could not understand his late arrival. The embassy staff suggested that we call as soon as he reached home or after a half hour if he had not turned up by that time. But Mother called again in twenty minutes, and the anxiety in her voice must have spurred them to activity. They said they would contact the Moscow police and get back to her if they received any information. After a short time, the embassy phoned again; the duty officer could not help revealing the alarm in his voice when he told Mother that the Soviet authorities, on hearing the news, had themselves reacted by taking immediate action and were now combing the city for any sign of my father.

There was nothing more we could do but sit and wait until, shortly afterwards, a young official from the U.S. embassy arrived at our house. We felt it was to keep us company and give us any assurance that he could possibly conjure up. He had only been with us about half an hour when we received a phone call from Moscow's city hall. In excellent English, the caller assured Mother that they were doing all they could to trace Father and that we need have no fear — because no one disappeared in the city of Moscow. Until that moment, the word "disappear" had not entered our heads; we had merely thought that there was some trivial delay. But now a real panic entered our hearts, a flood of fearful thoughts in all of us, including, we could see, the embassy official who sat anxiously with us.

Mother, in her anxiety, turned to both Kate and me and asked for the umpteenth time, "Did Henry say anything to you this morning or last night about whether he would possibly be delayed this evening, anything that might have forced us to cancel our night at the movies?" We again shook our heads; but the anxiety in her voice, added to ours, only served to increase the growing tension among us. The embassy official could do no more than anyone else, and he too was bereft of words as we sat there in the capital of this strange country with which we had been nominally at war, at least in the "cold" sense, since far back into the 1940s.

Shortly afterwards, the phone rang again, this time the Soviet official who had spoken to us earlier. All he could do was assure us that they were pulling out all the stops to do what they could and once more to say that no one could possibly disappear in Moscow.

"Where could they go?" asked Mother in some desperation.

The official said that it was a city they had under control. In any other context this would have sounded sinister, but now the words were meant to give us some degree of comfort. He said that they knew every street and road and corner, every apartment house, that they knew where to search for missing persons. He implored her, in a rather old-fashioned way, to rely on them because they were doing everything possible.

When she hung up, the three of us, plus the embassy official, sat and looked at each other and waited for the next phone call. And that was how the evening and night passed. Various phone calls, another visitor from the U.S. embassy, and passed-on reports from the Soviet authorities. We had no further direct communication from the latter, and we did not know which of their various strata of police or investigatory agents were involved. Whether they were the local police, the KGB, or even the army, we had no idea — but we stayed up all night. There was nothing more we could do than provide drinks and occasionally food for our visitors and ourselves. None of us went to bed.

When morning eventually came, we learned that the rivers had been dragged and searches organized in the parks throughout Moscow — anywhere there were lakes or ponds that bore searching. But Mother, Kate, and I were convinced that Father was still alive, and we were not at all surprised to hear that these activities had been unsuccessful. So far we had not visited the U.S. embassy itself. But now, as if to further convince us that they were doing everything that could possibly be done, the embassy sent a car to drive us all there, including Kate, who had insisted that she join us. Here we progressed as far as the ambassador's office; but he was away, and still there was no word, no suggestion, not even an idea offered to us as we went from office to office. Mother's request to go to the Moscow police headquarters was initially denied; but she pressed on with it and, after several phone calls, we were told that they had arranged for a high-ranking police official to meet with us at the embassy, and a room was set aside for that purpose.

Shortly thereafter, a Soviet official named Igor Gregorski arrived, accompanied by two younger men; he was dressed in civilian clothes, but we were later informed that he was in fact an NKVD colonel. After speaking with members of the embassy staff, he was led into the room where Mother, Kate, and I were waiting. He had arranged for a map of the city to be tacked on the wall, and using a ruler as a pointer, he showed us all the possible directions leading from the U.S. embassy to our home. He drew circles around each location they had searched and everywhere — he hesitated over the word — Father could possibly have been "delayed." Though we could see that he was going out of his way to give us all the assurance he could, nothing he explained to us gave us any comfort. We had nothing but praise for the way he was handling the situation, but he himself knew it was beyond his control. The embassy had offered us coffee, but, to our surprise, Gregorski had even brought with him a bottle of vodka and some caviar, in case — as he said — our embassy was not caring for us enough. He assured us that it was the most digestible sustenance in the world and would give us strength to carry on. So we gulped down some of the biting spirit and the fish eggs. When he rose to go, we rose with him; as he formally bowed over my mother's hand and gave her his last assurances, we smiled back at him and thanked him for his consideration. And as he left the room with his small delegation, the two members of our embassy who had been with us throughout the meeting had to agree that it was a convincing demonstration of the earnestness of the Soviet authorities in their search for my father.

"You can rest assured," one of them said, "that that man was not being insincere. From what we hear, they are greatly disturbed by what's happened. It's just the sort of incident that frightens both sides. I have to be perfectly candid that neither side fears anything more than a personal and insoluble mystery, when neither side can point the finger of blame clearly at the other. At least both can then sit down and try to produce a diplomatic solution."

There was no alternative but for us to return home. Escorted by the embassy official, we looked down every street as we followed Father's usual route home. But we learned nothing. There was nothing we could guess at, no clue even from our own discussions about what might have interested him, what he might have told us to look out for, or even anything he might have commented on in passing after he had returned home on previous evenings — absolutely nothing. We arrived home in despair, and we sat in silence with the embassy official who had accompanied us. Mother finally rose and offered us drinks, though none of us wanted anything but coffee after the vodka we had gratefully consumed at the embassy. The official followed suit, so we sat drinking hot coffee, as if that might stir further ideas in our brains. At last he rose and said, "I really will have to leave now, but we will go on — of course we will go on. . . ." Then he paused for a moment.

"May I ask you one thing, please?" We all looked up. "No word of Mr. Winthrop's disappearance is to be released to anybody. At the moment it is being kept absolutely secret, although, of course, there are enough people in the embassy who know about it. Others will guess that the concern we're showing must point to something. But for the moment it must be kept absolutely secret . . . and we certainly don't want the press getting onto it. They would have a field day with this."

Toward evening, after the intense pressure of nearly twenty-four hours, we learned from Washington that two FBI men had arrived in Moscow. But it was apparent when they came to see us that they too had little they could hope to find out, and they were perfectly open in their attitude.

"We're under orders not to reveal our presence here," one of the men said. "We're not allowed to interfere with the Soviets, and they're extremely guarded about us being here — if not downright hostile."

That evening and night passed almost as badly as the first one had, except that we all managed to get some sleep. By this time, both Mother and I had begun to feel guilty about involving Kate in this affair. But she insisted that her place was by our side, and we accepted that with gratitude. But Kate could not stay on in Moscow indefinitely, and our New Year holiday from school would soon be over. So after a few days Mother had to face the fact that the only wise thing for us to do would be to return to Washington. She insisted on staying in Moscow herself — at least until there was some sort of resolution. She said this in a neutral voice, and we could see that the strain was wearing her down; but she was absolutely insistent, and we felt that we had to follow her wishes. When she informed the U.S. embassy of this, they made arrangements for Kate and me to fly home together.

Back in Washington, I stayed with Kate and her widowed father, whose Georgetown home was only a couple blocks from our house. The only difference from our usual school routines were the visits from the FBI and the CIA, whose agents were desperately trying to stumble on any clues about Father's disappearance. They showed Kate and me photographs of the embassy, of the house where we had stayed in Moscow, and of various Soviet Foreign Ministry officials who may have talked with us (or whom we may have seen) while we were in Moscow. They even showed us photographs of the streets we had walked when we visited the U.S. embassy — or those we might have walked during our stay in the city. Although they insisted that we try to recall anything that might come back to us in the quietness of our Georgetown home, there was nothing we could add to the accounts we had given in Moscow, no matter how hard they pressed us.

Once or twice, rather to our surprise, we were visited by party politicians we knew had nothing to do with the State Department, the FBI, the CIA, or any police organization we could identify. We did not understand how they had learned about what had happened, but they also questioned us: it was in a more oblique way, harking back more to Father's previous activities in Moscow. They insisted that they were privy to the secret of his disappearance and were under strict orders not to spread it further; we dismissed their visits as rather unusual. My concern for Father's whereabouts overrode everything, and I waited anxiously for Mother's telegrams from Moscow, which came every other day or so. But she had nothing to add, and as day followed day, no further information was directly available from the State Department in Washington.

At last Mother was persuaded to return home to Washington. She arrived distraught, anxious beyond measure, and with nothing to show for the terrible time she had spent by herself in the Soviet capital. She told us that the Soviet authorities had instructed their embassy in Washington to offer all the help and sympathy they could; indeed, there were messages from them soon after she returned. With the agreement of the State Department, members of the Soviet foreign service occasionally visited — sometimes alone, sometimes accompanied by members of the U.S. State Department. But nothing could dispel everyone's total ignorance about Father's whereabouts. Sometimes a Soviet officer would cross paths with a CIA or FBI member as one or the other of them came to our house. But the only outcome was a desperation that eventually ended in despair, at least on their part. As for us, we remained convinced that Father was still alive and that the mystery would soon have some fairly simple solution.

In our high school, it became clear that news of Father's disappearance had spread through the city — at least the government and foreign service sectors. A number of students questioned us, though apparently the school staff had been given instructions to reveal nothing of what had happened. But they, too, were already privy to the so-called secret, which would only serve to spread it further. Eventually almost everyone we ran into — neighbors, friends, mailmen, and shopkeepers — was aware that something had happened to my father. There was nothing we could say or do — no way to duck questions — that could avoid the blank refusal on our part to add anything to what our questioners sought to know. In fact, some of them bluntly asked, "How did your father disappear? Was he assassinated?" We tried to field the questions, but the strain on us was only relieved when finally — as was inevitable — the newspapers themselves broke the story in headline banners. That made it easier for us to deal with the outside world, even though its immediate consequence was a siege by reporters and newsmen, television cameramen and reporters from the free world — even Russian reporters.

The Washington police put a guard on our house, and we had no alternative but to leave it to the administration and the State Department to handle the media questions; we didn't want to be interviewed ourselves, or make radio or television appearances, or be the subjects of special reports by the press. It was a difficult period. But soon the political campaign heating up in Washington rose to a rolling boil, and it drove my missing father's story off the front page, and at last things died down. In the meantime, there was no word from Moscow — let alone any messages from our own State Department — that might have given us some sort of hope that secret negotiations were taking place or, for that matter, anything that would have suggested some route leading to Father's reappearance. We were absolutely convinced by now that neither side had anything to contribute, either individually or together, and we could only wait in a vacuum of despair.

Mother went about her daily duties, but they were very slight because she was, after all, the wife of a diplomat, used to accompanying him on overseas missions. There was a limit to what she could do around the house, or indeed in Washington, and specifically in our neighborhood of Georgetown. The Soviet authorities offered her a return trip to Moscow, and the U.S. State Department suggested that she might wish to take advantage of it. But they also warned her that there was nothing to add, and that all she could do once she was there would be to live solitarily again in that largely empty house assigned to Father. In any event, Father's replacement, a younger diplomat, was due to take up his appointment shortly and move into that house with his wife, and Mother would again be returning empty-handed.

One or other of us continued to leap to the phone every time it rang, but it was with an increasing feeling of hopelessness when we lifted it to our ear. I racked my brain for something to divert Mother, to keep her from her worries and despairing thoughts. I shared those, but at least I had the daily occupation of going to school — where I had Kate and other friends with whom to talk and share extracurricular activities. Finally, at the suggestion of a friend, Mother started doing some volunteer work, which got her out of the house and gave her an opportunity to enter other people's homes and lives — people she could talk with and discuss problems outside her own anxieties. It was a good idea but, as both of us knew, only a stopgap measure.

One day in the cooling warmth of an Indian summer, we were having an afternoon cup of tea, a habit we had adopted in Moscow, in the den just off Father's study, where we often had sat as a family. Mother asked whether I wanted to know more about Father's family and its origins, much of which was a complete mystery to me. At the moment I wasn't sure whether she wanted to clear up some of that mystery or was bravely trying to divert herself and me from our immediate anxiety. But I was indeed curious, so I told her I was all ears.

CHAPTER TWO

My father, Henry Winthrop, was the son of a young physician, Harry Winthrop, who practiced medicine in Vermont, the state where he was born. He was a general physician, but he also held positions at the local hospital, which was a common practice out in the country. He had patients throughout the community, and his life was no different from that of thousands of doctors practicing in America. Not long after he had established his practice and had a reasonably steady income, he married a young woman he had met while visiting his aunt in neighboring Maine. They had one child, Henry, but the young mother died shortly after giving birth to him, which left Harry to bring him up a lonely child in a lonely house in Vermont. When the patients left in the evening, the house was empty and depressing. Grandfather Harry, in common with others in such circumstances, attempted to drown his loneliness and misery by plunging into his work: he took on the duties of other doctors at the hospital and probably accepted more patients than he could reasonably deal with — anything to distract him from the loss of his wife.

One evening, on another of his visits to his aunt in Maine, Harry sat in on a meeting being held in town to draw attention to the famine in the Soviet Union, which was sponsored by refugees from the Russian Revolution, many of whom were scattered throughout the Eastern Seaboard and in the hinterlands of the northeastern United States. Harry went to the town meeting more out of a need for something to fill his lonely hours than with any real sense of purpose or interest in the subject. In a half-full church hall, where a recent refugee from Petrograd was giving details of the famine conditions in that city, Harry found himself sitting next to a young woman, Maria, whose dark eyes were attractive to him. As they conversed, Harry learned that Maria was staying with relatives in an old house in Maine that had been left to the family by a distant relative who had emigrated from Russia toward the end of the nineteenth century. This earlier aunt had not been a victim of political persecution in Russia but had come to America after she had met and married an American engineer who was working in czarist Russia on the railways then being built. Americans, Harry learned, were almost wholly responsible for the Trans-Siberian Railway.

When the speaker from Petrograd had finished his address, Harry and Maria joined others for coffee and a general discussion, so their conversation stuck pretty much to the subject of the meeting; they parted on semiformal terms, certainly with no agreement to meet again. On returning to his aunt's house, Harry found a message from a patient who had to see him as soon as possible. So he cut short his visit to Maine, returned home to Vermont, and immediately plunged back into his practice and his hospital duties. For some weeks his life continued as before, following the busy course of his medical obligations.

A few months later, he had occasion to travel to New York City, not only to see a patient who had moved there but also to visit medical bookshops to acquire up-to-date medical resource books he needed, which were unavailable in his Vermont town. On leaving one of these bookstores on the second day of his visit, he saw a poster — again by chance — advertising the same kind of meeting he had attended in Maine: it was about starvation in Russia and the physical and economic conditions prevailing in that country generally. Harry decided to go, not necessarily with any intention or hope of meeting Maria again (since he was in New York rather than Maine), though the possibility that he might see her must have held some attraction for him. In any event, the first person he saw when he entered the hall was Maria, busily engaged in conversation with the same speaker who had given the talk in Maine. Harry waited for some minutes and, when there appeared to be a pause in their conversation, reintroduced himself to Maria. Her face lit up.

"Oh, I'm so glad you're here," she said. "What a surprise! How did you get here?"

Harry explained that it was a chance journey to New York and a chance glimpse of the poster. As if quite naturally, the two of them sat together for the lecture again, notwithstanding Maria's obvious close acquaintance with the speaker; they listened to a recital of the same appalling facts and figures they had heard at the earlier meeting. It seemed equally natural for them to go to a cafe together after the meeting was over, and Maria asked Harry where he was staying in New York. He said that he was in a small hotel not far from the meeting hall, and he wondered whether Maria would like to have dinner with him on her way home. She explained that she was staying with relatives in New York and suggested that perhaps he might find it more interesting if she took him home with her and introduced him to the family. The warmth of a family rather than the formality of a restaurant was a tempting idea to Harry, so they rode a trolley car some distance out to Queens. They got off the trolley and together walked to a house that was set back off the street in a quiet residential neighborhood.

Maria had a key to the front door, and when she let them both in, they were warmly greeted by a chorus of welcoming voices. Harry had half expected a house full of Russian speakers; but these people were, in fact, American relatives of the railroad engineer, the man who had married the Russian woman. Drinks were pressed on them, and then they all went in to dinner. Harry had the distinct impression that they, though very welcoming of Maria, were perhaps a bit wary of her. It was difficult to define, but he sensed that she represented a past with which they could sympathize, to be sure, but which they really failed to understand. But the conversation was wide-ranging and animated, and it was the first occasion in a long time that Harry felt he could get outside himself and his lonely world.

Later that evening he returned to his hotel and, before he retired, thought about the evening in its entirety. It certainly had been pleasant being in someone else's home again, despite the unusual company. And the evening had somehow stirred in him a curiosity about Maria that he had not previously felt. It was not necessarily a feeling of longing or desire, but certainly curiosity: he wanted to know more about her background. Before going to bed, he picked up a copy of the *New York Times* he had only glanced at that morning, and he scoured it carefully for any reference to the situation in Russia. There was little new that the paper was reporting. Since the Bolshevik Revolution in October 1917, the *Times* had largely been devoted to a continuing attack on the horrors of that regime, generally reflecting the views of its American readers. In 1917, following the toppling of the Czar, Americans had welcomed what they thought would be the coming of another democracy. But Bolshevism had become another matter, and the United States was coming to terms with what that meant. Harry read for a short time and then went to bed.

He had a few days left in New York, so he arranged to meet Maria for a visit to the theater and a dinner alone. He offered to come out to the home in Queens, but she said that she would be coming into the city herself. Three evenings after the visit to the family in Queens, during an after-theater dinner at a restaurant Harry had chosen for its quietness and anonymity, Maria raised her head and looked him straight in the eye.

"Would you like to know about me?" she asked in her thick Russian accent. When Harry responded affirmatively without hesitation, she placed her elbows on the table and rested her chin in her hands.

"I was born in 1890," she said, "on an estate in southern Ukraine. My father worked for the ministry of the interior and" — she smiled — "was technically a minor noble. My mother was the one who had inherited the estate, which they visited when they were not in St. Petersburg." She paused, and Harry eagerly nodded for her to go on.

"It was an idyllic place, the kind you read about in Chekhov's plays. We never had serfs; the servants were old retainers, and we lived at peace with our surroundings and our neighbors. I had no sisters or brothers, and most of my childhood friends were the children of the peasants. My parents were perfectly happy for me to run free with them, having confidence both in them and me. If anyone were to have asked, I could not have said whether they were of any particular class or occupation. They were just my friends. We spent most of our summers there when my father left his position in St. Petersburg, where naturally we spent the greater part of the year, particularly the winter."

Maria stopped for a moment, drank some coffee, and asked him, "Am I boring you?"

"Certainly not," he quickly answered, "but only so long as you want to go on. I wouldn't want you to get into matters that will upset you."

"It was a curious period in Russian history. Although I played with peasant children during the day, I was obviously lonely in the evenings. When the weather was bad, as it sometimes was in the summer at the estate, my readings were mainly in French — dictated by the fact that most educated conversation in Russia was carried on in French and its culture was based on the cultural tradition of Western Europe. At the time, what was being written in Russian was essentially radical and revolutionary. It wasn't that I was reading Marx or Lenin, but the whole tone of what I did read in Russian was that there had to be change.

"The assumption everywhere, from top to bottom — even the aristocracy knew it — was that something had to be done about czarist Russia. A general feeling of uncertainty ran through the whole of society. On the wilder fringes, if I can call them that, it was an idealistic assumption that involved terrorism and ultimately revolution itself. But that was not part of my literary diet. If anything, my reading and ideas were based on the possibility of an ideal rural community, and they failed to take any realistic account of the industrialization that was growing fast in Russia. To some extent, theories of industrialization were reflected in some of the writers who tended to be of a more radical outlook, yet were Western-looking and had assimilated ideas from Karl Marx and his followers."

What Harry heard as he sat listening to Maria tell her life story was all new to him, and it probably would have been to any American, new in fact to almost anyone outside Russia, except for those few who had followed Russia's internal history. By now he wanted to know everything.

"It was in this sort of atmosphere and literary surroundings," she continued, "that I met and soon found myself in love with my husband-to-be, at least I thought I was. It was strange, because he was not an intellectual, as we then knew them; he was a newly commissioned officer in the army, the czarist army. It was not one of the Guards' regiments, and he was certainly not in the cavalry; he was in a rifle regiment that drew most of its officers from the middle to lower-middle ranks of society. Thus his views were to some extent colored by the same outlook that had influenced me: a vague idealistic dissatisfaction with the condition of the country, a complete dislike of the aristocratic echelons of the army, which I then knew nothing about, and a desire to see change. Like me, he fondly anticipated that change and was certain it would come.

"His father was an army general who had worked his way up from a lowly rank and had achieved his position during our seemingly interminable wars against the Turkish Empire on the frontiers of Russia. The son, Alex, had no particular ambition, and it had seemed convenient to follow his father's career. His family and mine were both from St. Petersburg, and we met at a party that his father gave for Alex's coming of age. I was educated in St. Petersburg, of course, and thus the two of us had a very similar background. My father was a successful civil servant, his father the successful general — but neither had come from any great background. Perhaps in the distant past they had owned serfs, but there had been very few of them. They were not among the great landowners who still survived and whose peasants lived in bondage similar to the serfdom from which they supposedly had been released in 1861. Nor had either family undergone the extreme poverty that characterized the lives of many in the lower classes — at least not in recent years. We were what would have been a middle-class group and, had there been no revolution, would probably have developed into modern Russians.

"Alex and I met from time to time when he came home on leave or when I was in St. Petersburg. Eventually, almost as a matter of course, Alex was invited to stay with us on our estate in the country, and then, equally as a matter of course, we became engaged. I don't think that I had any particular ambition either. I certainly did not wish to teach, and there seemed to be little to occupy me after I had finished my education. Although a growing number of upper- and middle-class girls were going on to universities, it was never suggested that I should go, nor did I wish to. For a year or so I remained on the estate or would go to St. Petersburg when Alex could join me from his regiment. At last, both of us felt restless under this regime and decided to look for an apartment in St. Petersburg, which was then the capital of Russia. My mother was unhappy, and Alex's father was frankly worried, about the radical disturbances that were spreading through Russia. But we assured them that there was no danger in what we were considering.

"It was, in fact, quite a considerable move, and both parents were certainly justified in their worries when the sporadic outbreak of strikes by workers in the city's big steel mills served to remind everyone of the agitation that seethed beneath the seeming calm. More to the point, it was a reminder of the situation in 1905, when there had been what appeared to be the outbreak of a general revolution. The Soviets had taken over St. Petersburg, with Trotsky as their leader. The Czar had promised various reforms and had half-heartedly followed them; but he was determined to keep his position as an autocrat. So St. Petersburg was the home of, side by side, an increasingly extreme group of radicals and the aristocrats who knew that there had to be change.

"But Alex and I were not greatly concerned about this, perhaps not as much as we should have been, and our life together in the city was happy. He had a considerable amount of leave, and I did what could only be called 'good works': I visited families who were in need of food and amateur medical attention and received a nodding acquaintance with the life of the urban working class, which was very different from that of the peasants with whom I had spent so much of my time as a child in the Ukraine. Our apartment was not far from the Neva, the great river flowing through the northern part of St. Petersburg, which divided the working-class district from the government and ruling-class dwellings. Our apartment was small but comfortable, and our lives can only described as modest but enjoyable.

"We were not completely removed from the radical movements that were pulsing through the city, and occasionally we attended meetings. Sometimes, when Alex was on leave, I would go alone. Perhaps it was a bit odd for an army officer and his wife to do so, but there were quite a few like us. Some later joined the Red Army and formed the backbone of Trotsky's forces when they finally defeated the White Russians in 1920 — after that appalling civil war. We led our own lives, separate from Alex's regiment, separate from his side of the family, and to some extent separate from my side. We were, I suppose, by any standards like the new generation in every country, but in Russia the consequences were to be far more overwhelming."

Harry was totally engrossed in what he was listening to, and it was now clear that he was entranced by Maria herself, as he relived her life in her telling of it. Maria related most of this in matter-of-fact tones that seemed to put her at a remove from the person he had first met; but he probably would have accepted any recital of her life as she gave it. The narrative had gone on for some time, and the restaurant was threatening to close. Harry was due to return to Vermont the following day, and he suddenly felt a certain desperation when he realized that this might be the last time he would see Maria. He was about to take her to a late-night bar he knew about — really a speakeasy, since this was during Prohibition — where he could offer her a drink. But he felt uneasy doing so, and finally, almost as though admitting defeat, he told her that he would take her back to where she was staying with her relatives.

"Well, it's a long way out, as you know," she replied. "Why don't you spend the night there, and you can travel back to New York in the morning."

This took him by surprise, but he didn't turn down the invitation, and together they took one of the last trolleys out to Queens. Once again she opened the door, this time to a quiet house, and led him quietly through a darkened corridor into the kitchen, where she turned on a light and offered him coffee. He sank into a comfortable chair, and she stood by

19

the stove waiting for the kettle to boil. She asked him if he would like anything to drink, and seeing his surprise at the offer, added, "Don't worry, we have a little brandy that one of my cousins is occasionally able to bring in from France." When the coffee was ready, she put a cup on the table for him and settled herself in another chair. He could see that she was eager to continue, if not conclude, her narration; and he was eager to hear it, if only because he now wanted to know all he could about her.

He had wondered for a moment about her almost casual suggestion that he spend the night at this house; but later he realized that in Russia — at least in the Ukraine and outside the big cities — neighbors would have lived a considerable distance away from each other and would consider it normal to stay with their hosts rather than making a return journey the same day. Maria continued her narrative, this time looking straight ahead; he looked away from her as if to leave her in the privacy of her thoughts.

"You must understand that St. Petersburg — it was called Petrograd during World War I — was the capital of Russia, not only by the designation of Peter the Great but because it was the center of all culture and of all radicalism, and indeed it was the very heart of the country. The outbreak of revolutionary violence in 1905 was a precursor of what was to come; the revolutionaries who were sent into exile in Siberia, when they escaped, always returned to St. Petersburg. Side by side with the most magnificent opulence from the court downward existed not only abject poverty but something that was, curiously, shared by both — as I've mentioned, the unease that something had to happen. Alex felt it throughout the army, and I was aware of it in my day-do-day life of visiting others, and among my friends in the city.

"When World War I broke out in 1914, there was a great wave of patriotic fervor, and my husband was sent with his regiment to the eastern front, where the Russian Army intended to invade Germany before the Germans could overrun France. The campaign was, in fact, a disaster. It culminated in what many consider one of the Germans' great victories, at Tannenberg, under their eventual president, Hindenberg. The Russian generals quarreled among themselves, and their men died by the thousands — among them my husband, during the early weeks of the war. It was somehow as though he had never existed. He disappeared into nothingness — one among many, but each one an individual to each person who lost him. I was completely lost."

Harry could only sit in silence, joining her silence when she paused after describing her husband's death. Somehow he knew that he should not express sympathy; and she continued to look resolutely ahead as if determined to deliver herself of the vivid story that was nonetheless buried deep inside her.

"I took up nursing because the call for nurses was very urgent, and because I knew a little about first aid from the occasional work I had done in Petrograd before the war. I worked in a big general hospital in Petrograd, where conditions in those early days of the war were reasonably good. There were many of us young women who worked there; medically speaking, I don't think we were of much value, but we could at least offer comfort to the wretched men who were being brought in from the front. The work was hard, and everyone, from the surgeons on down, worked day and night, still bolstered by the patriotism with which the country had entered the war, even though the losses were now mounting horrendously. Many of the nurses had lost their husbands in the opening offensives. My parents were living in Petrograd because their estate on the Polish border was now a battleground. And even though my Polish ancestry might have marked me to a certain degree as someone who would sympathize with the Germans' cause — since their triumph might mean independence for the Poles — my loyalty was always with Russia, and no one ever questioned that.

"It almost seemed, in a way, that my marriage had never existed. I served for a while on one of the hospital trains that went up to, or close to, the front. That work was terrifying and dreadful; the conditions were primitive beyond belief."

Maria got up and poured herself another cup of coffee.

"The war got worse and worse. We could see it in the casualties now flooding Petrograd and the growing shortage of food and other necessities. At the same time, there was a most curious, almost feverish, excitement of ostentation and wealth as the war speculators grew richer and richer. Restaurants flourished, the theaters and ballet were packed to capacity, and life was a very strange mixture of the hell of the fighting man's world and the luxurious and sheltered comfort of those profiting from it.

"My experience as a nurse gave me a growing distaste — and eventually disgust — for what was happening. My earlier radical readings were now being reinforced by extremist literature that was circulating in the city: it called for an outright end of the war and an acceptance of peace — on whatever terms were available. In fact, this extreme view, which was Lenin's view, was that only through such a collapse would Russia find its solution. That eventually proved to be correct. Both my father and mother, as well as Alex's father, the general (his mother had died), disagreed with my views, of course, and there were many bitter arguments. My mother even feared that she would ultimately lose her estate and everything that she had become accustomed to in her upbringing and her life before the war.

"I began to feel isolated from my family. Nor did I have any particular friends among those who were seeking to end the war on any terms. I didn't like the radicals, and I certainly had no contact with the extremists. At the same time, I knew things were bound to explode. Conditions in the hospital were almost unbearable; the generals continued to call for further offensives; and men were being returned to their units who could scarcely move, let alone carry weapons and fight. My father-in-law, and my father to some extent, kept telling me that the army was on the point of victory, that they now had all the ammunition they wanted and one of the largest forces in the world. Perhaps they were on the verge of victory, but I had direct evidence to the contrary every day when I went to work in the city, where there were sporadic riots, occasional demonstrations, and attacks on food shops. If one could have stood back, one would have been surprised that life could continue in any kind of normal way. Gossip about the royal family filtered down, particularly the doings of Rasputin, and his murder failed to stop the accusations circulating about the German-born Czarina. The accusations that she was disloyal were now being directed against her husband, the Czar, who had taken command of the army and was thus bearing direct responsibility for all that was happening.

"My own private life amounted to nothing. I lived by myself, worked at the hospital — sometimes all night — and knew few people. There was no other man with whom I had any kind of friendship, though occasionally young officers would ask me out to dinner, and once in a while I would agree to go. I would sometimes stop to listen to radical speeches as I walked through Petrograd. I read the pamphlets that were handed to me, and of course I read the daily papers. And I increasingly noticed the terrible poverty around me. But I was in a blur . . . and had been since 1914.

"I felt no passion for anyone or anything, and, looking back on it, I am astonished that this blurred existence continued so long. Then one week something happened that did shake me to the core of my being, as it did everyone in Petrograd. It was the outbreak of the Revolution, the Women's Bread Riots, the troops in the city going over to the revolutionaries, and the collapse of the autocratic czarist regime. This startled me awake and toward some sort of purpose."

At this point Maria stirred in her chair and glanced at the clock. Harry also realized that it was well into the early hours of the morning, and he moved to get up, feeling that they could not spend the whole night talking like this. She must have felt the same, because she rose to her feet and said, "Well, perhaps I can go on in the morning."

"I have to catch the train to Vermont around midday," he said, "but perhaps we could meet as we did before — when I travel to Maine."

"That would be wonderful," she replied. "I feel I have to tell you everything. There is so much that I want you to understand."

This expression of intimacy pierced Harry to the heart because he realized how much he wanted — and needed — to know about her. She led him from the kitchen to his room and bade him a formal good-night, leaving him to retire with his own racing, though far from confused, thoughts. He knew that he wanted her whatever she had to say. He had come to a firm decision: rather than waiting for the chance to meet her in Maine, he would invite her to visit him in Vermont, introduce her to his son, and, if necessary, observe all the proprieties by asking someone from the town to stay in the house with them — even though they were widow and widower respectively.

In the morning, he dressed quickly, and when he came downstairs, Maria was already there. After a quick breakfast, she accompanied him to the trolley, which would take him back into the city. On the way to the stop, he made his invitation to her, and she accepted eagerly. She would give him a couple of weeks to settle back into his practice and to make whatever domestic arrangements were necessary. He bade her a formal farewell as the trolley arrived. On the ride back to New York, it was as though his mind was absolutely clear and he knew how he could plan the future. He was confident, too, that Maria sensed what was inevitably coming to both of them. He rehearsed in his mind everything she had told him the night before and realized that it had been the barest but most important essentials; there were few details of her marriage, her husband, even of her nursing years during the war. And he realized suddenly that he had no idea of what had happened to her after World War I. He knew that she had to have escaped from Russia and arrived in the United States at some point, probably with the assistance of her American relatives. There were many organizations set up to bring émigrés across the Atlantic, and he had no doubt that she had been assisted by at least one of them — perhaps with the backing of a distant relative. But he knew no more than what he could guess, and he hoped that more details would come to him as he came to know her better. In any event, his mind was made up and he felt at peace with himself.

*   *   *

Harry was buzzing with excitement as he returned to Vermont, and he decided that he could not wait for either Maria's visit to her Maine relatives or for her visit to him in Vermont. Indeed, he realized that, since the latter invitation had virtually amounted to a proposal of marriage anyway, there was only one thing he should do: call her as soon as he could on his return and ask her directly if she would marry him. If he thought about how this new turn in his life would affect his son, Henry, he would have undoubtedly realized that Maria, as a nurse, certainly would be able to care for a small boy; also, since Henry had never known his own mother, there was no question of her being replaced by someone else. He had already had a succession of relatives and nurses looking after him, and a permanent new one, having at least the virtue of consistency, would be an improvement.

On second thought, Harry thought that perhaps it would be wiser for him to write his marriage proposal in a letter than to phone Maria with it. Proposing over the telephone seemed precipitous — even for him. She would have her own problems to sort out, and he wanted to at least give her an opportunity to do so. He wrote that letter with an unconcealed declaration of his love and need for her, and then he returned to his practice, looking after those patients whom he had delayed visiting while he was in New York. He was quite confident that Maria would respond in the affirmative, but it was still with surprise and utter delight that he received her phone call after his letter had arrived. She agreed, firstly and promptly, to marry him; secondly, she felt there was no point in observing any delay. Accordingly, Harry arranged for a substitute to run his medical practice for a couple of weeks so that he and Maria could spend a honeymoon together. But he decided to take Henry with him to Maine; he was confident that there would be relatives to care for him. In his state of excitement and anticipation, Harry was able to tidy up his affairs quickly, and he soon departed for Maine with his small son.

When Harry arrived at Maria's relatives' home in Maine, he realized the extent to which Maria had already put in motion the wedding preparations, and what efforts had been made by her relatives to prepare a celebration and greet him as a new member of the family. His room was full of flowers, and there appeared to be fresh curtains in the windows; it even looked as though the room had been chosen for its sunny outlook. He was welcomed as a fellow American, and Maria herself seemed to have shed all her Russian attitudes, even to some extent her accent — though he knew this was improbable.

Nor was there anything Russian about that evening's dinner, which was quite a minor feast of plain American fare — solid but enjoyable. Harry came to realize that these relatives of Maria had come from Russia to America a good while back, well before the turn of the century, and that many of them were as American-born as he was. The conversation was lighthearted and looked to the future with happy anticipation. Maria herself seemed to be delighted, and Harry was almost taken aback by her warmth, which had not been apparent to him while she was telling her story. Young Henry was asleep upstairs on a cot in a small nursery, surrounded by a few toys. All of this was astonishing to Harry — but heartwarming nonetheless.

That evening, when the others had retired for the night, Harry took Maria in his arms for the first time and kissed her.

"Thank you," Maria said, a hint of her earlier formality returning. But then she laughed and drew her finger down his face and said, "You are the solemn one now. I am the one who is happy and content."

The following morning they were up early for breakfast, another exuberant affair, and then everyone departed on foot for the small church nearby. After the ceremony the couple, with their friends, returned to the house, where a wedding brunch had been prepared and brought it in by neighbors who had not attended the actual ceremony itself but who joined them for this meal, which progressed through the rest of the morning and most of the afternoon. Occasionally, Maria insisted that they go upstairs to see how Henry was doing, since they had left him at the house in the care of a neighbor during the church ceremony. They brought him downstairs for a short time at the beginning of brunch and then took him upstairs for his afternoon rest. There he must have lain, sound asleep, or staring with curiosity at his new surroundings.

As Harry and Maria prepared to leave on their honeymoon, they arranged for the care of Henry with Maria's relatives, who were prepared and only too happy to look after him. That wedding day and the honeymoon that followed began a new life of happiness for Harry, completely transforming his steady but lonely life of a widower with a motherless son. The couple departed for Florida, which was then still a largely undeveloped wilderness, but they could be sure of warm weather and comfortable accommodations. At the end of the honeymoon, the newlyweds took a train directly to Vermont, where Henry had been brought by Maria's relatives to await his new family. He greeted his father with some hesitation, but Maria flung her arms around the little boy, and from the very beginning he welcomed his new stepmother — not only as the return of some security to his life but also as a loving mother. She played that role to the fullest right from the very beginning.

CHAPTER THREE

I continued at school, becoming less and less of a curiosity as time wore on. It no longer made the headlines in the national papers: though there were occasional references to Father in the local Georgetown paper, the *New York Times* and the *Washington Post* had moved on and forgotten us. I graduated from high school in June, and it had already been decided that I was to attend Radcliffe at the beginning of the academic year in September. I insisted that I did not want to start right up in September, being unwilling to leave Mother alone. But at the beginning of summer vacation she was still saying that she did not want me to delay my first year of college.

We still received occasional messages and even visits from officials of the Soviet embassy, and at least one of those visitors, Emil Segalov, inspired a girlish affection in me. Emil paid an increasing number of visits to us, initially asking a few formal questions and then chatting amiably about his own home and his family. He was unmarried and had been living with his family in Moscow, where his father was some official in the economics ministry, so he told us. Emil seemed genuinely pleased to be able to practice his fluent English on us. We, in turn, felt that we could talk more or less freely to him; but, of course, he had nothing further to tell us about Father. Sometimes his questions seemed a bit too focused on Father's past in Moscow, but we couldn't really accuse him of being too probing. As for me, I think he was genuinely interested in the American school system, in my own schooling, and to some extent in me personally.

An occasion arose when he asked Mother and me to a reception at the Soviet embassy. We were both immediately inclined to accept, but before we did so, we checked with the State Department. They told us to go ahead, perhaps hoping that we might learn something further about Father or at least get additional material for them to work with. On the evening of the reception, a very obsequious chauffeur arrived in a black limousine to take us to the embassy. Indeed, though Father did not hold a very senior post in Moscow, they treated us at the embassy as though we were a visiting ambassadorial family. Mother and I — either separately or together — were introduced to the most important guests, and we found ourselves speaking with ambassadors from the rest of the world, mainly from Eastern Europe.

I had Emil by my side throughout the introductions as a member of the conversational trios and quartets that followed from these introductions. I could detect curiosity on the faces of the diplomats to whom I was introduced; but they had either been primed ahead of time or took their cue from Emil's presence. Mother was escorted by an older man, someone I had not seen before but who appeared to be greeted with deference by other members of the embassy staff. The Russian ambassador himself was absent. When dinner was served, Mother and I were not seated together: she was still accompanied by the older man, and Emil remained by my side. Another member of the embassy sat on my other side, and, after greeting me warmly, he asked whether I had ever been to Russia. I told him of my visits to Moscow, but he only shook his head.

"Ah, that's not what I mean," he said. "It is a beautiful country, a very large and beautiful country! Have you ever visited Crimea? You should. It's like the Riviera along the Black Sea coast. It had wonderful resorts, particularly Yalta, the playground where the old czars had their villas, and now it is where we have many health clinics. Stalin himself had a villa there just along the coast." All I knew about Yalta was a vague recollection that it had been the meeting place of the Allied leaders at one point in the last few months of World War II. I was about to say that I would like to visit Yalta sometime, but I became cautious — not from the mention of the name, but from the fact that any return to Russia was still obviously overshadowed by my father's disappearance. So I proceeded cautiously to raise that subject with my dinner neighbor.

"I would like to return one day, but before anything else I need to know where my father is. We have lived knowing nothing about him for so long. . . ."

His face saddened. "You know we have done all we can. It is an absolute mystery to us as well as to your people, and I am sure that both of us are doing our very best. He will appear one day, and all will be well." He said this with no particular conviction, but I smiled at him in thanks for his reassurance. Then he added, "I am sure you will be most welcome when you do come." He returned to his food as though he had finished a prepared statement.

Emil took up the moribund conversation. "It is very pleasant living here in Washington; you have a very fine capital city. I don't expect that you saw a great deal of Moscow, but one day it will be easier to get around there. We have so much to show you — the Kremlin, of course, our center of government. But there are other great cities — Leningrad, Gorki, Kiev, and many out to the east, such places as Samarkand. The empire stretches as far to the east as it does to the west." He hesitated when he said that, somewhat uneasy at suggesting that the eastern European countries were part of the Soviet empire. I nodded. The conversation felt forced and trivial, and I became aware of the tedious proceedings.

But shortly the tables were cleared, and a small band entered the room; to my great pleasure, it became apparent that there would be dancing. Emil naturally asked me to be his partner. He was a good dancer, and we circled the floor effortlessly. But to my surprise, he returned to the subject of my father.

"Can you tell me something about your father, about his life? I know that both American authorities and our staff have asked you questions again and again. But as I'm getting to know you, I would like to know more about your family. I have met with your mother frequently — with your father, of course, not at all. Where was his family from?"

"He was of old colonial stock," I replied, using the stock language of the formal biographies of him that had appeared in the press. "His father was a doctor, and his grandfather was also a doctor, I believe. In the background there was someone who served in the Civil War, but if it was as a doctor, I simply don't know. I could go further back, but eventually one ends up with merchants who sided with Washington against the British during the Revolutionary War."

"So your father was a doctor?" he asked.

"No, no, *his* father was a doctor."

"Ah yes, ah yes — and what was his mother?"

For some reason I felt on guard. We were sitting down at the table again after the first dance, and I merely shrugged my shoulders: "She died when my father was very young."

I knew immediately that it was a mistake to assume that would answer his question. His rejoinder was quick and obvious:

"Did your grandfather remarry?" I realized now that his conversational focus — or line of questioning — was narrowing and seemed to be
a deliberate and specific form of inquiry. I felt uncomfortable and started
to look around the room to see whether I might espy someone who
could rescue me by asking me for a dance. Emil must have caught my
glance, because he stood up, bowed slightly and said, "If you will excuse
me for a moment, I just saw someone I need to speak with."

One of the younger members of the U.S. State Department who
had been invited to the reception came over to me and asked me to
dance. I immediately told him about my conversation with Emil, since
the whole department obviously knew the full story.

"Naturally they know that your father's stepmother was Russian,"
he said, "but I suspect he wanted to know whether you, as a member of
the family, have more information about her than they do."

"Do you think her origins had anything to do with my father's disappearance?" I asked him suddenly.

He looked at me curiously now, and I thought he was rather slow in
shaking his head. "I don't really see how she could have had anything to
do with it. After all, she died before your father was assigned to Moscow."

"But that needn't have been the end of her influence," I replied.
"She may somehow have led to something we're totally unaware of."

"I don't think so," he responded. "Even though she came to this
country as a refugee from the Soviets, she was completely Americanized
by the time she died. I can't believe that her influence would have extended to Moscow or anywhere else in Russia after all those years. In fact,
the opposite is more likely: she would have been what the Soviets themselves refer to as a 'former person' — one of the bourgeoisie who for all
ideological purposes has ceased to count, or even to exist."

That made me resolve to press Mother for further information
about Father's stepmother, since all I knew was what Mother had told me
recently, which had ended with Maria's life up to the time of the
Bolshevik Revolution. I knew that Father was absolutely devoted to her;
he had said this to me, and he had even hinted at the suffering from
which she had escaped. But I had few details and assumed, along with
Mother, that, in coming to America, Maria had fled from the horrors following the Bolshevik Revolution. Emil returned and we danced again,

but I had become impatient and wanted to leave the reception. I did dance with another member of the Soviet embassy and with one European ambassador before the time finally came that Mother and I could courteously depart.

When we got home, I surprised Mother, who was preparing to go to bed, by asking her whether we could perhaps have something to drink together because there was a lot about Father's stepmother that she hadn't yet told me. She agreed, and we sat facing each other companionably as we sipped our cups of cocoa.

"Do we know exactly what happened to Maria after the Revolution and before she came to America?" I asked.

"No," she said, "as I've told you, there was the starvation, typhus, civil war, the cold. I don't know the specific details any more than anyone does — other than Maria, of course. She put all that behind her when she came to America. It's true that she supported Russian immigrant groups. But as far as the family was concerned — at least as far as I gathered from your father — she threw herself into being the busy wife of a doctor and the loving stepmother of a young boy."

"Did she leave notes or a diary or memoirs?" I asked, somewhat desperately.

Mother laughed. "She wasn't that kind of person. She had been a nurse and, I suppose you could say, had picked up some scientific knowledge and was used to medical notations. But she certainly wasn't a literary kind of person. No, she left nothing of that kind that I know of."

"Do you think she told Grandpa — or even Father — about things we don't know about?"

"It's possible," said Mother, looking puzzled. "Something upsetting you? What started this off — something Emil said?"

I was silent for a moment. "He was certainly rather pointed in asking about her," I said finally. "He seemed to know more about her background than we do — almost as much as Grandpa and Father did."

Mother refilled my cup. "Don't forget, your father was very young when your grandfather married Maria. He would not have been in the least interested in the events of Soviet Russia or anything else outside his own immediate world at that age."

I was still puzzled. This sudden interest in Maria in itself bore no immediate or obvious significance. But from what I had heard, everything about her life in Russia seemed to have ended with the Revolution. This had been the case with most immigrants: they had been faced with the problems of how to escape, legally or illegally. When she came into my grandfather's life, and more importantly during my father's younger years, everything had to have been fresh in her mind. I desperately wished that I had asked Father more about her when he was around. And then, of course, I wished even more desperately that he would somehow reappear — and that I could see him again.

The idea, absurd as it now sounds, was gradually formulating in my mind of undertaking my own search for my father, though I didn't for the moment consider or even guess what that would involve. Both Mother and I were still waking up every day with hopes that somehow he would reappear, that the news would come through that he had been found. Though those hopes were gradually diminishing, we had not given up hope altogether. It was only that we knew the silence was almost as bad as the sightings that had proved to be false.

"I've got some thinking to do," I said to Mother, and she nodded.

"Yes, of course, dear, but please, please don't let this business worry you more than it has to. Try to get some sleep, and at least put tonight out of your mind."

That evening, for the first time, Emil had asked whether he could see me again, that is, away from my mother and such public occasions as the embassy reception. Perhaps we could go to the movies together, he'd said. I lay awake wondering whether to accept the invitation, or at least to offer to accept it. In the long run, it was up to the State Department, of course, which still ruled everything I did.

The following morning I had made up my mind, and I told Mother at breakfast that I would accept Emil's invitation — if the Department approved. She realized that there was no stopping me and, though unhappy about my decision, she reluctantly agreed. But the State Department was adamant that the daughter of the U.S. diplomat who had disappeared in Moscow should certainly not be seen at a theater alone with a member of the Soviet embassy. And if the press were to get wind of it, they told me, it would be a public relations disaster. I had to admit that they were right, and I had to call Emil to tell him that the decision was negative and was out of my hands.

But what other lead could I follow up? I asked my mother about any surviving relatives of Harry Winthrop — brothers, sisters, sons, daughters, nephews, nieces, anyone I could think of. His family was unusually small for those times: Grandfather almost seemed to have grown up alone. I asked Mother about the town where he had practiced medicine in Vermont. She agreed that there might be people living there who would remember him, who might even remember my father. But it was not long after his remarriage that Grandfather had moved to New York, in an effort, no doubt, to start a new life for himself and his new wife. In any case, it was hardly likely that the townsfolk of a small town in Vermont would know the kind of intimate details I was searching for, and I certainly could not see myself searching through the changing neighborhoods of New York in such a pursuit.

Then Mother remembered. "Your grandfather did have a cousin who lived in Chicago; I remember Henry saying that he met him once when he was young." Fortunately, he had the same surname as Grandpa Harry and we did — Winthrop — and that sent me scurrying for an up-to-date Chicago telephone directory, which I knew we had in the house as part of my father's State Department material. I searched for the Winthrop name and found five of them, which I scribbled, along with their numbers, on a piece of paper. For some reason I didn't want to make these phone calls in front of Mother; but she failed to understand my desire for privacy.

"I don't think you need to do this," she said. "Of course, I hope you find something, but what we really need to know is the present whereabouts of your father — if he is still alive. Can't you think of anything we can do in that direction?"

In spite of the look in her sad eyes, I went up to my room and was about to dial the first number when the phone began ringing on its own. I assumed, correctly, that the call would be for Mother, and I resisted the impulse to listen in. Soon I heard her hang up the phone and call out to me urgently:

"Come down, Lorina . . . your father . . . he's been found!"

I ran downstairs to find Mother standing in the den looking confused, elated, and anxious all at the same time.

"Where is he — how is he?" I demanded.

"The curious thing is that Emil and Edward Wilson — that's the young man from our State Department you were dancing with last night — are coming here together to tell me. I don't understand why one or the other couldn't have told me on the phone, or why both of them need to come here at the same time. All Edward would tell me was that Henry was found — and that they would be here in a couple of minutes."

We stood looking at each other in astonishment at this development, hopeful that it was completely good news. But obviously neither of us could guess, and we were basically in a state of shock. It was, indeed, only a matter of minutes before Emil and Edward arrived in the same car; when they came into the house, they looked at each other and hesitated as to which one should speak first. Then Emil said, "He is now in General Hospital Number 5 in Moscow."

"Is he ill?" Mother immediately asked.

"He is alive and as well as the circumstances allow," said Emil. "We think he has something wrong with his heart."

"But how did he get there?" I asked.

"That," said Edward, "is what we do not understand. As soon as medical checks have been made on him in Moscow, he will be flown back here to Washington. All regulations have been cleared, and a plane is standing by."

Mother gestured for us all to sit down. She and I sank back in our chairs — relieved, worried, and still completely confused by this development. Emil turned toward Mother.

"I can assure you we are doing absolutely everything we can to look after your husband. He is getting the best treatment that we can give him, and we will bring in any doctor that you wish to send. I came here with Edward because it was in Moscow that he was found. But of course as soon as he is ready to travel he will be completely in the hands of U.S. authorities." Emil stood up. "I don't believe I have anything more to add, and so perhaps you will permit me to leave. We felt that we should be united in giving you this news."

We thanked him warmly, and I accompanied him to the door.

"Thank you, Emil," I said. "It was kind of you to come with Edward, and I'm sorry we can't go to the movies. But thanks very much, and please see that they do all they can."

"Of course, we will," he responded, and with that he departed. I watched him walk quickly down the street, leaving behind the car I presumed the State Department had supplied, and which Edward would take later. When I returned to the den, I heard Mother repeating the question:

"How is he, really?"

Edward shook his head. "We know absolutely nothing. From what we do know at this moment, there is clearly something wrong with his heart. Otherwise, he appears well. He is unmarked and unbruised. . . ." He slowed on those words. "In all respects, I wish to God I could tell you more, but we are frankly as much in the dark as Emil is."

"His father had a weak heart," Mother mused aloud. "In fact, he died at the relatively young age of fifty-seven. But I never knew of any trace of such a condition in Henry; in fact, as you know, he served in the Navy during the war. Now that was some time ago, of course, but anything would certainly have been discovered since then, because he took good care of himself."

"I simply don't know," Edward repeated. "I sure wish I did."

We knew now that we could only wait, and I asked how long it was likely to be before we saw him.

"Not very long," he said. "The plane standing by has doctors on it and will probably fly, with a break somewhere such as Frankfurt, across the Atlantic and directly here to Washington — probably the naval hospital at Bethesda."

Edward shifted nervously in his chair. By now he clearly felt that he should leave; at the same time, he did not want to leave us alone, and he asked whether there was anything further we needed to know.

"Only when he will be back," said Mother, "and you have already told us that." Her tone was exasperated, almost one of irritation — not so much directed at Edward as at the circumstances that had thrown us once again into a state of doubt and suspended animation.

"You mean back in the service again?" Edward's weak joke served to relax the sudden tension that had arisen between us. "He'll be in the hospital, but of course you'll be able to visit him immediately. I hope we'll soon find out what happened in the months between his disappearance and this sudden reappearance in a general hospital in Moscow."

Edward, who knew nothing more, saw that the moment had come for him to leave.

"You have my number — and my extension. All you have to do is call me. For the time being, you will see nothing in the press about this. Both of us, the U.S. and the Soviets, really must sort things out before any announcement is made" — he added softly — "if it is made at all."

After he left, we stood looking at each other incredulously. Then I joined Mother on the sofa, put my arms around her, and we sat sobbing together. This extraordinary discovery was almost more than we could bear after all the months of waiting. We sat there, close together, for some time, silently holding each other's hands. Neither of us had an answer for anything the other might ask.

CHAPTER FOUR

Moscow, 1960

It was only a short time later that the phone rang again, and it was Edward again. He had just gotten back to his office.

"Your father is leaving Moscow in one hour's time," he said, "and he wants you and your mother to know that he'll be home soon. I warned you that they want to check him at the military hospital in Frankfurt before he comes across the Atlantic. So I'll be able to let you know more when he has reached Frankfurt. I know that Emil wants to call you again, but I assured him that I've spoken to you. I'm grateful to him for giving us this news, but for the moment at least, I think it will be only the State Department that contacts you." After I thanked him, he added quietly: "Are you sure there's nothing else we can do? Can we send someone over?"

"No, thank you," I replied. We hadn't wanted anyone else around the house with questions they didn't dare ask and we didn't have answers to. When I hung up, Mother and I sat in silence for a while, and then we went into the kitchen and made ourselves a cold meal, which we ate quickly before going upstairs to bed.

The next morning, the call we hoped would inform us that Father was back in the United States came at about ten o'clock, this time from the hospital. No doubt Edward had requested that they call us immediately. They assured Mother that Father was as well as they could reasonably expect, that they were sure there was no immediate danger to him. When she asked how soon we could visit him, she was told that he had to be debriefed by the State Department, and they asked that we delay our visit until the following morning. Mother called again in the afternoon and was told that he was doing reasonably well but was sleeping now, and it would certainly be better if we did not disturb him until the following day.

Although we had been warned not to call anyone about Father's reappearance, I did call up Kate under the strict promise of secrecy. I wanted her to share in our knowledge because she had been in Moscow with us when Father disappeared. I could see that Mother was also desperate for someone she could talk to about it. She called the State Department to talk with Edward again, but he was not at his desk and they did not know when he would return. At one point I almost called Emil at the Soviet embassy, but then decided that it would be unwise. With all the secrecy and conspiratorial attention concentrated on Father's disappearance and reappearance, I thought that perhaps our telephone wires could be tapped. That day was a waiting game, and we scrounged around for what little food we had in the house.

An early phone call woke us up the following morning: a considerate nurse at the hospital was eager to shorten our anxiety as much as possible.

"You can come and see him this morning," she said. "But please don't expect to stay long." She was obviously limited in the amount of information she could give us. Mother thanked her, and after a fast breakfast we took a cab to the naval hospital. When we arrived at the reception desk, a young doctor came down to escort us to Father's room.

"Please don't stay long," he advised us, and then added in a cautionary voice, "And please don't be too surprised by his appearance."

Father was not thin or even gaunt, but his face was terribly strained and his eyes looked almost deadened — though they lit up when he saw us. There was a nick or two on his face where a hospital orderly had attempted to shave him before we arrived, and I thought that it would have been better if they had used an electric razor. As Mother bent over to embrace him, the only words I could actually hear were "I'm sorry," and then he was silent as she held him as close as she could to herself. I went to the other side of his bed and laid my face against his; but he said nothing, and I could tell that he was exhausted. But he raised his dull eyes to me and whispered, "You want to know where I was, don't you?"

I nodded and whispered fiercely, "Yes, very much."

"I want to tell you . . . but I'm so weak I can hardly talk. . . ."

The young doctor, who had been hovering in the background, stepped forward.

"I'm afraid you can't stay long," he repeated as we settled by Father's bedside and looked at him. We didn't ask any questions ourselves, only indicating that we were healthy and very happy that the ordeal was over. Toward the end he said "I'm sorry" once more, and we could see that it was all a terrible effort for him. The young doctor came forward, and we both immediately stood up and leaned over to kiss Father good-bye — both of us repeating that we would come back as soon as we could.

In the corridor outside we met Edward, who looked more somber than I had ever seen him before.

"I have spoken to the doctors," he said to Mother, "and we feel that it would be best if you left Henry here for a while before you see him again — not long, mind you, just a few days, say. Then he will be able to come home. In the meantime, we'll help you get the nursing help you'll need and make all the necessary arrangements."

Mother and I were overwhelmed and somewhat confused by the condition Father appeared to be in. So we merely nodded in agreement and were driven home in silence, each in our own turmoil of thoughts. We did not, in fact, visit Father again in the hospital. But we did make the arrangements the doctors called for, and he was brought home to us after a few days in the hospital. But before that, Edward, who was eager to allay our terrible curiosity, paid us a visit and told us what the State Department had learned from Father.

It appeared that, on the evening of his disappearance, he had left the embassy at the usual time and was walking home when, as he passed one of the huge Moscow apartment complexes that had been constructed in the 1930s, he was suddenly struck by a terrible pain in his chest and an impending sense of doom. Scarcely able to keep his balance, he stumbled into one of the doorways of the housing complex and lurched toward what he took to be an open door. In fact, it was an elevator with its gates drawn back, with a resident about to emerge. He collapsed across the entrance, and as the gates began to close and press on his legs, the occupant, a woman, pulled him onto the elevator, with the gates quickly closing behind him. They ascended to what he later learned was the fourth floor of the building, and the woman dragged him out of the elevator and into one of the apartments, which consisted of two very small rooms. He remembered being heaved up onto a sofa, at which point he lost consciousness. When he came to — he had no idea how long afterward — he saw the woman leaning over him, a look of horror on her face.

Within a day or two he learned the reason for her horrified expression. In recovering consciousness, he had apparently murmured some words in English, and those words had caused her consternation, which was to govern his life for his months of captivity. The woman who saved him, whom he knew only as Felina, had worked for a very short time during World War II at the British embassy in Moscow; now she shared a tiny apartment with her widowed sister-in-law, whose husband had been a chauffeur at the American embassy during the war. After the war, Stalin had initiated a wave of terror to obliterate all Western influences on Russian citizens, particularly those who had had any contact with the West. The NKVD had reached down to the very bottom of the list in rooting out these "dangerous" Soviet citizens, and Felina's brother had been arrested, sent to a labor camp in Siberia and, as they both subsequently learned, shot on some trifling pretext. Felina and her sister-in-law now faced the terrible dilemma of having a sick American in their apartment. For some years, since the end of the war, Felina herself had lived with the fear that her record at the British embassy would be used against her. Now Henry's falling into her lap was a nightmare beyond her wildest fears.

From the beginning, it appeared, the two women looked after Henry with such rough, amateurish nursing as they could think of, totally ignorant of what could be wrong with him. He could scarcely move around the apartment, and they were certainly not going to allow him out of it. They were terrified that news of his presence would somehow reach their neighbors. On the other hand, he lived in terror himself — of being imprisoned indefinitely by these two women — though his mind was clear enough to understand their terrible fears. On one occasion they contemplated trying to move him out to the country, to the dacha of a friend, and they sought someone they could involve in the plan. This he encouraged, desperately hoping that he would then have a means of escape, though his state of health was such that he could scarcely move away from them no matter where they were.

On another occasion Felina, through a friend, managed to get a Soviet doctor to come to see him — under an oath of absolute secrecy. The physician took one look at Henry, shook his head, and murmured that he should be in the hospital. He then fled the apartment, desperate to avoid being involved in this "plot."

Stalin had been dead for about seven years, and the current leader of the party, Nikita Krushchev, had already revealed to party delegates in closed session Stalin's tyranny and had denounced Stalin in his own campaign of de-Stalinization. But this was not the general sentiment throughout the country, and it certainly had not reached Felina and her sister-in-law; even if it had, it would not have been sufficient to convince them of their own safety. At times Father was seized by delusions, unable to distinguish between his nightmares and the nightmare of his existence. On one occasion, he thought he heard an American voice. He became convinced of it, and he attempted to croak out some kind of response; but he was immediately silenced by Felina. In order to eke out an existence for themselves and him from their limited food, one or the other of the women traveled to the peasant markets on the outskirts of Moscow to buy vegetables and sometimes a little meat. (Although the nutrition in his diet was scarcely adequate, he was never near starvation.) But there was always one of the sisters in the apartment, and though they did not watch over him night and day, he was really never alone.

The doctor who had fleetingly visited him had mumbled something about a heart condition, but Henry was no more aware of what was wrong with him than the two women were. All he knew was that he suffered from an overwhelming weakness, which left him unable to move most of the time. Occasionally, with their support, he would stumble for a few steps around the apartment. His only way of telling the passage of time was to observe the lengthening of the daylight, and eventually he saw the leaves forming on trees outside his window pane. He learned that the Soviet security police paid occasional visits to the apartments, not so much as searches but merely to pick up one or another of the residents they wanted for questioning. Those occasions were enough to induce a sense of terror in the women. On one occasion they covered him with sheets and blankets to make it appear that there was no one else in the room.

The strain of hiding him was now clearly taking its toll on the two women, and they at last, reluctantly, took into their confidence another widow who lived in the apartment complex. Her husband had been a junior officer with the Soviet forces that met up with the Americans at Tolgare, when the two fronts came together toward the end of World War II. As a consequence, he had come under the abiding suspicion of the security police; they eventually dispatched him to a labor camp, and he was never heard from again. His widow — because that was almost certainly what she had become — naturally had an abiding hatred of Stalin. She was somewhat younger than the two women guarding Henry, and though she understood the terror of Felina and her sister-in-law, she realized that their situation could not last indefinitely, nor was she entirely convinced that it had to.

The plan they finally hatched involved taking Henry by some means or other to an area close to one of Moscow's hospitals and leaving him there for a passerby to find and report to the hospital. The plan was for the third widow to ask a taxi driver she knew whether he would help some neighbors of hers with a sick friend who needed to be transported to another apartment that was conveniently situated near the hospital. Henry, whose appearance and clothes in no way distinguished him from any other Russian citizen, was told to be absolutely quiet throughout these proceedings. Late one evening, the taxi drew up in front of the apartment, and the three women took turns supporting Henry from the building to the taxi. The driver was evidently curious about why he was not being taken directly to the hospital, but Felina had concocted a story: she explained that it was the hospital itself that wanted him nearby, and the sisters had fortunately located an apartment temporarily vacated by a friend who was visiting relatives in the Ukraine.

Henry had no way of knowing which direction the taxi went or how far they traveled. All he knew was that, when the vehicle stopped, he was assisted out of it by two of the women while Felina paid the driver. They all waited until the taxi had turned the corner, and then Felina turned back to the three huddled on the pavement. Between them they staggered along for what seemed an incredible distance to Henry, but was probably only a few yards when — with the utmost tenderness and, in Felina's case, tears streaming down her face — they lowered him so that he lay on the pavement, well away from the gutter but near enough to a streetlight for any passerby to see him. With a final good-bye, they hurriedly left him; the last thing he heard was their footsteps disappearing down the street. He did not know how long he lay there — not very long, he felt — and at least two or three passersby stepped into the gutter to avoid him. But at last someone paused and stooped over him.

"Tovarishch," she said, "are you ill?"

"Yes, please get me to the hospital," he immediately replied in Russian. "Please, please," he begged, "I am very ill."

The woman disappeared, and he thought that she had left him alto-

gether. But soon she returned with two men who were obviously orderlies from the hospital. They were carrying a stretcher, and they lifted him
onto it and carried him to the hospital. For the moment he didn't know
whether he should speak in Russian or English; but then he realized that
the sooner he announced his nationality the better. Though the orderlies
did not understand English, when one of them seized on the word
"American," he quickly left to seek further assistance. He returned with a
man Henry took to be a doctor: he was wearing a dirty white coat but
had a stethoscope suspended from his neck.

"I'm an American," Henry repeated. "I'm an American and I'm
very ill."

The doctor appeared to understand that, and he spoke rapidly to
the two orderlies; they remained at Henry's side while the doctor disappeared. The doctor's immediate reaction, he learned, was to call the police: shortly thereafter, three plainclothesmen arrived, one of whom
spoke reasonable English and was clearly senior to the others.

"You say you are American?" he asked Henry.

"Yes, yes," Henry repeated wearily, now beginning to tire dramatically. "I come from the U.S. embassy . . . they know about me there.
Please, get in touch with them as quickly as you can."

The three policemen had a quick conversation out of his hearing,
and then the senior one disappeared, feeling the need to call the Soviet
Foreign Commissariat, which in turn phoned the U.S. embassy. The duty
officer who took the message was aware of the unexplained disappearance of Henry Winthrop, and he called the senior officer without hesitation. Henry's photograph had been shown to every incoming member of
the embassy, and full details of his disappearance had been circulated to
new arrivals and kept up to date.

Eventually, a senior secretary from the U.S. embassy appeared at
the hospital. When he immediately recognized Henry, he bent down and
whispered quickly and fiercely, "Don't worry now, you're safe." The secretary disappeared with the doctor, but another officer, whom he had
brought with him from the embassy, now stood by Henry and gave him
continuing assurances of his safety. After a short time, the senior secretary reappeared and spoke once again to Henry and the Soviet embassy
official.

"We obviously can't move Henry in his present condition without
full preparations to fly him home. So I have arranged for him to stay here

overnight and for as long as it takes for Washington to make the necessary arrangements. A plane will be standing by for him, so I don't think those arrangements will take long. Perhaps, Henry, we will be able to get you into our hands a bit sooner than that."

He must have seen the look of fear that involuntarily crossed Henry's face, because he put his hand on his shoulder and said, "Don't worry, I will leave someone here with you for as long as you stay in this hospital, which I pray to God will be as short as possible." He lingered for a moment at Henry's side, gripped his shoulder again, and said, "You're all right . . . it's going to be all right. Just bear with us a little while longer, we won't waste a moment."

*   *   *

The rest, of course, we already knew. The American doctor who visited Henry in Moscow was a cardiologist, and after a relatively short time, he transferred him to the waiting U.S. Air Force plane, which was medically equipped and had been flown in from Frankfurt. The cardiologist accompanied him back to Washington after further tests had been conducted at the base in Frankfurt. Henry then told his story to the State Department and CIA personnel during his stay in Bethesda. Because of his complete exhaustion, the authorities felt that he should be guarded from all outside concerns until he was eventually brought home. With the cooperation of the hospital, we arranged for a room to be prepared and for nurses to look after him around the clock once he got home.

We heard nothing further from Emil Segalov, nor did we expect to. We guessed that an intense diplomatic activity had taken place just before Father's return from Moscow; we were informed that the State Department had been surprised at the ease and speed with which the Soviet Foreign Office Commissariat had accepted his identity when he miraculously appeared at the Moscow hospital. Though they were always suspicious of strangers and hostile to foreigners, in his case they had not assumed that he was a dissident trying to escape.

While we were waiting for Father to come home, we received another visit — this time not from the State Department but from a CIA agent. He asked us whether we would consider the possibility of their taking Father into hiding so that no word of his return to the United States would get out to the press. The agent was clearly testing the water for our reactions, and Mother and I were appalled at the suggestion. We began to feel as though we were in a fight for Father and that, unless we dug in our heels, we had little or no chance of living with him in any semblance of an ordinary household. We flatly refused the suggestion and pointed out that — as must have been obvious to the CIA and any other agencies involved in this affair — the Soviets, at the very least, knew what had happened, and that already one of the more inquisitive investigative journalists had linked the as-yet-unnamed sick member returning from the U.S. embassy in Moscow with the name Henry Winthrop.

To our relief, the agent dropped the suggestion. Right after he left, we called Edward Wilson at the State Department to demand that the request be formally withdrawn; but we learned that Edward had been taken off the case. Upset by this unexpected development, we grabbed a taxi to the State Department and demanded to see the Secretary of State himself. We failed in this, of course, but at least we were assured that Father would be returned home so that we could care for him during what now appeared to be the relatively little time he had left.

It was not until he was safely ensconced in our house, with a nurse in attendance and a cardiologist examining him regularly, that our fear abated to some degree. But Father's reappearance at home also posed a problem, because it was now clear that some parties had connected his reappearance with the earlier disappearance. The sensation caused by his disappearance more than six months earlier had by now faded from the headlines; but his reappearance had leaked out to a few people, which is probably why the CIA requested that he assume a new identity and disappear altogether. That was the best interpretation we could make of it. Naturally, the Soviets were not eager to give prominence to any report that suggested a reign of terror in their country, even if it was the memory of Stalin's terror; and the State Department, in turn, was embarrassed by what seemed to have been one of their own men disappearing into thin air under their very noses.

Thus we received all the assistance we needed in resisting the press, and not one journalist was allowed to enter our house. The State Department did issue a statement to the press, after considerable deliberation, giving the unadorned facts of Father's case — which were certainly incontrovertible by either the Soviets or the Americans. Once they issued that statement, the pressure from journalists diminished. Even so, the

Department guarded us against them and controlled all our incoming calls. We could only hope that the interest would die down or that some other event would divert the attention of the media.

In the meantime, Father got good nursing care at home, and we watched him regain a certain measure of his strength. Essentially, he was suffering from a cardiological condition, a heart muscle enlargement, that was incurable at that time; he could only be offered palliatives to alleviate his weakness and exhaustion. Mother and I sat by his bed and talked to him when he had the strength to talk; we listened and followed him through whatever subjects he chose to bring up. Sometimes they were trivial domestic matters, some aspects of the running of the house, and we managed to smooth those over as well as we could. The State Department had provided us with a tape recorder in case anything relevant to their investigation might come up. But our chats with him were really the bedside conversations of a father with his wife and daughter, and we did not bother to turn the machine on.

To some extent, Father seemed to think he had betrayed us by what had happened in Moscow; we tried repeatedly to convince him that that wasn't true and that neither of us felt it was his or anyone else's fault. We had occasional visits from representatives of the State Department, but we saw nothing of Edward. Why he had been removed from Father's case was a mystery to us. We heard no more from the Soviets, and media interest in the case declined.

Then one afternoon, Father seemed more animated and restless than usual. Mother asked him whether he wanted her to call the doctor, and one of the nurses came in suggesting a sedative. Father shook his head and said that it was only Mother and me that he wanted with him, and he seemed to feel an urgency to tell us what was now preying on his mind. Apparently he had been thinking of his early years, and of his stepmother, which brought to his mind the time his stepmother spent in Russia prior to her arrival in Maine. Since I only knew about Maria's life up to the Bolshevik Revolution, what came next fascinated me.

CHAPTER FIVE

The beginning of the Revolution in March 1917 had not, of course, ended the war with Germany. There was still fighting all along the front, and the casualties that kept coming into the St. Petersburg hospital meant that Maria's nursing work was as taxing as ever. There was a movement, however, to take Russia out of the war; and it was clear that, once the fighting ceased, the hospital would no longer be needed and Maria's employment would come to an end. That would mean no income at all for her whole family. She had lost touch with her father-in-law, the retired general, and never heard from him again. He was no doubt among the millions who disappeared in the massacres and starvation that came with the Revolution and accelerated to a fever pitch during the civil war that followed. But when Lenin seized power in November 1917, he immediately instigated moves to bring the war with Germany to an end; in March 1918, the Treaty of Brest-Litovsk declared Russia's peace with the Germans.

Even with the end of the war, the worst did happen in Maria's family: her father was dismissed from the war ministry because he was bourgeois, and thus he lost his entitlement to any food rations. Maria herself was dismissed from her job at the hospital, leaving the family without money, food, or warmth. It was toward the end of the winter of 1918, but the temperature was still plunging well below freezing. Everyone in Petrograd was waiting desperately for the ice to melt on the Neva River, and for spring to bring both warmth and the possibility that perhaps grain might come to the city on the river in sufficient quantities to feed those who had no entitlement according to the Bolshevik conglomeration of orders. Those people were just barely existing on small bits of food illicitly given to them by friends and neighbors, and also by selling their possessions one by one in order to purchase goods on the black market, which in itself was an offense that could mean imprisonment or even death.

Those early months of 1918 were almost indescribable. Civil strife had broken out throughout the country. The White Army, made up of counter-revolutionaries, was determined to do all they could to advance on Petrograd and Moscow (the new Russian capital) in order to reinstate the Czar, or at least to throw out the Bolsheviks. Peace with the Germans had certainly not brought peace to Russia. One day, during the early months of that spring, a man who called himself a representative of the Red Army came to Maria's family's apartment and told her that, since she had been a nurse for the army, she was now being called on to resume her duties for the revolutionary forces. Giving her scarcely enough time to bundle a few clothes together, the soldier led her away and drove her to one of the hospitals that had previously served the imperial armies. He led her, without any kind of uniform or information, to what had previously been a reasonably organized ward but was now in utter chaos. The beds were overfilled, and many casualties lay on the floor. Harassed doctors, many of them without medical overalls, their clothes streaked and stained with blood, worked among the casualties. Maria was led up to one of these doctors, who was bending over a casualty and silently shaking his head.

"Here is Maria," the Red Army representative announced to him. "She will work with you now." With that he abruptly turned on his heel and left.

She crouched down next to the doctor, and he whispered to her, "There is no hope here!" As he straightened up, she stood up with him. "Do you have any qualifications?" he asked desperately.

"Yes," she replied, "I have been nursing since 1914. I only left the military hospital last December."

"Thank god," he said. "Anything is better than nothing." He smiled an apology. "I'm sorry . . . my name is Boris. There is little that either of us can do in the chaos you see all around you." He pulled Maria to one side and continued to whisper. "Are you one of them?" he asked, nodding toward the red star that had been plastered on the wall at the end of the ward.

"No," she said, taking a chance. "My husband was an army officer who was killed in the first weeks of 1914."

"I joined the army in 1916 when I qualified as a doctor," Boris said, "and I've never been released. The only good thing is that my parents live in Kiev, which is now occupied by the Germans, as you know — since they control the whole of the Ukraine. And your family?"

Maria began to tell him briefly about her parents, but their quick exchange was interrupted when they had to turn to the next casualty, who had fallen to the floor from a bed already occupied by two other victims. That's the way Maria's work began, and it continued like that night after night. Most nights she simply slept at the hospital, but occasionally she managed to escape home — only to find her parents in an increasingly emaciated and despondent condition. She smuggled hospital food to them when she could, but she was thereby risking her own life, and they tried to dissuade her from doing it. Sometimes Boris gave her some of his rations to take home to her parents. She was envious that his parents were in the Ukraine living safely under the Germans and wished that somehow she could arrange her own parents' escape; and yet she knew they had nowhere to go, and, in any case, their health meant it was out of the question.

With Boris she shared companionship and intimacy, but they both knew it could not be called love. It was as if they were huddled together against the forces of violence and evil. They could only struggle to cling to each other — emotionally and occasionally physically — desperately seeking to shield themselves from anything that threatened their own existence. From time to time doctors and nurses would be taken from the ward and, they presumed, shot for being guilty of counter-revolutionary activities. One night a rattle of gunfire startled them: some hostages were being shot up against the outside wall of the hospital.

The casualties brought into the hospital were, of course, solely from the Red Army; there were no White Army troops — no so-called bourgeois counter-revolutionaries — among them. The two sides were slaughtering each other indiscriminately. Occasionally the hospital admitted a czarist officer who had joined the Red Army and was considered trustworthy; yet he was treated with a kind of suspicious respect, and the staff knew that his family was being held hostage in case he proved to be a traitor.

Maria's concern about the plight of her parents grew when her mother came down with some unspecified illness that could only be attributed to malnutrition. Knowing that she could do nothing for them,

Maria became desperate. At one point she considered deserting the hospital and concealing herself at home so that she could care for them. But she realized that this would prove impossible because she would soon be found out and the whole family would be condemned to death. Each day she left home with a feeling of hopelessness, trudging through the frozen streets back to the hospital to plunge feverishly into the activities that never seemed to cease.

One day in the early fall of 1918, she was surprised to find a line of horse-drawn carts drawn up outside the hospital. She could see figures carrying boxes and equipment from the building and loading them into the carts. One or two motor ambulances were among them, and as she entered the building she asked one of the drivers what was happening.

"They are forming a unit up at the front," he said, brushing past her with a heavy box. She made her way to the ward, which was even more chaotic than it had been, looking desperately for Boris. She could not see him among the figures moving back and forth among the patients, who watched this new activity silently from their beds with dull, uncomprehending eyes. Suddenly Boris was at her side, silently grasping her hand.

"They are moving us up to the front," he said.

"I know," she said, "but what good will that do with the lack of equipment and drugs?"

"It may help a little. At least we will be nearer to where the casualties occur, and first aid on the spot will save more lives than bringing them here."

"Come on, hurry up!" a commissar shouted at them. Maria followed one of the men to a storeroom, where he piled equipment onto her arms and half-pushed her out of the room toward the horse-drawn carts at the hospital entrance. And she continued loading equipment, following orders to ignore the patients as they lay unattended on their beds. One moment she saw Boris leaning over a bed, but the next moment someone shouted at him to move away and get on with loading the equipment. The hospital, it appeared, would continue to exist, but, with most of the equipment and nearly all of the doctors and nurses transferred to the front, it would not be able to offer any services that would pass muster as a hospital in any civilized country.

At last she was told to climb over the tailgate of one of the motor ambulances, and the convoy moved off, bumping and rattling over roads that the freezing winter had left cracked and full of potholes. She prayed that Boris would be in the convoy somewhere. He was young and healthy, not one of the elderly doctors who had been pressed into service back in Petrograd. Yet, even though she had assumed he would be coming, there was a terrifying possibility that he had been left behind. Maria now realized with horror that she had become inextricably a part of the Red Army, fighting the White Army, which was advancing on Petrograd with a certain amount of success. She had been forced onto the wrong side and into supporting a campaign that was being waged against her own people. She could not imagine that she would be caring for any White Guards who would be captured by the Red Army units fighting in front of them. The Red Guards usually did not take prisoners, and if by some chance a wounded White Guard were taken, he would probably be executed or stabbed to death on his stretcher.

All of Maria's semi-radical and liberal thoughts for the future of Russia had evaporated. She realized that it was now a stark, merciless question of survival — no quarter taken and none given.

The immediate reason for moving the hospital forward was the threat to Petrograd posed by the White armies under the control of General Yudenich — with the support of the British fleet in the Bay of Finland. In the meantime, Joseph Stalin had been appointed to oversee the defense of Petrograd and to take charge of operations. His initial step was to seek to wipe out all so-called conspirators against the Red Army — "counter-revolutionaries" — in short, a summary execution of as many of the bourgeoisie as he could lay his hands on. Boris had told Maria some of the stories he had heard, stories of whole families taken out and shot on the merest suspicion of treason, or, more likely, the word of a neighbor. Those executioners were the people, and Stalin was the man, on whose side she was now arbitrarily and forcibly stuck. As her supply truck bumped along, she wondered desperately about any possibility of escaping to her own side. Her parents were still alive; but her mother was desperately ill, and Maria could not imagine that she could survive another year.

At last the convoy came to a halt, and Maria and others were pressed into assembling a makeshift camp that consisted largely of tents and a few huts. The motorized ambulances were also to be converted into "operating theaters" because the unit was far enough up toward the front line that they could not be used as mobile ambulances: casualties would be brought in on foot or, more likely, left to die where they fell. Suddenly Maria saw Boris working among the crowd of people and vehicles, and she felt — irrationally but with a rush of joy — that with him nearby, there was at least some hope of her retaining an element of sanity in this brutal life.

In the distance the steady booming of gunfire could be heard, and Maria was informed that it was the British Navy shelling the Red Army over the heads of the White Guards. There were some units on the islands in the Bay of Finland that had gone over to the counter-revolutionaries. Now, in addition to their hatred of the White Guards, the Red Guards also hated the British and the French, indeed the Americans and even the Japanese, all of whom had sent units to Russia in an attempt to dispossess Lenin and his Bolshevik supporters.

"If only we could get across to one of the islands, we might stand a chance of escaping this inferno," whispered Boris, who had managed to get to Maria's side and — as if guessing her thoughts — inclined his head toward the sound of the firing.

They both jumped as someone's scream rang out in the air. Boris moved to investigate it, but he was stopped by one of the Red Guards.

"It's only a spy among the nurses," he said, and left them to guess what horrible fate had been hers. He ordered Boris to get back to his work, and Maria returned to unpacking what medical equipment she had been able to bring with her. She had to stifle her impulse to burst into tears because she knew that any such sign of weakness would immediately bring her under suspicion as a sympathizer with the Whites.

Once they had erected the tents, they were allowed to sit down for a meal of the limited food they had brought with them. This gave Boris a chance to come back to Maria, and they sat silently exchanging their identical thoughts, but not daring to voice them. The booming from the British warships' bombardment continued, and the Red Guards scowled every time a gun thundered out.

"Damned British . . . damned English . . . damned British," they kept repeating. "They're the ones who've brought the White Guards so close to our city."

The meal was brought to an abrupt halt when casualties were carried into the tents in various stages of mutilation. Backed by the British guns, the White Guards had attacked, and the Reds were getting hit hard.

"See that one," said one of the Red Guards, pointing to a man whose cheek bone was bared of all flesh. "That's what the White Guards do to you if they capture you."

From what Maria could see, it was a classic flesh wound caused by shrapnel; she had seen enough of that throughout the war with Germany. Boris and she leaned over the man, and Boris asked him quietly how he had been wounded.

"Oh, a gun from the other side," he said, fainting as Boris did what he could to stitch his wound with the minimal amount of anaesthetic he was allowed to use.

As night fell, the bombardment ceased and they worked quickly and quietly among the casualties until, exhausted by a day that had started with packing the convoy and leaving Petrograd, they finally collapsed on the straw mattresses that had been provided as their beds. The following morning, a deputation arrived from Petrograd, sent by Stalin, whose authority in the defense of the city seemed largely to consist of exterminating counter-revolutionaries. Maria, who was standing at the flap of her casualty tent, momentarily gasping for fresh air as a relief from the putrid atmosphere inside, watched a group of men stalking between the tents. She saw them abruptly stop at one tent and go inside. Somehow she knew instinctively that it was the tent where Boris was working. Sure enough, within minutes two men dragged Boris out of the tent. He was protesting violently. Maria could not hear what they were saying, but she didn't have to guess what they were about to do. They took him to the edge of the encampment, stood him against a tree, and shot him.

Maria almost collapsed as she edged back into her own tent and sat for a moment, savagely biting her tongue and fighting against an explosion of grief that would have brought down the savagery of the Red Guards on her as a co-conspirator. For a few minutes she was left undisturbed, until she was suddenly prodded in the back with the butt of a rifle.

"Get on with your job," the guard said. "They have simply dug out another damned bourgeois trying to reinstate the old régime."

"What did he do?" she managed to ask, thinking it was probably unwise.

"They know who they are," the guard replied. "There is no need to find any particular action. Their motives are bad enough. This one obviously showed he was an enemy of the people. And what about you?" he asked suddenly. "You were a nurse throughout the war. Who were you nursing?"

"Who were we all nursing?" she said. "There was only one enemy then — the Germans."

He stood there confronting her, but he had the grace to smile.

"Yes," he said, "and now we kill each other. It's rather more difficult to guess who is an enemy and who is a friend. But you can tell a bourgeois pretty quickly, and they will tell you that they can guess who is a Bolshevik."

The conversation was palpably absurd and terrifying, and with a nod to him, Maria stood up and went across to one of the casualties who was crying out for her. As she held the tin cup to his lips, the image of Boris against the tree was all that she could see. She was certain that he would not have been crazy enough to have revealed his beliefs. It must have been some specific action, and she knew she would have to find out what had caused this sudden savage act. Boris was, after all, one of the very few doctors available at that location as the fighting continued. She waited until the evening meal and chose a moment as they were lining up for their food at the ration tent to ask one of the other nurses what had happened. According to the nurse, Boris had been tending one of the wounded when the interrogators reached him. One of them pulled him up for questioning in such a way that made Boris's scalpel slip, wounding the man even further. He had managed to keep quiet, but the interrogator accused him.

"So you are what the damned bourgeois call a doctor, killing your own side."

At that, Boris swore at him and turned on him with his fists doubled and his face contorted in fury. The words "murdering swine" rang out through the tent. By this time, all the occupants of the tent — nurses and those wounded who could rise up from their stretchers — were watching what was happening. For a moment it appeared as though the interrogators were about to seize Boris again, but they stepped back.

"Oh, let him get on with his work," one of them said. "He is almost the only doctor we've got here."

A quarrel then broke out among the interrogators themselves, and Boris returned to his patient. As he did so, however, the interrogator who had originally seized him appeared to push against him deliberately, so that once again his scalpel plunged further into the flesh of the patient.

The nurse who had been whispering to Maria abruptly moved forward to get her rations, and Maria heard no more about it. But it was not difficult to guess what must have followed. The bourgeois doctor had amply proved his counter-revolutionary behavior to warrant his summary execution.

With Boris dead, Maria seemed to have even less to live for, and for a time her determination to escape was sufficiently weakened that she simply endured the régime she was under. But the savagery of the conflict continued: the killing of prisoners, the occasional shooting of so-called counter-revolutionaries, the discovery of so-called spies. The whole horror of the civil war engulfed her. But her strength and determination gradually returned, and she realized that perhaps she could take advantage of the fact that the front had fluctuated considerably as the White Guards advanced from the Estonian frontier and then fell back again. She later learned that even the Estonians, who had regained their independence from Russia, were quarrelling with the White Guards. Their sole purpose was to establish their frontier as far forward as possible before the fighting ceased, because Estonia itself, once part of the great Russian Empire, was now supposedly a free country — free of imperial Russia and free of Bolshevism. The White Guards' objective was still Petrograd, the former capital, St. Petersburg. Lenin had now transferred the capital to Moscow because of the threat to Petrograd from enemy forces.

If Petrograd were to fall, the morale of the Reds would be greatly shaken, and Maria knew that they were determined to do everything possible to defend it. Maria had a sneaking temptation to fall back with the Red Guards to Petrograd; at least she would be near her parents. But her other emotion was that she had to flee and do all she could to save herself. The chaos of the front meant that her medical unit was constantly on the move: huts were quickly erected, and tents were just as quickly taken down and moved, with casualties often left to die in the fields by themselves. Maria debated with herself whether to take anyone else into her confidence. Though she knew that she could by now trust a great majority of the nurses, many of whom would be only too glad to flee, she felt that it would be safer if she kept her intentions to herself. Once she could sneak away into the surrounding forest, her disappearance would not be as readily noticed as that of two or more.

At last, early one morning, when the camp was being struck in haste because the White Guards had achieved a further advance, she slipped out of the tent where she was supposed to be stacking equipment and simply ran — ran from the outer edge of the camp into the mercifully close forest. She ran through the birch trees, deeper and deeper into the woods, aware only that she had to keep to one direction and not lose her sense of compass. She ran interminably, gasping and panting and weakened by lack of food and the long hours she had been working month after month. She stopped occasionally to gaze up at the sky, making sure that she was still running in the same direction. No one seemed to have followed her: there was no sound except her own crackling of branches and rustling of leaves as she ran between the trees.

When exhaustion finally overcame her, and she could run no more, she collapsed on the trunk of a birch tree and sat with her back against it. Her head drooped forward, but she resisted the impulse to fall asleep. She had to stay awake until she was sure she was free — across the Estonian border. So she rose to her feet as soon as she could, and ran on through the forest that was enveloping her — on and on toward sanctuary. When it was obvious that she had no alternative but to keep moving in the same direction, suddenly the trees thinned out and she found herself in an open field. She could hear voices, and she saw a farmhouse on the far side. Taking a chance, she stood up and waved; the man in the field waved back and came slowly toward her. She quickly told him where she had come from, and he told her that she was now across the border. He took her back to the farmhouse, which was no more than a primitive hut, thatched almost to the ground. Once inside, he handed her a bowl of milk and crouched on the ground opposite her, watching as she thirstily slurped it down. When she had finished it, she told him her story, more to relieve herself than to give him the information. She wanted to clear her mind, at least of the immediate impression of the dreadful days, weeks, months, and years that she had endured.

When she came to the end of her tale, he stood up.

"We must decide what you do now," he said in heavily accented Russian. "You can stay here for a few days and help us, but I'm afraid there is nothing we can offer you, and then you'll have to move on."

"I can try getting to Sweden," she said. "From there I will have to decide where to go. I do have relatives in America, and maybe I can find someone in Sweden who will help me get there."

"It's terrible for you," he said, nodding sympathetically. "I was in the Czar's army during the war. But the moment we heard about the Revolution, I came home. Now we have our freedom as a country of our own, and I have no wish to return to Russia."

He described the fighting against the Germans, the conditions in the army, and she saw that he, too, was all too eager to leave his past behind.

"It's strange that you are here," he said, "because the major attack against Petrograd is coming from the south through Gatchina and Tsarskoye Selo, but they have been thrown back." He shrugged, took the empty bowl from her, and went outside the hut, where she heard female voices joining his. He returned with his wife and three young children. Maria was tired — very tired — and they gave her a rug to lie on in a corner of the room. She slept for hours, through the rest of the day and through the night, indifferent to the noise of the family around her.

When she awoke and saw the family around her, she thought of her own mother and father back in Petrograd. She considered trying to go back to rescue them. But she knew there was no hope of succeeding; and once back in the city, she knew, she would be trapped. Instead, she tried to recall as much as she could about members of her family who had immigrated to the United States. But she could only recall with any clarity the one who had married an American man. She returned to her thoughts about how she might reach Sweden, wondering whether this family could pay her in any way for her helping them on the farm. But a glance around the room told her that they could afford nothing. She had to get to the nearest railway station, if there was one, and somehow get on a train that would cross the border into Sweden.

After a day of helping out with perfunctory tasks on the farm, Maria decided that it was time to depart. As the family gathered together in its one-room hut for the evening meal, sharing from a bowl of cooked vegetables, she stood up and formally thanked them for their hospitality. She told them of her resolve, and they nodded in agreement. The father offered to accompany her the next day as far as he could in the direction of the nearest railway station.

CHAPTER SIX

Part of my stepmother's story seemed sketchy even to me, Henry continued. I was never very clear on the details of how she got to Sweden and from there to the United States. It was her experiences in Russia that she was eager to describe to me, so she made light of that part of her journey. But she must have made it to Sweden and then to America, or she couldn't have met and married my father. I did learn that she managed to get on a train out of Estonia that got her close enough to cross the border into Sweden; once there, she contacted a refugee organization that, in turn, put her in touch with her relatives in America. And so she arrived in the United States in the spring of 1919, where she was, for a short time, supported by one the many charitable organizations that raised money for and provided for émigrés. But as soon as she learned a smattering of English, she looked for work — with the condition that it not be in nursing. Though that would have been the obvious source of employment for her, she later told me vehemently that she would never work as a nurse again. When she met my father, the doctor, she was actually working in a library, where her facility in Russian, French, and English stood her in good stead. But when she married my father and came to live with us in Vermont, she threw herself wholeheartedly into the role of housewife and mother. Later, when my father's experience and contacts were such that he moved his practice to New York, she adapted herself to the busier life of a city practice and a greater cultural life that the city offered her.

During all this time she maintained contact with various émigré groups and organizations, such as the one where she had met my father. Occasionally she had some of her Russian friends over to the house, and she always brought me in to meet them; as I grew older, I became involved in some of those conversations. While I was in grammar school in New York and then during my vacations from prep school, my stepmother was my constant companion. Together we would explore Central Park, the public library, the museums, and other fascinating parts of the city — often in the company of other émigrés from Russia and Eastern Europe.

This was the period when Russian grand dukes were driving taxis in Paris or presenting themselves as waiters in New York restaurants. At the same time, however, influential refugees were organizing continuing resistance to the Bolshevik regime; curiously enough, some antagonists of the Stalinist doctrines were represented by Trotsky and were now themselves refugees from the country where they had successfully brought about revolution. These latter were not a part of my stepmother's circle of friends and acquaintances; but she did follow the activities and tactics of the Bolsheviks closely, and she described to me Stalin's step-by-step grasping of power and his elimination of political enemies. And she told me in detail about the political trials and the terror he used to gain an iron control over her country. I, in turn, astonished schoolmates and teachers alike with my detailed knowledge of Russia's current affairs; and as I advanced in school, I found myself opposed and contradicted by those who took a rather more lenient — perhaps even liberal — view of what was happening in Russia. Naturally, my stepmother had nothing but scorn for the journalists and others who had any kind of tolerance for the Stalinist government, and I naturally was developing the same reaction myself.

My father seemed to tolerate a fairly steady stream of Russian refugees coming and going in our house, immersed as he was in his successful and expanding New York practice. One of those in particular stuck out in my memory: his name was Vladimir Stefansky, and he was a curious mixture — by Russian standards — of someone who seemed to be a member of the nobility and at the same time of the merchant class. He had fled the Crimea at the very end of the civil war, and had come to the United States, where he had investments in the sugar business; it had not taken him long to become established as a merchant and broker in sugar and other commodities. Though I wouldn't have known about it then, as I look back on it, he seemed to be developing close connections over the years with senior members of the Roosevelt administration, that is to say, the New Dealers in the Democrat Party. I do remember that, at our home, his conversations were a mixture of diatribes against Stalin and confident hopes that one day the régime would collapse, possibly under pressure from the United States.

When I went off to prep school, I only saw Stefansky — who seemed to be known by almost everyone as Vlad — on infrequent vacations from school. Naturally, I had other interests and occasionally stayed with school friends. But my life changed in May of 1939, near the end of my junior year at Yale, when I was suddenly summoned home with the news that my stepmother was seriously ill with septicemia. Unfortunately, I didn't get home in time; she died before I got off the train in New York. My father was, of course, devastated by my stepmother's death, and I spent most of that long summer vacation of 1939 as close to him as his medical practice would allow. Occasionally, some of Maria's relatives would visit us; but almost all of the Russian refugees fell away, probably because my stepmother had been the magnet and the focal point of the activities that drew them to our home. My father and I were pretty much left to grieve alone.

My senior year at Yale coincided with the outbreak of World War II in Europe. Though I shared the general revulsion that the nation felt for the Nazi régime, I could see no reason for America to become involved in the conflict. That situation changed, of course, with the fall of France: public opinion became clearly divided between those who realized that direct support of Great Britain was necessary for the defense of the United States and those who were America-first isolationists; the latter still thought that the United States could stand back from the European turmoil and retain its freedoms and its own way of life. Although my sentiments were not with theirs, I still felt that there was no reason to become fully involved in the conflict. My views at the time were not out of line with the majority of students at Yale.

But the German invasion of Russia in June 1941, at the end of my first year of graduate work, did alert me to the possible consequences of the hostilities in Europe. I found myself sharing the views of Senator Harry Truman of Missouri, who said that he would be happy to see both sides destroy each other. I certainly did not want Hitler to succeed, but at the same time I had been so indoctrinated by everything my stepmother had told me that my desire to see the collapse of the Soviet Union was far greater than that of my peers at Yale, of those who shared Truman's opinions, or even of most Americans.

Just a few months later, on December 7th, Pearl Harbor made the position of the United States decisive, and I immediately enlisted in the Navy. After my initial officer's training, I was granted a commission and assigned to the Navy yards at Norfolk, Virginia. While there, I found myself in a chance conversation with another "hostilities-only" man, who told me that the Navy was looking for Russian-speaking officers. After making a few inquiries, I got myself a preliminary interview in Norfolk; then I was flown up to Washington and questioned by a panel of two naval officers and a civilian about my knowledge both of the Russian language and of Russia itself. It was easy to satisfy them on my fluency in Russian, because my stepmother had done her work very well. And even though I was not as up to date as I might have been if she were still alive, I impressed them with my knowledge of Russian affairs. Because of the interest in all things Russian that she had instilled in me, I had kept myself abreast of the Soviet régime, and it was probably more that knowledge than my Russian language skills that convinced the board that I was the man they were looking for. For two years I worked in Washington, not always for the Navy itself; occasionally I was on loan to the State Department. It was in that dual role that I was sent, in the late summer of 1944, to the U.S. embassy in Moscow, whose chief ambassador was Averell Harriman.

The Americans in the Moscow embassy, as far as I could judge, were seen in a rather ambivalent light by the Russians. One moment they were welcomed as allies, as the providers of Lend-Lease equipment, and indeed as fellow human beings; the next moment they were as good as ostracized because the second front had not been opened and they were suspected of going after a separate peace with the Germans. In fact, some Soviets went as far as suspecting that ultimately the United States and its British allies would side with the Nazis in their attempted destruction of the Soviet Union. But on the whole I enjoyed life there. I went skiing on the outskirts of Moscow, visited the Bolshoi ballet and opera, and toured the city as much as I could. The ambassador did his best to make life tolerable for those working at the embassy, and there were occasionally gatherings of other Americans — diplomats, journalists, and the like — who had been assigned there. Then, after the massive invasion of Europe on D-day, Americans were genuinely welcomed in Moscow. Those of us at the embassy shared the great admiration the Russians felt for the vastness of the operation and its initial success.

Shortly after D-day, however, I was informed that my father had died — suddenly and unexpectedly — of heart failure. I was granted a leave, and I flew home to New York. The congregation at the funeral was a reflection of the sparseness of my father's family and friends. There was a sprinkling of patients and medical colleagues that I expected to see; but few appeared from my father's family, and there were none from my stepmother's side. Presumably, those American relatives of hers had either not heard of his death or, if they had, had chosen to ignore the funeral. Toward the end of the ceremony, a handful of those relatives did appear, apparently having lost their way in New York. They were the ones who had originally vouched for Maria when she fled from Russia to America in 1919.

On my way back to Moscow, it occurred to me that I might perhaps use the occasion to visit Leningrad in search of what might be left of my stepmother's relatives. But the occasion never materialized. The city was recovering from its terrible three-year siege, which had wiped out hundreds of thousands of its residents. I could not banish from my mind my stepmother's descriptions of life during the civil war and of her grief over leaving her parents starving and probably dying in what was then Petrograd. I wished that I could atone for her feeling of having abandoned them when she fled Russia. But I realized that it would be highly unlikely for me to ever find any trace of Maria's family — even if they had survived the civil war, the starvation, and the subsequent great terror. And I was again reminded of the clear class distinctions that had been the propulsive force of the Revolution and the civil war. I also realized that the one or two vague inquiries I'd made about those former members of the bourgeoisie had aroused nothing but suspicion among my opposite numbers in the Russian corps, and that could only cause problems for the American embassy. So, for my own sake and the embassy's, I decided to keep that interest to myself.

Life in the embassy had become increasingly hectic, and the last fling of the German army — when it struck for Antwerp and was held at the Battle of the Bulge — meant that it was necessary once more to turn to the Soviet Union for assistance. The Russians had promised to accelerate their advance into Germany to ease the pressure on their Anglo-American allies, and I found myself engrossed in my duties.

*   *   *

YALTA, 1945

For some months there had been a flurry of wires in our embassy between Roosevelt and Stalin, and between Churchill and Stalin, and then
from Stalin in return, as those three leaders made plans for a conference.
Churchill had traveled to Moscow himself before the end of 1944; but
that meeting had been indecisive because Roosevelt had instructed Ambassador Harriman to sit in on as many meetings as he could so that no
commitments would be made on behalf of the United States. Churchill
had agreed to this, much to the surprise of Stalin, who was curious to
know why the meeting had been arranged at all.

The Big Three conference, though, was slated to resolve as many
of the outstanding points as Roosevelt felt needed to be settled with the
Allies, and particularly with the Russians, on whom he appeared to base
his hopes. Roosevelt and Churchill made every effort to dissuade Stalin
from his insistence that the meeting be held in Russia. They suggested
Scotland, the Azores, and North Africa; after all, Roosevelt was a sick
man, had suffered from polio for most of his life, and the distance from
the United States to Russia was extreme. But Stalin insisted that his doctors would not allow him to travel outside Russia and that his presence
was required to direct the Russian armies (which were now advancing
deep into Europe). He added that the Crimea represented a convenient,
if not ideal, meeting place. He did not, of course, mention that he was
terrified of flying and was unwilling to repeat his experience of flying to
Tehran. But perhaps what counted most to him was the prestige of being
host in his own country to the other two powers, which in the past had
snubbed him and taken little, if any, account of the Soviet Union as a
power to be reckoned with in the world. By now his armies were su-
preme: they alone were fighting and suffering to an extent far exceeding
the participation of the British and American armies, who were just now
struggling through France and into Germany. After all, hadn't the West
asked for his help when Hitler, in his last fling, had thrown them into
such disarray in December 1944?

Yalta itself was the principal resort on the shores of the Black Sea: it
enjoyed a Mediterranean climate and a mild winter, and it had been the
favorite summer escape of the Czar and the pre-Revolutionary aristocracy. Following the Revolution, the Soviets had turned the royal family
palaces into sanitoria and rehabilitation units for the workers. But most

of these had been destroyed when the Germans, under Field Marshal von Manstein, cleared the peninsula and set up his headquarters in a villa just outside Yalta. The fighting had been savage on both sides, particularly in Sevastopol, which was the main port and noted for its role in the Crimean War. The determination with which it was first defended by the Soviets and then later occupied by the Germans was reflected in the destruction of the city, which by 1945 lay almost flat.

At the U.S. embassy in Moscow, the numbers and names of the personnel who would make up the American delegation were filtering through. I did not see myself as part of the American delegation; no one had mentioned the possibility to me. Then one day a wire arrived from President Roosevelt asking Harriman to ensure that there would be adequate interpreters and other Russian specialists at the conference, something for which the ambassador was already preparing. My knowledge of the language did make me a strong candidate, and one day I suddenly found myself listed among those who were to travel to Yalta. I was told that I would be involved in a mixture of tasks: translating documents, personal interpreting, and proofreading papers to ensure the exact meaning on translations already prepared. The instructions grew as the conference approached. I guessed that I was to be a general dogsbody, but with a Russian slant.

Roosevelt's main Russian adviser, Bohlen, also a fluent Russian speaker, would be attending the actual high-level meetings. But I certainly hoped that at some point I would be able to at least see the Big Three in action. I was excited by the proposition, though I now found myself in an anomalous posture: I was a very junior naval officer with a semi-departmental position in the State Department among service personnel older and more senior in rank, including State Department officials of some standing. But they put me at ease, and I realized that they were curious about my knowledge of Russian and of Russia itself. They would confront me with a variety of questions, some of which I was unable to answer and some of which I was even unable to understand why they had been asked.

One day at the embassy, I met with Ambassador Harriman himself. He took me into his office and told me that this was an extremely important conference, one that would probably decide the fate of Europe for at least the next fifty years. There were, as he saw it, two conflicting views: one was that peace could be maintained only with the agreement and the active cooperation — or even the joint surveillance — between the Russians and the Western Allies, predominantly the United States; the other was that the world had to learn to live with — and understand how to live with — the Soviet Union, yet guarding itself against its totalitarian view of life and its opposition to standards that were common among democratic nations. We had already had trouble over the provision of Lend-Lease material, and their cooperation in that strategic field had been absolutely nil.

Then the ambassador told me that I'd been promoted to the rank of lieutenant commander so that I would at least be able to rub shoulders with senior members of the delegation and not merely be treated as a humble "hostilities-only" hanger-on.

"Thank you, sir" was all I could manage to reply to Ambassador Harriman as he moved toward the door. I left the room bewildered by this sudden turn of events, but at the same time exhilarated at what seemed to be a development in my life in a direction that had been shaped in my early years by my stepmother. Here I was, in Russia on behalf of Maria, as it were, with a certain amount of authority to at least help in negotiations with the monster Stalin — as she had painted him during my formative years.

When I returned to my room, I again went through the list of those slated to attend the conference, especially those who were expected to come from the United States. Now, to my surprise, I came across a name I hadn't expected to see: Vladimir Stefansky, the Russian-American who had come to our home while I was growing up, and who apparently had organized many of the protest meetings and demonstrations against the Bolshevik régime since he had immigrated to the United States. I knew of his business-related connections with some in the Roosevelt administration; but I could not understand why he was included in this important conference. Was he coming as a businessman?

The decision to hold the conference at Yalta had been an almost last-minute one, and the ambassador's daughter, Kathleen Harriman, went down to Livadia Palace, just outside Yalta, to make sure that everything was in order for the reception of the President. When the ambassador joined her there, he said that the set-up looked extremely good: the Russians had worked hard to make the accommodations as suitable as possible. The various delegations were scheduled to be housed in the converted villas that had once been the Czars' palaces. The lines of communication from U.S. Navy vessels stationed offshore seemed to be perfectly adequate. And Harriman noted that the President had arrived safely in Malta aboard the warship *U.S.S. Quincy,* and reports indicated that he seemed to be in remarkably good spirits. This would later be contradicted when we learned that he had actually arrived almost exhausted, complaining that throughout the ten-day crossing of the Atlantic he had never been able to, as he put it, "achieve a satisfactory sleep-out."

As I lay in the sleeping berth that first night on the train down to the Crimea, I recalled once again my stepmother's descriptions of the behavior of the Red Guards, leading, of course, to the murder of Boris. I wondered how the democratic nations would be able to come to any kind of basic agreement with such a group of people. Although the wires from Washington were consistently optimistic about what would be achieved in this second face-to-face meeting between the President and the Soviet dictator, I knew that there was also strong — indeed growing — resentment among State Department and War Department officials in Washington concerning Roosevelt's trip to the Crimea, in fact, concerning meeting with the Soviets at all. It seemed to me that the overwhelming opinion was that the President should not go and that the Soviets could not be trusted one inch.

I arrived at Livadia Palace, where the U.S. delegation was to be housed: it had a glorious position about 150 feet above the sea, and there were fifty-two rooms in the palace itself, as well as two other buildings on the grounds. The U.S. State Department had certainly been provided with reasonable accommodations, and I was given a room of my own in which I was later joined by a roommate. The Russians were in Corice Palace, about six miles away, and the British were to be stationed another six miles further down the road at Vorontzov Palace, perhaps the most interesting of the palaces. The Soviets had cleverly stationed themselves between the Americans and the Brits.

It was about six o'clock on the evening of February 3rd that President Roosevelt reached Livadia Palace, having traveled by car up from Saki, where he had landed in the *Sacred Cow.* With him, in the cars following his, came the senior members of his delegation, including, of course, his daughter Anna. Activity in the palace became intense as he was settled in his quarters on the first floor, where he had the rooms originally occupied by the Czar; they were adjacent to the vast ballroom that was to serve as the conference hall for the main meeting. Senior members of

Roosevelt's staff were installed on the second floor, which had been the Czarina's quarters; and of course it became an open joke that General Marshall had settled into the Czarina's boudoir. I saw nothing of the President's arrival, but I knew that the Washington contingent had arrived because at about nine o'clock, after we had had a more than adequate meal, I almost stumbled on Vladimir Stefansky. Although I had not seen him for several years, I immediately recognized him passing me in the corridor.

"Vlad," I called out.

He stopped and turned with a look of curiosity, which then changed to one of astonishment.

"Henry," he said, coming toward me with outstretched hand. "What on earth are you doing here?" He looked me over in my naval uniform and said, "Well, I guess it's obvious you're part of the naval delegation."

"In a way," I replied cautiously. "I've actually come from the embassy in Moscow, to which I was assigned from Washington."

"So you are not sea-going?" His voice had a trace of sarcasm in it.

"No, I'm here because I speak Russian, I suppose. But you know very well the origins of that."

"I know," he said. "I will always respect — and I will miss — Maria, your wonderful mother. And I was very sorry to hear about your father's passing just a few weeks ago."

He took me by the arm to express his sympathy.

"Is there anywhere we can go and talk — of old times and how things have developed?" he asked.

"It's almost impossible here," I said, "we're so packed in."

But we did find a small room that was, for the moment at least, unoccupied. We sat facing each other, curiously, at a small table in the middle of the room, a room obviously set aside for meetings of a lesser kind.

"Done pretty well for themselves," he said, spreading his arms as if to embrace the whole of the palace, the whole of the Crimea, the whole of Russia. "When you think that they destroyed almost everything and then built the country up in their own image. . . ." Then he added bitterly: "And they've done it over mountains of corpses and rivers of blood. . . ."

I couldn't help but agree with him.

"You probably didn't know, by the way," he went on, "that I came out of Russia from here — the Crimea — in 1919. British destroyers took a lot of us out as the Bolsheviks were temporarily held back, including the Dowager Empress and the Czar's sister. We were taken to Constantinople, which the Allies had occupied since the collapse of the Ottoman Empire. And from there I was lucky enough to hop a ship to the United States on the strength of my American business connections."

"You were lucky indeed," I said, thinking of Maria and especially of Boris, who had never achieved such an escape. "You were very lucky."

"Oh, I know, and it hasn't changed my mind one iota about what I think of the whole present régime." He leaned forward, an earnest look coming over his face. "I don't know what sort of feeling you get in the embassy in Moscow, but I can tell you there are an awful lot of people in Washington who didn't want to come here at all. They hate the Russians and they hate Stalin, and they regard the whole set-up as frankly abhorrent. Come to think of it, they're pretty wary of Roosevelt, too."

"He is our commander-in-chief," I said, rather weakly. Stefansky nodded.

"I know all that. He's the commander-in-chief of all the forces. He's head of the country, but that doesn't mean he's up to dealing with this meeting. Have you seen him?"

"No," I replied. "He got here this evening, but went straight to his quarters. No doubt we'll see him in the next few days."

Stefansky shook his head gravely. "He's ill . . . terribly ill. I think he's really near death. Those who saw him giving his inaugural speech in January said he was shaking and trembling — almost dropping with exhaustion. How can he deal with people like Stalin? Not only that, he now seems to include Churchill, if not among his enemies, at least among his opponents, in his schemes."

"Who are you talking about . . . ?" I asked.

"Roosevelt," he said. "After all, he's all the Americans have in negotiating with Stalin. The chances of disabling Stalin have to be pretty remote, surrounded as he is by the security he's built around himself. If he has survived this long, it's not going to be easy to crack through his defenses."

The conversation had now taken a rather astonishing tone, I thought, and I could only sit for a moment and look at him with profound and somewhat shaken curiosity.

"What exactly are you driving at?" I asked.

He shrugged his shoulders. "Don't you remember anything Maria told you? Or any of what you must have learned from the other victims of the Revolution? Are you, too, a Stalin lover?"

"Don't be absurd," I said. "She was right — because she didn't have a theoretical argument. She told me about facts and events, and everything I've learned since then has confirmed what she told me, has verified her hatred of the whole system and indeed of its leader. We also have seen enough, by the way, in the embassy to have our share of doubts about the policy now coming out of Washington. But so what! What exactly are we going to do about it, except hope to God we can keep them from sweeping through Europe, reaching the Channel, and eventually achieving their long-term goal of conquering the capitalist world?"

Stefansky stood up and paced around the narrow room.

"Oh, we can achieve a lot," he said. "Stalin has his enemies within his own entourage. He may rule as a despot, but that doesn't mean there aren't those who wish to topple him and" — he added, looking away from me — "there are those among us who are willing to help them. He's done with his work, as far as we're concerned: he's beaten the Germans, and he's within forty miles of Berlin. But where the Soviets are at the end of the war is of vital importance."

I looked at my watch, if only to bring this conversation to an end, and to confirm that I had no more time for this conversation. Even as a small boy, I had guessed that Vlad was an intriguer and a conspirator. Children can somehow sense that, and now I had the sense that he was roaming around Livadia Palace, lurking in the background as these momentous meetings were taking place in the conference room on the first floor, cooking up some kind of plot.

"Well, I must go now," I said, standing up. "I'm sure I'll see you around the palace sometime." And I left the room without turning back.

That evening the President, exhausted by his air journey from Malta and the drive from the airport at Saki, ate quietly in his rooms with a few of his advisors. When they retired, we were left with a sheaf of papers to prepare for the actual start of the conference. It was to begin the following day, after Stalin's personal visit to Roosevelt, which would precede the formal proceedings. Stalin was cunning. We knew that, before meeting with Roosevelt, he would be paying a visit to Churchill, and we couldn't help wondering about his motives in jockeying between the

Prime Minister and the President — playing them off against each other. Though Churchill's loyalty to Roosevelt was never in question, Stalin seldom lost an opportunity to undermine — if not to downright insult — his Western allies.

The military delegates and civilians had a mess together, as well as a bank where we could exchange our dollars for rubles, on the second floor. After our first night of translating, I was forming a friendship with a member of the civilian group from Washington, Philip Goldsworthy, who was attached to the State Department. We both had a balanced view of affairs, I believed, though I didn't reveal to him my own personal antagonism toward Stalin and the Bolsheviks. Goldsworthy had what I would consider a traditional view: Be on your guard against the Soviets, but take from them what you can while you can, and hope that you get something in return.

The next morning Stalin arrived for his private meeting with Roosevelt accompanied by Foreign Minister Vyacheslav Molotov and his interpreter, a man who was — curiously and amusingly — named Pavlov. We wondered to what extent his master had conditioned him, and Philip suggested that he no doubt salivated over the best translations during the high-level meetings. We didn't see any of them, though the flurry of activity and security was reflected throughout the palace; but we did find ourselves bumping into various leading members of our delegation: General Marshall of the U.S. Army; Leahy, Roosevelt's chief of staff; Admiral King, head of the Navy; and the general who was standing in for General Arnold, commander of the Air Force.

The first plenary session of the leaders was convened at five o'clock in the afternoon. We had already prepared the papers, but I had been asked, along with other junior members of the delegation who could interpret, to stand by and be ready to receive any notices or documents that came back for immediate translation. They told us that we might even to be called into the conference room should one of the official interpreters need assistance.

When that first meeting ended in the early evening, we were released from duty. Philip and I went for a walk in the gardens, which descended dramatically to the sea down below. In the background were mountains covered with vineyards, cypresses, and tropical plants that had been gathered from all over the world during the previous century and planted there for the Czar's delectation. The weather was not as warm as we had anticipated, but the crisp air off the sea was a welcome contrast to the sometimes stifling atmosphere of the palace. Below us, in the harbor, two small American minesweepers were anchored; the principal support ship, the *Catactin,* was harbored off Sevastopol, along with two more naval vessels, some eighty miles away. Landlines carried messages to this ship, from which they were wired out via Radio Iran to Washington.

We understood that the British had a much quicker service: their Mosquito aircraft flew daily from London, carrying that day's newspapers along with all the official documents, of course. We envied them their up-to-date communications system. There were also, we understood, some Russian-speaking American naval officers on the support ship in Sevastopol whose role was to deal with local Russian contacts and to maintain the lines of communication. I hoped I could meet them and find out what role they played outside their naval duties, if any. I suspected that they were fully sea-going officers who had been chosen on the basis of their linguistic abilities.

President Roosevelt was giving a dinner that evening for Stalin and Churchill that was essentially American in character, though it was preceded by the ubiquitous caviar and accompanied by the inevitable toasts — one after the other. We later heard that Stalin spoke aggressively of the need for the smaller nations to be gagged if the three great powers were to rule the world effectively when the war was over. But Churchill spoke up on behalf of the smaller nations, and there appeared to be a certain amount of mumbling from Roosevelt. After he and Stalin had left the table, Churchill and Anthony Eden stayed to continue arguing the point.

CHAPTER SEVEN

From almost the day of his return from Moscow, Father had been in the same medical hands. A team of cardiologists had visited him, all of whom we respected and liked and whose judgment we were absolutely satisfied with. Thus we were not too upset when we heard that a new view of his situation and condition was proposed, which entailed a visit from a man we had not heard of before. However, we did notice that our regular cardiologist, who told us of this proposed visit, seemed uneasy, even unhappy, about this prospect — though he did nothing to oppose it. We asked him whether he could be at our house when the newcomer arrived, but he said that, unfortunately, his duties at the hospital prevented him from being there.

When the new cardiologist, Dr. John Berg, arrived, he was guarded and impersonal toward Mother and me, but we attributed that to his late arrival on the scene and the fact that he was entering an established routine that was new to him. He examined Father — somewhat superficially, we thought — and then announced in peremptory terms that he wanted Father back in the hospital for further tests. We asked what these tests might amount to, but he said that he could not go into detail: they were quite complicated and would be difficult for us to understand without some knowledge of cardiology. We both had a pretty good grasp of Father's condition, indeed of some of the medical details, and we had continued to learn about it from his visiting physicians. So for a time both of us stood firm. Could we please have details of what they were looking for? He refused to answer — adamantly and almost rudely. So, without consulting each other, we said that we flatly refused to let Father return to the hospital.

"You are risking his life," was Dr. Berg's reply. "Time has passed, you know, and there have been advances in medicine. You know perfectly well that his life at the moment is limited; but I'm sure you want to take every step to lengthen it — perhaps to save him. You don't have any new proposals, except to stand in the way of these further tests."

Neither Mother nor I were convinced by these "arguments," so she went upstairs to call a member of our existing team of cardiologists. Unfortunately, he was unavailable, and she came back downstairs looking miserable and defeated. But by this time I had found my resolve.

"I am speaking for my mother and for myself," I announced to Dr. Berg, "and frankly I don't think I like you."

He looked astonished.

"I certainly don't trust you," I added. He was absolutely mortified.

"And we want written evidence, with a second opinion, that these tests are necessary."

With that I basically pushed him out of the room and toward the front door, opened it, and he quickly shuffled out.

Mother was trembling in her chair when I returned, and I sat on the arm of the chair and put my own arm around her shoulders.

"This is absurd," I said. "We know that Father is being cared for by the leading doctors in Washington — the leading doctors in the nation. Who is this man who is supposedly superior to all of them? Absolutely no one has suggested that there was such a person."

I went upstairs to Father, who was bewildered by the new turn of events, and asked him openly, "Did you trust that man?" He shook his head.

"No, I don't want to return to the hospital unless to relieve you and your mother from the strain of having me here."

"You won't go," I assured him, "and neither Mother nor I want you to leave us unless it's absolutely necessary."

It suddenly dawned on me that Kate's father, Jerome Harris, was the president of a large health insurance company. I thought that he might be able to put us in contact with someone who could give us an impartial assessment of this new doctor and his supposed superior ability. Fortunately, Kate was at home when I called, and she promised to have her father call us back as soon as possible.

"There is something going on here," I said to Mother.

We had nothing to do now but wait for Mr. Harris to call, so Mother and I allowed Father to fall asleep. We were hoping that he would sleep for some time in order to regain some strength, and also because we did not wish to be disturbed once he could continue with his story. All we needed to know was that his medical care was adequate, unless we were informed that there really was some recent medical development that could make an impact. We did get one telephone call that afternoon from one of the regular cardiologists, who asked that we allow Father to be readmitted to the hospital.

"It would be in his interests really, to take the strain off him and off you," was his rather lame justification. We detected a note of caution in his voice, and since we had set our resolve on the question, we merely thanked him for the call and said we had not yet made up our minds.

Later that evening Kate called back and put her father on the line with Mother. She told Mr. Harris about the visit that morning and expressed our determination that Father not return to the hospital unless it was absolutely necessary and could be shown to be in his best interests. Mr. Harris then gave her the name of perhaps the most senior cardiologist in the country, Dr. Ben Johnson, and advised her to call him direct and authorize him to conduct a separate examination of Father at home. Then she should contact Dr. Berg, our morning visitor, and, unless Dr. Johnson agreed with him that it was absolutely necessary, we should not allow Father to be removed from our home on any pretext. He added that Mother and I could call on him whenever we needed any help — or indeed comfort — and I realized how much we were missing male support in this confrontation with the mysterious "authorities" in Washington. Mother asked whether she should call the cardiologist right now, and he said, "Yes, by all means. He has an answering service, and if you don't get him immediately, he will call you back as soon as he gets your message. I have already spoken to him."

Mother did call Dr. Johnson right away, but it wasn't until just about midnight before he called back. Though both of us were in bed, we were wide awake, and Mother was ready to explain the whole situation to him. But Dr. Johnson assured us that Mr. Harris had given him the whole story — from what Mother had related and, of course, from the earlier press coverage of Father's return to the country. He was brief but considerate: he told her that, although he had a very busy schedule ahead of him, he would come to see Father at about 7:00 the next morning.

"Don't you ever manage to sleep?" Mother asked, trying to bring to the conversation a lighter and more personal tone.

"Oh, I get what I can," Dr. Johnson replied, "and this looks like it's an emergency — though slightly different from the kind I'm usually faced with."

Mother was effusive in her gratitude. As for me, I was by this time convinced that there was some sort of convoluted political scenario into which we were both stumbling, knowing nothing. I suspected that every part of Father's narrative from now on would somehow involve intrigue, or at the very least turmoil, for which we were totally unprepared, considering our ignorance of what lay behind it.

Dr. Ben Johnson was even more prompt than his promise: he arrived at quarter to seven, but Mother and I had been up, dressed, and breakfasted well before that. He spoke to us before he went up to see Father.

"You realize, of course, that I can't really do much merely by looking at your husband here. But I can at least give an initial impression, and the notes, I gather, are very full because of the nursing that's been taking place."

He went upstairs to the nurse who was on duty, and Mother and I left him to make his investigations. We were now quite determined that, unless there was the faintest hope that Father would benefit from being transferred to the hospital for any reason whatsoever, he was to stay at home with us.

When Dr. Johnson came back downstairs, he said, "I've looked at the case notes on your husband, and they are up to date. They reflect the views of the last cardiologist to visit him, Dr. Berg, and the day-to-day nursing conditions that the nurses have recorded. It's a straightforward, almost routine, case for this particular affliction. And there is nothing, I'm sorry to say, in the least bit new that could be tried on your husband. I'll tell Dr. Berg that under no circumstances will I sign any joint recommendation that he be transferred to the hospital. If you want me to fight any attempt by him to do so, you can rely on me."

We did not expect such resolve on his part, and it was especially astonishing in that it was coming from someone whom we had just met an hour earlier and even then through a somewhat remote connection. Only later did we come to realize that Dr. Johnson was far more aware than we were, engrossed as we were in looking after Father, of the political implications surrounding Father's reappearance in Moscow and how that had become the talk of Washington again.

"I am very, very sorry that there is no more I can actually do for your husband, but I can give you one piece of advice: if you have a lawyer, get hold of him now. If you don't have one, the sooner you get one the better." Then, as he rose to go to the door he said, "I am always available if you need me."

Mother and I were left in almost the same state of confusion we had been in when Father disappeared in Moscow. We wondered how long we would have to wait to hear the outcome of what would undoubtedly be a confrontation between Johnson and Berg.

We did not have to wait long. Later that morning, without any prior notice, we received a visit from a State Department representative, who was courteous, bland, and smooth. After expressing the usual sympathy and considerate wishes for Father — which was no more than we expected — he launched into what we figured was a prepared speech.

"You realize, of course," he said to Mother, "that your husband is still a member of the State Department and technically on sick leave. Just as he would have a duty to us in the days of his good health, so we now have a duty to him in his sickness. You see, we look after our own, and the recommendation of doctors advising us is that he be readmitted to the hospital for further tests. Therefore, you are to a certain extent obstructing the State Department in the performance of its duties."

I scarcely had time to be astonished by this new tack when Mother replied:

"I'm prepared to take that risk, and if necessary I am prepared to put every obstruction in your way. In short, I will fight you. I am here to protect my husband. That's my primary purpose and my duty — and it ought to be yours as well. I have no faith in the last doctor you sent us; frankly, he appears to be acting on your behalf and certainly not in any medical interests that I'm aware of. My husband stays here under our own care and with the medical arrangements we've made — in cooperation, I might add, with the hospital and with your department and, indeed, with the whole of the administration, as far as I know. If you want him, you had better get yourself a court order."

"You may well be faced with one, I'm afraid," he replied. "So if that's all you have to say, I have no more to say except to add that we are genuinely trying to act in your husband's interests."

This platitude, following the threat he had just uttered, was too much for Mother and me, and we stood up to order him out of the house. He went as blandly and smoothly as he had come, his rehearsed mission unsuccessful, but he personally not in the least deterred.

We decided to contact an attorney immediately. The problem was that, because of Father's periods overseas, neither he nor my mother had a family lawyer. But she remembered a friend of her father who was an attorney, and she looked him up in the telephone book. When she got him on the phone, he recalled the family and agreed to take on the case. Though fully engaged himself, he told us that he had a younger associate, Alan Clarke, in whom he had complete confidence and that he would arrange for Clarke to visit us. Fortunately, the law firm was in Washington, and he said that he would try to get Mr. Clarke over to the house sometime that afternoon. He told us that in the meantime we should try to recall everything we could so that we could brief him as fully as possible.

At about 4:30, a young, tall, and fair-haired man appeared, perhaps in his late twenties or early thirties, and very friendly in his manner. We immediately felt that we could speak freely to him because of his sympathy for our problem. We told him the whole story from beginning to end, including the doubts we — and Dr. Johnson — had about Berg's advice. But we realized that our suspicions of Dr. Berg could be unfounded. Clarke listened without comment, taking full notes and from time to time questioning us where he felt he had not gotten the details down. Eventually he gave us his advice:

"I think you should sit tight and ignore any immediate threats," Alan Clarke said. "There is no power on earth they can use to have Mr. Winthrop forcibly transferred to the hospital, and I believe you have trumped what appears to be their blackmail charge by bringing in your own eminent cardiologist — though of course we'll have to wait and see what happens when they confront each other. Should it come to a demand for his return, we'll have to look at it again. But I think I can say with some confidence that your father stays here as long as you wish him to. Here's my number. Call me whenever you may need me, twenty-four hours a day if necessary — and I really mean that."

It was three days before we heard anything further, and then it was a phone call from the State Department representative who had threatened us earlier.

"I have taken instructions," he said to Mother, "and I have also spoken to Dr. Berg, who, you may recall, came to see your husband. He appears to be, for the time being at least, very heavily engaged with other patients and thus would not be available to conduct any tests if your husband were in fact returned to the hospital. I would have preferred him to tell you this himself, in the event that he had raised your hopes that the transfer of your husband to his care, at least temporarily, would possibly have been of benefit to him. . . ."

I could see that Mother was turning white with anger and would be unable to speak coherently. So I snatched the phone from her trembling hand.

"My mother has noted what you had to say," I said into the receiver, "and we don't wish to hear from you again under any circumstances. I gather that would be most unlikely anyway, and if Dr. Berg wishes to contact us, he can set up an appointment and do it in person. As for communications from the State Department in the future, we would like to deal with someone of higher authority and frankly of more common decency than you."

I gave him an opportunity to reply, afraid that, driven into a corner, he would threaten some new and even more appalling action. But he was still the same bland and imperturbable smoothie as ever.

"I will see that Dr. Berg receives your message, but of course you must realize, as I have said before, that your father is still under the jurisdiction of his employers, the State Department — and ultimately the administration — and they will have the final word."

"I fully understand that," I replied, "but please try to understand that he is also a father, a husband, and a human being."

"We do of course understand that," he said, "and that's why I said that the Department always looks after its own."

My impulse, like Mother's, was to slam down the receiver, but I allowed him to finish his sentence. "Thank you" was all I could say as I hung up.

We wondered how long we would be left in peace by the State Department, or by any other government agency. Clearly, Dr. Berg had been thwarted by our cardiologist, Ben Johnson, and the State Department had equally been shaken by the force with which our lawyer, Alan Clarke, had apparently made his case. Clarke told us on the phone that if the matter became a public issue, he would release information to the press that would undoubtedly be on our side.

*　　　*　　　*

On some days, when his health allowed, we would get Father up and sit him in a chair; with the help of the nurses and occasionally additional assistance, we would move him downstairs. On one or two occasions we put him out in the garden, small as it was, to enjoy the sun and a change of scenery. He continued to get visits from the cardiologist who had originally attended him when he came to Bethesda from Moscow; but he said nothing about Dr. Berg's attempt to override his opinion and treatment. We, in turn, did not raise the subject, wishing to convey no suggestion that Berg return to the fray.

One day, however, we received a phone call from Alan Clarke, who told us that he suspected that the State Department was about to make a further attempt to have Father returned to the hospital. It seemed that Dr. Berg had sought out yet another cardiologist, with whom he had prepared some kind of report pointing to the necessity — according to them — of Father's taking advantage of recent advances in treatment.

"I've already contacted your man Johnson," Clarke said. "He told me that, with the speed of modern medical progress, it's becoming increasingly difficult to resist those demands."

Mother and I agreed with Clarke that an outcry in the press would be difficult at this moment. But what he said beyond that concerned us.

"It's beginning to look," said Clarke, "like this has become essentially an inter-party conflict, and I'm starting to think about bringing in politicians on our own side. A few confidential inquiries by a well-placed senator might help — so that's what I'm considering right now."

Mother and I were once again beginning to feel under siege, and Clarke's remarks only confirmed our suspicions that Father's case and fate were somehow going to become a subject of controversy in the upcoming election campaign.

"Do you think there is anything one side or the other really wants to know about Henry?" Mother asked.

"I don't know," he said. "I'm afraid that remains with your husband, and perhaps a few Russians who remember what went on . . . and of course those who are now making their inquiries."

The thought that Father's fate depended on the scurrilous exchange of political insults going on in Washington made the situation more tense.

"There must be someone who can help us," Mother said in distress as she hung up the phone after her conversation with Clarke. I thought again of Jerome Harris, who had so successfully produced a cardiologist in our defense some time earlier. I decided to call and see whether he could perhaps come to our aid once again. When I called, Kate and he were out, so I left a message for them to call as soon as they got home. In the meantime, in an attempt to do something with my nervous energy, I went to the bookstore on the Georgetown University campus and bought two more books on the war, one specifically devoted to the U.S. role at the Yalta conference. I sat down to devour them as carefully and quickly as I could, looking for clues about Father's life and possible role at the Yalta conference.

Mr. Harris returned our call that evening, and Mother spoke to him. He couldn't give us further advice, but he did confirm that we should hold the line with the medical profession and demands from the State Department. He added that if Father was returned to the hospital, we were to insist that it be in Washington and that Mother occupy a room there during his stay. He dismissed any suggestion that Father could be, as he said, "whisked away" into the unknown. That, I'm afraid, did not convince either Mother or me, and we had our doubts how sure he was himself of the strength behind his words.

For a few more days we were undisturbed, and with the weather turning very warm in Washington, we took Father down to the garden, and on one occasion walked him in a wheelchair through the neighboring streets in order to cheer him up. Perhaps he had caught something from our general mood of apprehension, or perhaps it was a growing anxiety about the next segment of his recollections, but he seemed uneasy. We knew somehow that the key to the next step in his narrative had to involve Stefansky, because it was in connection with that name that his anxiety seemed to increase.

We had used the tape recorder for ourselves, keeping the tapes of Father's narrative under lock and key, and giving the State Department the tapes of only such general comments as Father might make about day-to-day household management. Sometimes we would play back our own tapes to make sure that they had some semblance of a logical sequence and to ensure that we would be able to follow the tale Father was telling. We both wondered when we would hear from Dr. Berg again, convinced that we had not seen the end of the Department's attempt to get their hands on Father. Alan Clarke, we knew, was prepared to proceed immediately with an injunction, should that be necessary, and his latest ploy was what he called a preemptive move: he had established contacts with the leading Washington and New York papers, indicating that he was ready to break this story if it became necessary. He gave the editors no indication of the nature of the information he would give them; this we kept within our own very closed circle. But if worse came to worst, he said, he would tell all, and we agreed with that decision.

It was after one of our wheelchair trips around the neighborhood that Father seemed to gather the strength to take up the thread of his narrative again. He seemed to have a certain apprehension about doing so, yet also a compulsion to continue. It was as though he knew about the political threat and was telling us as much as he could before there was a further attempt to monitor him.

CHAPTER EIGHT

YALTA, 1945

The principals attending the Yalta meetings were closely guarded. They moved only with a retinue of troops and police, and on the whole they kept very much to themselves. The papers that came out of the meetings were equally guarded and only filtered through to the underlings after they had been considered — and in many cases censored — by those who initially received them or reported them. And there were meetings of lesser standing, though of equal importance, going on in the other villas, where the foreign ministers met to further wrangle over matters that had been discussed in full session the day before. On more than one occasion, I accompanied the Secretary of State, Edward Stettinius, to either the British or the Soviet villa; but he did not sit in on any of the Yalta meetings himself. He seemed to have the role of checking and double-checking everything that came out of the meetings, and he longed to see the participants actually speaking and in action.

While I had an inbred hatred for Stalin, I was astonished to find that some in our own delegation really disliked Roosevelt. A number of the members of the U.S. delegation, particularly those who were involved with me in interpretation and translation, were refugees from the Bolshevik Revolution who, if they did not have firsthand stories of the horrors of the civil war, had recollections of what their parents and relatives had told them. Of course, those stories only confirmed what my stepmother had told me. Somehow Hitler seemed to dissolve into the background as the archenemy among these émigrés, and Stalin took center stage. But the antagonism of many of them toward Roosevelt was what I found shocking. I had been brought up in the atmosphere of the New Deal with the general feeling that at the very least Roosevelt had averted revolution in the United States. Even in the wires that had gone

82

out from the U.S. embassy in Moscow warning the White House of its attitude toward the Russians — even in them I had not seen quite the personal antagonism toward Roosevelt that I now could hear.

We knew that Churchill was on his guard against Stalin, of course, since he had been a consistent opponent of Bolshevism from the beginning of the Revolution. In fact, he was almost entirely responsible for the Allied intervention in the Russian civil war. Unfortunately, this had done nothing but lead to a bitter hatred of the Western powers by the new Soviet ruling company. It all was "like a three-cornered fight," Churchill had said, "and it was impossible to tell who was right." Of course, I had my own very thorough grounding from my stepmother, and I was inclined to give Churchill the benefit of the doubt in any contest he might have with Stalin. And, of course, he represented America's closest ally.

On the morning after the first plenary meeting of the conference, which had been devoted almost entirely to reports on the military situation, we were working hard on those reports in order to provide the background of what would follow. They essentially involved accounts by the Russian and American chiefs of staff and our own of the military fronts as they were situated at that time. As such, they had little, if any, political content; but they were interesting and at least produced a kind of competitive material from both sides. Seeking a break from the somewhat stale air inside, I walked out onto the grounds and looked out across to the sea. It was a gloriously crisp morning, with the sun casting a clear light over my vista, and it was hard to believe that humanity could do anything to disturb the peace that seemed to reign. At the same time I knew that the most appalling atrocities had been carried out in the Crimea, especially when the Bolsheviks cleared the area of their White Army opponents. I also brought to mind the terrible fighting that had taken place between the Germans and the Red Army just a year earlier. But now I put that out of my mind as I gazed down on the Black Sea and then at the flowers, shrubs, and trees in the foreground. I wanted to be alone, but I heard someone approaching me. I turned around to see Stefansky coming toward me.

"Hello, Vlad," I said, somewhat discouraged to see him approaching, hoping that he was out on a brisk walk himself and would leave me alone. But he came up close behind me, and I could see that he was determined to talk.

"It's a glorious sight, isn't it?" I said, hoping to keep the conversation on a neutral basis.

"It's stained with blood," he said bitterly. "I'm sure you know that last year Stalin transported all the Crimean natives from here to Siberia, shipped them out in cattle cars. God knows how many of them died on the way — at least half, I should guess, if the past is any guide — and then they were dumped out to fend for themselves in Siberia. That's exactly what he did to the Poles when he marched in there in 1939 — that is, those he hadn't already shot or thrown into his labor camps."

Stefansky seemed to be in a quiet fury, and I was curious to know what had led to his line of conversation.

"I've just been talking to one of the entourage," he said with a laugh. "A man who appears to think much as I do. He has just learned through underground channels that some of his family — distant, it's true — have been taken from Moscow by the NKVD and have disappeared into a gulag. He hopes his membership in our delegation will give him a measure of protection and that he won't be included in what is the usual family cleansing that Stalin engages in. But it's not certain — they may well ship him out in a box.

"It must be possible, it must be possible," he went on, kicking a stone down the pathway as he turned to face me again. "Someone really must get Stalin — it can't go on indefinitely. This complacence by a country of millions with a . . . a despot.

"You wouldn't want to help us, would you?" he suddenly asked, turning toward me. By now it seemed as though his monologue had reached almost a fever pitch.

"Help you do what?" I asked.

"Oh . . . to somehow stop him . . . somehow. We know there are Russians opposed to him, and we know there are Americans who cannot stand the concept of him at any price. I know that about myself first-hand, and surely you do — among the embassy officials."

"I can't see anyone, from the ambassador on down, joining in an assassination attempt, if that's what you are hinting at," I said sarcastically. He ignored me. "Really, Vlad, you must get a grip on your feelings. We all understand what you've gone through, and we understand what you must feel. But surely there's some sense of balance you've got to reach."

"We've got quite a lot of support, if you think of it," he said. "The Poles are on our side. Even though the Red Army is supposed to have liberated them, they are slaughtering all the underground fighters, all those who resisted the Germans from 1939 onward. There is almost civil war in

Poland, and only those who have been trained in Moscow are supporting the Red Army units."

"What about all of Stalin's cabinet?" I asked, trying to keep the discussion on some level of sanity. "Molotov, Vyshinsky, Mikoyan, Voroshilov, plus his military leaders — Zhukov, Koniev, and the rest. There are enough of them, and they all owe their positions to Stalin. They're not going to throw away everything they owe him by assassinating him or removing him or whatever you have in mind."

"Ah yes, but these aren't the old days when Lenin led a group of what are now called devoted revolutionaries. These are all just yes-men fighting as much for their lives as they ever were and doing it beside Stalin. Take him away and they'll all crumble . . . the whole edifice will collapse, I hope to God. Don't think in terms of the United States, where, if and when Roosevelt dies, Truman and the rest of Roosevelt's cabinet take over running the country for the Democrats. There would be changes in policy, and there certainly would be changes in foreign policy, thank God. But there would be no revolutionary change, no collapse of an existing order."

"I know that," I said wearily and turned to go. The sunny brightness of the morning had been completely overshadowed by his incredible tirade. And the awful thing was that I felt his hatred for Stalin and the Bolsheviks almost as much as he did, as the memories and reminiscences of my stepmother came back to haunt me.

"But do we imagine that they know what we are doing? Have we the slightest inkling of the nature of those we are dealing with?" Stefansky was determined to get in the last word as he accompanied me along the path back to the palace. "Take Marshal Rokossovski," he insisted. "He's one of Stalin's leading generals — in charge of the armies approaching Berlin. He's a Pole and has already been arrested by Stalin and released to go back to the army. There are plenty of people like him around."

"I'm fully aware of that," I said, "but I don't believe there's anything you or I can do in the internal affairs of the Soviet Union." I changed the subject: "You seem to have prospered very well in the United States since you immigrated there, isn't that correct?"

"Oh yes, I've been very successful and very happy. But we Russians have long memories, and there were those among the slaughtered whom we loved and whose graves are in Russia. We have our roots. Once a Russian, always a Russian."

"What exactly is your role in this delegation?" I asked.

"Well, I'm an adviser to some extent on Russian affairs, but also on supplies and Lend-Lease, of course. That's the main connection between the United States and Russia, and it was so from the beginning: Harry Hopkins flew to Moscow, met with Stalin, and reported back to Roosevelt that the Russians would hold out and that they were worthy of being supplied, even at the expense of the beleaguered British. He was right, of course, as it turned out; the Russians have in fact succeeded in shoving back the Germans, and they continue to advance. But what Hopkins didn't realize was that Roosevelt bought the whole package, as it were, and now is as entrenched in his support of the Soviets emotionally as he was when he ordered the extension of Lend-Lease to include them along with the United Kingdom."

At last we parted, and I returned to the room where I was working with Philip and some others on the preparation of papers for the full meeting that afternoon. The subject was to be Germany and the treatment the Allies would mete out to that country after the war was over. The Germans had already been told that they faced unconditional surrender; but once the occupying powers were there, there would need to be a plan on how to administer it and — more importantly — how the Allies could protect themselves from aggression in the future. The lesson of 1918 had been burned deep into the souls of those who were facing the Germans now.

As I reread the papers that had been prepared for President Roosevelt, which would form the basis of the U.S. contribution on the subject, I couldn't help thinking back to Vlad and his passionate denunciation of our ally in the East. I knew we were dealing with an ogre, and with a terrible régime, and it was difficult to look at the papers in front of me, with their calm proposals that seemed to assume that the Allies were united members of a long-standing alliance of similar-thinking and similar-speaking people. We had only been thrown together because of Hitler's aggression; otherwise, there was nothing to show that any two of the three parties to this meeting had anything in common. Even the Brits, according to many Americans, didn't have much in common with us, living their mysterious lives on an island moored just off the coast of Europe.

There were certainly those among the Russian refugees in America who so hated the ascendancy of Stalin and the Red Army that they would almost risk a successful outcome of World War II by plunging us into some terrible conflict with our Eastern allies. And Vladimir Stefansky was one of them, though he seemed to think that it could be done without risking an ultimately successful conclusion to the war we were already in. He had referred to the Poles, but the Polish government in London accounted for nothing, nor did any of the anti-Soviet committees that occasionally appeared in the United States. I wondered how the conference would go as it discussed Germany's future. My own feeling, and certainly that of my whole generation, was that the best thing to do would be to hold the Germans down by whatever means were available, while looking to our defenses against another threat that Churchill, at least, saw looming over us once the war came to an end.

Philip and I and the others in the room were suddenly faced with a mass of papers brought in from the main conference hall of Livadia Palace, where another plenary session was now taking place. We had yet to see the room, but we had been told that we might get an opportunity to go around to the various state rooms, as well as this main hall. Perhaps, in the haste of requiring retranslation, some of the papers reaching us should have been held up by the censor. Philip and I remarked that we were beginning to get the flavor of a meeting full of sharp divergences of opinion on what to do with Germany. Roosevelt, we knew, was for complete disarmament and had expressed himself as even more eager for revenge on this occasion than he had earlier in the war. He sided with Stalin to some extent; but Stalin at least had an understandable desire to protect his eastern front. Churchill was also suspect: he wanted to build up France in order to have a strong ally on the continent against Germany. He was clear in his mind that, however much he might have quarreled with de Gaulle personally from time to time, he wanted a rebuilt France. Stalin, in turn, was doing all he could to prevent this, though he himself had signed a treaty of alliance with de Gaulle only a few weeks earlier.

At that meeting with de Gaulle, Stalin had followed his usual practice of discussing matters late into the night and then insisting that his visitor sit through a movie show. Most visitors were dropping from exhaustion by the time at least two turgid Russian films — or an occasional Western one — were shown as they sat at awkward little tables with refreshments in front of them, already wearied and possibly half-drunk from the banquet that had preceded this entertainment. De Gaulle had called it quits after one film and gone back to his headquarters, only to be called out at 2:00 a.m. by Stalin to sign an agreement, wherein the latter had artfully restored conditions to which de Gaulle had objected earlier. All of us in the Moscow embassy knew the story.

At last the conference ended, and Stalin and Churchill departed for their separate villas. I caught a glimpse of Churchill: he was dressed in a British Army uniform and had a black fur hat on his formidable pate that was sharply pointed fore and aft. I didn't see Stalin; no doubt he had been smuggled out the back, surrounded by his guards. Roosevelt would be dining alone that evening, we were told, with his advisers. I left the translation room somewhat disheartened, feeling what it must be like to have the weight of the world on one's shoulders. I went downstairs to the front of the palace and out into the open air. The guards nodded as I walked by them into a darkness that was broken only by the lights surrounding the building. I had started to walk down the road away from Livadia when I heard someone approaching me from behind.

"So your friend Stevens wants to knock off Stalin," said the voice behind me, and as I whirled around, I found myself walking along beside one of the senior U.S. delegates. He was, in fact, one of those who had attended the conference that afternoon, and I had the feeling he had followed me out of the palace. I was surprised to find myself accosted by him, but even more astonished by the familiarity with which he opened the conversation.

"Is that what he calls himself now?" That was all I could say in immediate response, referring to the anglicizing of Stefansky.

"I think he is gradually slipping into that name," he said, "but let's call him whatever you want to call him. Vladimir is his given name, as the Russians say."

"Vlad," I said.

"Curious fellow. He has done very well in the States, but we've always known that he had kept up his Russian contacts. But somehow he seems to have been able to take advantage of the régime, even though his initial success in trading ventures was well known before the Revolution. We've always been worried that he would cause an incident because of his hatred for the régime — and of course for Stalin. But he seems to have been able to convince the administration of his value to us, and here he is now, supposedly a Russian expert. Well, he's fluent in Russian and has an up-to-date knowledge of the régime that is sometimes superior to what we have gotten through the OSS and the other agencies. He claims to have many contacts in the ruling Soviet régime, even among those here in Yalta.

"We would like to know who they are, of course," the delegate went on, "and I'm wondering whether you can help us. We know that there are those among the Soviets, largely of Polish origin, who expect us to go to war with the Soviets right away. In fact, they are ready to take the Germans as allies in such a conflict. What we really want to know is, who — among Vlad's so-called contacts — is really setting out to assassinate Stalin. Whatever they intend to do will probably lead to the disintegration of the whole Soviet Union. He has no doubt already told you that he regards the war as successfully concluded and that the use of the Red Army is now at an end — which he's got right. But we need to know more details about this: what exactly is being planned and, naturally, what is Stevens' role, if any? Of course, he may be just another bigmouth. Lots of these Russians are — they talk big until they are threatened. But we need him and he seems to need us. Anyway, let's keep in touch."

He patted me on the shoulder and disappeared into the evening. I felt now as though I had been thrust into the middle of the behind-the-scenes machinations going on at the conference. I continued to walk past gutted and burned-out buildings, the shells of vehicles destroyed by gunfire, wrecked tanks and trucks — the whole detritus of war. The Germans had certainly ravaged the countryside in their advance, and then they had done it more heavily in their withdrawal, when they deliberately destroyed everything as they retreated. The evidence that the battles for the Crimea had been savage lay all around me. Eager to get away from this reality of war, this backdrop to the confusion of the talks and the documents and the cables that we were dealing with daily, I turned back to the palace. Showing my pass to the guards, I went up the stairs to the second floor, where a meal of both Russian and American food was available. I looked around to see whether the delegate who had approached me a few minutes earlier was there, but he was not. I wondered whether he was with the small group dining with the President. Perhaps he was simply up in his own room working with whatever unit he represented — likely the OSS.

Our conversation, naturally, had disturbed me. I agonized about where my sympathies lay: were they with Vlad and his intense hatred of

Stalin and the Soviet system, or were they with the U.S. delegation's vague accommodations and what was now becoming apparent — a shadowy alliance with Stalin and acceptance of him as a convenient ally? I believed that, in the final analysis, though I had a historic but uncertain emotional kinship with Vlad's position, I had to be on the side of my own country, my President and commander-in-chief.

CHAPTER NINE

Mother poured glasses of wine for both of us, and we sat drinking them, feeling rather like solitary drinkers.

"I wonder how long his story can go on," she said. "He seems to be bursting with it. It can't be doing him any good, yet I suppose it offers him some sort of relief."

"It sounds like it was a turning point in his life," I said. "Now at this moment" — I hesitated over the words — "when his life seems like it's drawing to an end, maybe that turning point has become the most important thing for him."

For a moment I longed to get away from everything, not to go to college but somehow to escape from the intensity of the emotions that surrounded Mother and me as we dealt with Father's remembered emotions. Then the moment passed, and I went over and sat next to her on the couch.

"I know we're doing the best thing by listening to him," she said. "We're not encouraging him to dredge up those memories, but if he wants to talk, all we can do is listen and try to understand."

Father slept through most of the following day, but that was not all that unusual, and it was only in the evening that the nurse became alarmed.

"He is not at all well," she told us, "and I don't think he should be here — at least not at this moment." Mother and I looked at her in consternation. "We can call in the doctors," she added. "But they'll want him in the hospital, I'm certain of that."

We could see that she did not want the responsibility of anything happening to him while she was on duty. Before we could stop her, she moved toward the phone.

"What are you going to do?" I asked her.

"I'm going to call Dr. Johnson right away, and tell him that in my professional view" — she straightened herself up — "we've got to get him back to the hospital."

I saw Mother raise her hand to stop her, but then she let it drop again and shook her head. We both knew there was nothing we could do except agree with the nurse, and there should be no delay. When our nurse made the phone call, the message must have gone through directly to the cardiologist on duty, because when she hung up the phone, she nodded and said an ambulance was on its way.

The nurse had Father ready for the ambulance ride by the time it arrived, so the emergency men got him into the vehicle very quickly. They waited briefly for us to say good-bye to him, but Mother insisted on riding with him to the hospital. I went back into the house and back to contemplating Father's future. It was hard to know what to think: at one extreme there was, of course, the possibility that he would die. We had been warned by his doctors that his hold on life was hardly strong, and he had been under great emotional strain telling his story. On the other hand, once he was in the hospital getting the superior care of their staff, he might well be exposed to interrogation by State Department or CIA officials, and where would that lead?

I started to pace restlessly around the house and ran into the nurse as she carried fresh sheets and pillowcases into Father's room.

"Is he very bad?" I asked her.

"Well, you know how it is," she replied, "it goes up and down. But this time he seemed so strained, so tense . . . and it's obviously hard on his heart. Did you notice anything that might have affected him badly?" She said this with a certain degree of hesitancy and embarrassment, clearly not wanting to seem like she was accusing her employers of distressing her patient.

I shook my head. "He wants to talk. He's had a long and active life."

"Not all that long . . . ," she blurted out.

"Well, what I mean to say is, it has been an active one. Anyone who lives through the war and afterwards, particularly in his position, has obviously been involved in all kinds of things."

She nodded in understanding. "Of course," she said, "but I hate to see him go down like this."

I was so grateful for these words that I clasped her hand, and she put her other hand on my shoulder as we stood there silently.

"Don't worry," she said. "He's in the hospital now, and they'll do all they can. I'm sure they'll manage to make some improvement, and he's got your mother with him." This, I realized, was not something that particularly assured her. Perhaps now that she seemed alert to the possibility that somehow Mother and I could be putting a strain on Father, we had to watch ourselves around her and the other nurses. I released my hand and smiled.

"Thank you," I said, "you're very good to us."

Mother called a couple of hours later, but only to say that Father was now sleeping peacefully after his initial examination and a sedative. They would set up tests for when he woke up in the morning. These no doubt would include whatever Dr. Berg had thought up; but they would at least bring the specialists up to date on his current condition and give us some assurance about his immediate future, with which I was most concerned. I realized that he was now exposed, as we had always feared, to the close surveillance of the State Department. In addition, some politicians might find an excuse to visit him in the hospital. And I remembered the representative of the CIA who had suggested that perhaps Father should be moved away from Washington altogether. But I dismissed that as an immediate possibility: he was sure to be safely ensconced in the hospital, and Mother was watching over him. I wondered whether he would feel compelled to continue telling his Yalta story to Mother in the hospital; but I came to the conclusion that the hospital activity — the tests, the comings and goings of doctors, nurses, and others — would make him converse in a more general and relaxed way with her and them.

Later that evening, Mr. Harris called. He had contacted the hospital officials and my mother, and she had asked him to get in touch with me for my own reassurance.

"There really is a grand conference of cardiologists in that hospital now," he said, "and I don't think Berg or any other Department appointee will be able to get away with anything that is out of line with current thinking or the best practice. Not only have we brought Ben Johnson in again, but he's brought himself in; by the time they're finished, we'll know exactly your father's condition and what the future holds. My own hunch is that he'll be back with you at home soon. I've also taken another step: with your mother staying at the hospital, I've put pressure on the administration — frankly through the strength of our own orga-

nization, which underwrites the insurance of so many of the doctors —
to let one of our people visit the hospital. This will give your father another guard, so to speak, in addition to your mother."

This was a totally unexpected development to me, and most com-
forting, and I thanked him from the bottom of my heart.

"Wouldn't you like to come over and stay with us?" he asked.
"You'll find it lonely in that house with only your own thoughts and anxieties as your companions. Kate has been away for a few days, but she's
coming back tonight. So why don't you pack your things and come tomorrow morning . . . or tonight right away, if you'd like."

He seemed to have made the decision for me, and I thanked him
again — sincerely. It would indeed come as a relief to be with others who
had other topics of conversation to distract me from the double anxiety
of my father's condition and the effect his revelations were having on us
all. I decided that it was only fair to Kate's father for me to go there in the
morning. So I retired to an early bed and fell asleep immediately.

The following morning I was much more refreshed than I had expected to be. After a quick breakfast, I packed the few things that I might
need at the Harrises', and left for their house. Kate greeted me with the
warmth of a true friend, and she suggested immediately that we go out
shopping together to get some things she had suddenly discovered she
needed while she was out of town. I guessed that she was making up
most of her list for my benefit, but I readily fell in with her plans. We
planned shopping for the morning, a lunch out, and then a visit to my father and mother in the hospital that afternoon. The morning passed
quickly but happily; it was good to be back again with people in the
shops and on the sunny streets, and to talk with Kate about her trip and
about our various activities since we'd last been together. Despite my
protestations, she treated me to a splendid lunch at the Mayflower, and
afterwards, buoyed by the meal, we both left for the hospital. When we
arrived, we were questioned quite carefully, to establish our identity —
which did not surprise us. But soon we were in Mother's room, and she
immediately took us to see Father.

He seemed much more alert than he had been in the last few days
and greeted us warmly. Perhaps, I thought, they had given him some sort
of minor stimulant or, alternatively, a sedative that had worked to relax
him.

"I don't think I'll be here long," he said. "There have been swarms of people in and out, and none of them seem to have anything to tell me, except to take things as they are and to go on as before — as if I am doing anything now." He laughed. "Empty sort of life, when you think about it."

He seemed to have regained a good deal of his wry humor, and we all thought he'd received something in the morning that was helping his outlook. I thought instantly about the possibility of some sort of truth serum that might have been administered; but I dismissed that from my mind immediately as a wild figment of my imagination run amok. While that was flitting through my brain, Dr. Berg came in. He motioned to all of us to stay seated and then addressed Mother:

"I don't think Henry will be here long this time. We've done almost everything we can. I'm sorry if I disturbed you with my earlier suggestion of more tests; but now that all of us here have had an opportunity to examine your husband and to go over some blood samples, I really don't think there is much more we can do right now."

He had taken his defeat — or so it seemed to us — remarkably well, though he naturally added a caveat regarding the tests they had done.

"For the time being," he went on, "I think that he should be here for a few days. It will do him good to have our specialist nursing, and of course the constant attention of the doctors may prove of some use. It will certainly be valuable to have them standing by." He turned and smiled at me. "And how are you, young lady?"

I bristled, but bit my tongue. "Very well, Dr. Berg. It's good to know that my father can come home very soon."

I wanted him to confirm that, but he refused to be nailed down, and shortly after that he left the room. Dr. Ben Johnson himself came into the room minutes later.

"I suppose that was Berg assuming superiority," he said, "but you needn't worry. He wasn't the one who brought Henry back in here — it really was that downturn in his condition. But he seems to have recovered remarkably well, and I think you can leave him safely to us and disregard any other threats."

In fact, it was after a stay of only three days that Father was returned to us, certainly in better condition than when he left. The nurses were obviously glad to see their patient in better shape. Mother and I were also somewhat less strained after that break. We took care to steer Father away from any contentious subjects — certainly from any mention of the name or subject of Yalta. And it was as though he himself had retreated from the subject to give himself a rest from what had been a compulsive preoccupation. The couple days I spent with Kate were peaceful and enjoyable, and now she was staying with us for a few days. My invitation to her was somewhat tentative because, I said, it was rather like living in a hospital. But she said she would enjoy it and offered to do all she could to help us. She also proved to be a good diversion for Father, almost a suppressant for anything secret he may have wanted to bring up if Mother and I were the only ones around.

When she left for home, she promised to return the moment we asked for her; and she also invited me back to her house whenever I might need a break. As she was leaving, I somehow felt that we were on the verge of getting the next disclosures from Father. They were soon to come.

CHAPTER TEN

Yalta, 1945

Yalta really was a glorious place. There was the town well above the Black Sea, and the wonderful palaces, with gardens leading right down to the sea, their paths twisting and turning through the beautiful trees and shrubs, some of which must have been blooming throughout the spring and summer. Livadia Palace, though it had been looted by the Germans, was now packed with our delegation. The formerly ornate rooms had tall windows with expansive views out to the sea or, on the opposite side, up the mountains where the vineyards climbed, producing the Georgian wines of which Stalin was so fond.

The Russians were incredible drinkers. The routine at banquets and dinners was their insistence on proposing toast after toast; at the end of each toast one was supposed to up-end his vodka glass, so there was no alternative but to drink the entire contents. On one occasion, however, someone noticed that Stalin had a glass of water by the side of his vodka glass, and when he had drunk the vodka halfway down, he would top it off with the water — thus effectively halving his consumption. He had a habit, which other members of the delegation mimicked, of standing up at the table and walking across and insisting on clinking glasses with the recipient of the toast, if it was an individual. When he toasted the proletariat or the Allies or victory in general, however, he stayed at his seat.

With some junior members of the department, I was invited to accompany a meeting of the foreign ministers that was convened at Corice, the Soviet villa; afterwards, we junior members had lunch together because we were not actually invited to the meal of the ministers' conference. One of the Russians remarked on my curious position as a naval officer and asked me whether the U.S. government was controlled by the armed services. I had heard that, from Stalin on downward, the Soviets

97

had little, if any, understanding of the democratic processes of the U.S. government, and I was quick to emphasize that that was not the case — that I was merely sent to the conference because of my knowledge of Russian and to some extent of Russian affairs. Saying that proved to be something of a mistake, because he immediately started questioning me about how I had learned Russian and why I should be particularly knowledgeable about his country's affairs. I told him, perhaps naively, about Maria, her nursing throughout the civil war, and of her eventual immigration to the United States. After all, I thought, the Russians were quite accustomed to émigrés returning as U.S. citizens.

I told him frankly that my interest in Russia had been inspired by her, and that I had followed its history throughout my education and into my service years. Naturally, I did not add that this was because of my hatred of the communist system and of Stalin himself. He nodded his understanding and introduced me to another member of his delegation, who appeared to have some knowledge of English that he wanted to try on me. I was seated between the two of them, and I soon realized that they were engaging me in something deeper than I had suspected. At first, as they delved into the affairs of their country, I thought it was merely for conversation's sake — just because I spoke Russian and had expressed an interest in its history. But after a while, I began to wonder whether they were deliberately guiding me into expressing some kind of position. The questions became more and more direct: "What do you think of General so-and-so?" and "What do you think of Marshal so-and-so?" and, eventually, "What are your views of Molotov?" For the moment they kept Stalin out of the conversation. I would have liked to answer some direct questions about the terror in Russia, the famine following the collectivization of the farms, and the show trials. But they were hardly likely to bring those up. The personal questions about their generals and cabinet ministers were difficult to comment on, though they were pressing me for answers.

"Some things I cannot respond to," I said, "because I am a guest in your country." I cast my eyes around the room, feeling somewhat concerned about being asked my opinion of Molotov, their foreign minister.

"Oh, you can say what you like," said my first questioner. "You are not only among allies, you are among friends. And we perhaps have some questions to ask you because we also need to know the opinion of those in America. Some of those in your delegation have already spoken to us very frankly."

It was on the tip of my tongue to ask the identity of those in the U.S. delegation he was referring to; but I remained silent, wondering whether he would continue this line of conversation.

"Oh yes," he said, "we have several friends from among you, and they share our views."

"What views?" I asked, without thinking.

"Well, for one, we do not like Stalin," he said, suddenly and emphatically, plunging straight into what must have been behind their approach to me. "Many in your delegation loathe him intensely — to an extent we had not realized. You know, sometimes we discuss what can be done about the whole situation."

His companion nodded. "He has us all under his thumb, you know. I'm sure you've noticed that, when he speaks, everyone remains silent and has no opinion until he has expressed his."

"I've never been at any of the full conference sessions," I replied. "In fact, I've never even seen Stalin, let alone spoken to him."

"Oh, you can take it from me that all such meetings on our side are the same, except that some of the military leaders will speak up tentatively and a little more freely, because Stalin's experience in the early years of the war — when he made so many terrible mistakes and lost so many millions of our people — has led him to listen to them, sometimes very carefully. But he makes it clear that his will be the last word. He really dictates all our military moves. Ultimately, everyone has to report to him with every detail, and his is the final yes or no."

This, I knew, was the opposite of Roosevelt. Although nominally commander-in-chief of the U.S. services, he pretty well left everything up to his generals and admirals, subject to any overriding political necessity. Churchill clearly had led his embattled nation from the jaws of defeat to ultimate survival, but I could not believe that even he had anything like Stalin's control over the whole of his military. As I sat there listening to them, my mind raced in confusion, remembering, from my own studies of Russia since the Revolution, the various attacks that Stalin had made on members of his own party and his ultimate success in wiping out all opposition. I was beginning to worry about where this conversation would lead.

"Perhaps, to begin with," said one of my lunch companions, "you might like to meet some of your own delegation who are our friends. They can give you a clearer idea of how things are going. You might be

99

confused, and it would be difficult to ask you to join us at this time. I will see what I can do to get some of your people to meet with you."

He turned back to the table and then rose to his feet to propose a toast, as if to signal the termination of this strand of our conversation and to indicate that we should now behave normally, like members of the regular service at a diplomatic luncheon party. But he did make one brief but important reference to the gist of our conversation toward the end of the meal.

"Perhaps afterwards, if you stay long enough, we can give you a glimpse of Stalin — it's a good idea to recognize your . . ." He hesitated over the word and then said it in a lower voice, ". . . your enemy," as if to drive home the whole purpose of our lunch conversation. When we left the table, and as we mixed and talked with others in the friendly and normal way of allies, my mind was buzzing with their extraordinary remarks, indeed, their assumption that I was now party to — or at least ready to join — a conspiracy against their leader. I wondered how much Stefansky had to do with this, whether he was, in fact, one of the Americans who was to be introduced to me to explain what was happening. But I had a feeling that there were others they had in mind, and that worried me.

A signal from one of my lunch companions beckoned me to a window, and I went to look down on the entrance to the villa, where several large Packard cars stood. I had learned earlier that the Russians had imported Packards from America before the war in order to copy them and initiate their own auto industry. Armed guards stood on either side of the entrance, forming a narrow corridor leading to one of the cars, and men in plain clothes, undoubtedly NKVD members, moved between them and appeared to be jostling around the entrance to the villa. Someone took my arm and led me toward the center window, where I could look down directly on the departure for Livadia Palace, where the afternoon's full conference was to take place at its usual time of five o'clock.

Suddenly there was a stirring among those below, and a stocky, thick-set man with iron-gray hair emerged. I could not see his face fully, but as he walked out to the car, I noticed how solid he seemed. Harry Hopkins, I believe, had said he was like a football coach. That day he wore a simple peasant's shirt, breeches, and highly polished boots, though sometimes, I had heard, he appeared in the full uniform of a Red Army marshal. Beside him, almost trotting, was another man, perhaps a little taller and bald, dressed in a Western suit and wearing pince-nez spectacles. This, I guessed, was Vyacheslav Molotov, the foreign minister and so-called deputy prime minister. The two men separated and quickly disappeared into two separate cars with darkened windows, which drove off immediately. Already ahead of them on the road to Livadia were identical cars with darkened windows, which was common practice for Stalin: a would-be assassin would thus not be able to tell which vehicle he was in. Other Packards drew up one by one to the front of the building, and the remaining members of the delegation who were to attend the conference climbed into them: Vyshinsky, the deputy foreign minister and the chief prosecutor at the Terror Trials; no doubt Pavlov, the interpreter; and others who either flanked Stalin or stood behind him at the full conferences to occasionally give him whispered information.

When the whole procession had left the palace grounds, we moved away from the windows. Further drinks were offered, as if some sort of toast were called for. Luckily, no one proposed anything more, and after we had finished them, the U.S. delegation members went downstairs to return to Livadia. It was an interesting moment: I had seen the person who had been forever identified as the enemy; but, like any other encounter with someone who has played a part in one's imagination, the reality did not have the impression on me that I had expected. On first sight, Stalin appeared to be just another Russian, though our hosts at the Russian headquarters had certainly expected my glimpse of him to have some great symbolic importance.

Our car followed the mountain road back to Livadia Palace; and once we got there, I felt that I was, at least for the time being, back home — not in downright hostile territory. But where was it more dangerous? At least I knew where I was in the Russian compound: if the necessity arose, I could deny the whole lunch conversation and seek diplomatic immunity, whereas in my own delegation quarters it was now going to be difficult to distinguish friend from foe, or at least friend from opponent. I went to the room I shared with Philip, lay down on the bed, and smoked a cigarette, wanting to assemble the jumble of my thoughts into some kind of order. The effect of the several toasts we had drunk took hold of me, and I fell asleep, not to awaken until I heard someone entering the room. I was startled back into consciousness by Philip, who looked down at me and said, "Well, you've certainly been working hard — time to get up. They're working through this afternoon's conference, and papers are coming in thick and fast."

"It's Poland again," someone said when we returned to the translation room. "They keep returning to it, at least Roosevelt and Churchill do, though it's quite clear Stalin regards the whole thing as settled. He's got his armies in there, and he has a government installed. He's certainly not going to let us persuade him that the government that fled from the Germans and is now in exile in London has any right to return — or even to form any part of the composition of a new government."

"But the British have a hundred and fifty thousand Poles fighting on our side," I said. "There's no way they're going to be sold down the river; it would be absolutely catastrophic. Imagine civil war, even mutiny, among the Western forces."

"Regardless of that, I'm afraid Poland has had it," another translator chimed in. "Once the Red Army is in, they'll do their damnedest to stay, and we can't expect to throw them out now anyway. It would mean another war, and we certainly haven't got the forces to go into Poland. God, what a crew, what allies for us and for everyone in the West."

One of the translators, who had been poring over a sheet of paper in front of him, said, "I think Roosevelt is putting up quite a fight, I'll give him that. He didn't really give a damn about Poland, or even Europe, before he came here. But I think the message has sunk in: with the Soviets' strength in Europe, there is going to be little peace if they decide to go out and conquer the world."

"No, no," another delegate countered. "Roosevelt thinks he will have his peace with Stalin, and then between them they will settle everything. They are including Great Britain among the so-called peace men. But they know that the British Empire is nearly finished, and between them they have got the happy job of running the whole show."

"I wonder just how many of the Russian military men are behind Stalin," I said, musing aloud and feeling like I was taking a chance. "I mean the top men: usually they give the impression of being yes-men, though they are obviously capable. The generals who relieved Stalingrad and those who are driving across Europe — some of them must have minds of their own." I looked around the room to see if anyone would respond to this remark, but initially there was nothing more than a murmur.

"Oh, they're used to being led," said one of the interpreters. "Who was it that said Russia is controlled by the knout?"

"What's that?" someone asked.

"Oh, it's a whip — more a rope than a whip — used to flog the peasants pretty well to death . . . not very different from Stalin's methods now." For a moment my eyes met those of the definer of "knout" across the room, and I thought I recognized a look of mutual comprehension. It may merely have been that we were both thinking along historic lines; on the other hand, maybe he was part of the group that at some point I was supposed to be introduced to.

We were under pressure to keep the flow of paper moving. The differences between Roosevelt and Stalin continued, but it was now Churchill who had taken over and was speaking in support of the Western Allies. Neither Roosevelt nor Churchill would give in to Stalin's demands, that his so-called puppet government would be recognized as the interim rulers of Poland until a proper constituent assembly had been elected and a regular government installed.

It was a long and exhausting session. Churchill at his best was brilliant: sometimes he could be long-winded, and he tended to recapitulate historical backgrounds that were known to everybody; but on this occasion he advanced the case formally and forcibly. The United Kingdom could not possibly accept the imposition on Poland of a government that they regarded as representing either minority interests or those purely of the Soviet Union. Both he and Roosevelt had already given way to Stalin on the question of Polish frontiers when Stalin had taken back the entire portion of Poland that he had seized following the outbreak of the war in August 1939. It was true that the compensation to Poland would be to give her East Prussia and large chunks of Germany in the west. But this did not change the fact that a good part of the Polish population, which had existed independently of the Soviet Union before the war, would now once again be under Russian rule.

The man who had asked the meaning of the word "knout" — though I doubted that he was as ignorant of it as he appeared to be — looked up again.

"Of course, the trouble with the President is, he thinks that a free election is a free election. He hasn't the slightest idea of what occupation by any other country means, let alone the communists. He takes for granted that the Germans will squash everybody. But to have the Russians in Poland and to expect there to be free elections is frankly insanity. I told you he didn't give a damn about Poland or Europe before. I doubt if he knows anything more of the world than he gets from his postage stamps, which he sits pawing over evening after evening, so I'm told."

"Oh, for god's sake, shut up!" came a voice from the corner. "For heaven's sake, we are U.S. citizens and he is our President. That's a pretty rotten way to be talking while we are working here at his side, supposedly trying to bring some sort of peace to this cock-eyed world."

We returned to our work without further comments, until eventually someone said he had finished and proposed that we all clear out and have a drink. I chose not to follow them, deciding that I needed some fresh air instead. It was dark now, and I took a few steps onto the garden paths that twisted and turned down to the sea. I didn't want to go far, just to get away from the building, and I knew it would probably be unwise to go out the front since it would be surrounded as usual by guards. With the burned and destroyed villas all around, it was too upsetting.

I hoped that Stefansky would not approach me again, but by now I was somewhat apprehensive about anyone coming up to me. They all seemed as likely to be friend or foe, with curious and conspiratorial threats appearing to emanate from everyone. I sat down to think, and lit up a cigarette. The faint glow of the tip or the smell of the smoke must have drawn it to someone else's attention, because out of the darkness I heard a voice saying, in accented English, "Good evening, comrade, how nice seeing you to enjoy our wonderful country." This seemed a harmless enough introduction, and as the man approached, I rose to find myself facing a young Soviet army captain. He sat down next to me, and I offered him a cigarette.

"Thanking you very much," he said, shaking his head. "But I may give you perhaps some of ours — we have very good cigarette. Even Stalin himself sometime smoke them when he is not smoking his British Dunhill type."

This was a detail we had learned in the embassy as part of the general briefing.

"Your armies are doing very well," I said. "They must be almost in Berlin by now."

He nodded enthusiastically. "I hope so — and that will be the end of the war."

"Certainly in Europe," I replied, "but we still have to beat Japan."

"Oh, we will settle that also," he said, thus confirming that the U.S.S.R. had promised to come into the war against Japan within three months of the end of the war in Europe. That was all being kept very secret, because if the Japanese were to get a hint of it, they might well make a preemptive attack on Russia from the east and possibly from Siberia, and that would not have helped the Russians' progress toward Berlin. We both smoked in silent companionship until he reached into an inner pocket of his uniform and brought out a piece of paper, which he silently handed to me.

"Can you read this?" he asked. "Is enough light?"

"Yes, thank you," I said, glancing down at the sheet in front of me. It was a page from the list of members of the delegations, which we had all received. I assumed that copies had been passed out to the Russians as well as to our British allies, and I saw little on the list of any particular interest.

"Can you remember the date of the year?" he asked.

"Nineteen forty-five, of course," I said.

He nodded and said in Russian "Da da" (yes, yes, that's right), as if there was some special significance in that. "That page you have in front of you — I expect you to know several names on it?"

"Of course I do," I replied. "They are all members of our delegation and some of them . . . I run into some of them from time to time."

"Only to remember the date of the year," he said. "Those numbers correspond to the names on this list who understands what we are talking about. They are friends of some of us — among the Russians as well as yourself."

I suddenly realized that he was giving me a coded list of certain of the conspirators who were, it was now clear, fairly well organized. I glanced at the sheet and committed the names to memory; only four of them were coded on the page, though I wondered how many more there were. I handed it back to the captain, and he put it back in his pocket.

"See what you think of them the next time you meet them," he said in an idiomatic English that surprised me considering his Russian accent. "I expect you will find that interesting. Well, good-night, comrade." With that he was gone.

This seemed to me an extraordinary assumption and imposition, and I wondered exactly how far Stefansky had persuaded his conspirators that I could be relied on to forward their agenda. I felt, in spite of myself, that the obvious thing would be to seek out and report this incident to the OSS agent — or whoever it was who had approached me a day or so earlier. I returned to the palace intending to do so, but I didn't know his name and wasn't sure that he would be immediately recognizable. In our work room I found a further pile of papers waiting for me, and I started to work through them, putting the problem out of my mind for the next hour or so. But, suddenly startled, I realized that one of the four names on the sheet I had been given, Alexander, was the man whose eye I had caught when we'd had the discussion about Stalin and Roosevelt in that room earlier. The obvious thing to do, I decided, was to approach him first and ask him about whether there was any truth to what I had just been told. At least I could find out something far more concrete to be able to tell our U.S. agent when I found him. I chose my moment, and as I stood up to go to the mess for dinner, looked across the room. I saw that he also stood up, but so did Philip; so the three of us went upstairs to the mess together.

With Philip there, I realized there was nothing I could say, and for a time we ate our food in silence. Our work of rendering the correct reading of words and nuances was generally exhausting, and all of us were tired. I hoped that perhaps Philip would be the first to suggest that we retire for the night. Then, perhaps, I would have an opportunity to speak with this Alexander, or Alex, as he introduced himself. It was a name that was not all that common in the United States but was very common among the Russian émigrés. It was Alex who stood up first.

"Anyone feel like a stroll before turning in?" he asked. "I always think a breath of fresh air helps you sleep better."

"Count me out," said Philip. "I'm hitting the sack right away."

That left me, though my heart sank at the thought of yet another clandestine conversation on the paths in front of the villa, which I had begun to see in my mind with a bit of dread. I remained seated for the moment, and then said, "I think I'll just have another drink."

Philip left us, and Alex resumed his seat.

I knew that he was a civilian from the State Department, and as he sat there in his mufti, I wondered whether he was "hostilities only" or a career diplomat — or perhaps hoping to be one once the war ended.

"They are going over Poland again tomorrow," he said after a short time. "I've seen the agenda for the plenary meeting. Then there's a dinner at Corice Palace, where Stalin and Molotov are staying. I would be curious to know how they get on. It's all soft soap on the surface, but there are damned large principles at stake here . . . terrible stakes." Then he continued in a completely different tone: "I gather you are quite an expert on the Russians, fluent in the language. You must have picked that up somewhere."

By now I was convinced that he knew my background perfectly well. I shook my head. "Old family attachment — I learned it from my stepmother."

"I see," he nodded. "Is she Russian?"

"Yes, she was," I replied. "What about you?"

But he pressed on with his questions: "Were you born in Russia?"

"No, nothing like that. I'm from old Yankee stock. My father remarried after my mother died, shortly after I was born. It just so happened that, when he did remarry, it was to a Russian emigrant, and I was young enough to learn Russian at my stepmother's knee. I also learned a good deal about Russia as it was when she fled from the Revolution. And you?"

"Yes, I'm from Yankee stock too — a little west, though . . . Chicago. I'm here as part of the liaison team between the State Department and the White House, you know, the one set up by Stettinius because he thought the White House was off on a track of its own . . . almost off its trolley."

"Well, to some extent it is," I ventured. "After all, the President seems to have all the power in his hand in expressing himself — but that's what presidents normally do." I was not eager to show my hand so early in the game.

"Oh, we all know his hand," said Alex. "It's Stalin who's the important one at the moment, and there sure are plenty of people who want to close out that for good."

I was beginning to tire of the opening gambit, so I said to him, "You're on a list, you know. I was given a copy of it this evening. What do you have in mind? What are you doing now?"

He looked around the room, back at me, and then down at the cup of coffee in front of him.

"I'm on the side of the Russian-Americans. Some of us are, you know, and it's not the official side."

"What on earth do you expect to do?" I asked. "Is someone going to assassinate him — or something like that?"

"Don't be absurd," he replied. "There's more than one way to skin a cat."

"Have you — or they — got many supporters?" I asked, referring to the Russian side.

"Oh, the Russians obviously outnumber us; we are just a few. But throughout the country — Russia, I mean, and the Ukraine in particular — there are hundreds of thousands, if not millions, who would thank us if Stalin fell, and everything he stands for. With him gone, frankly, the U.S. interests would be served best. Then democracy would rule the world. Soviet Russia would disintegrate, and the power would be totally in our hands."

"It's a roundabout way of doing so," I said. "It would be like the British trying to stir up dissent among the colonies during the Revolutionary War. If they had, they might have broken us up. Good thing they didn't. But this is much bigger."

"It's not a parallel case," he said angrily. "Don't you realize what can happen? The Soviets will be at the Channel ports before we know it. The only way we can stop them is to stop their leaders. We certainly can't block their advance, and we have nothing in the way of troops with or without the British — with or without anybody — that can stand up to them. They are rushing across Europe now."

"So, what is the plan?" I asked. "What are you going to do? And how are you going to help the Russian dissidents? You can hardly take over the State Department — and Stettinius is certainly not on your side. He sure wouldn't be in on this kind of project."

"We can count on the Russian dissidents far more than you think," Alex replied, "far more than you can really guess. Are you going to help us?"

I realized now that I had gotten myself into a trap. The research they had done on my background — and presumably from what Stefansky had added — seemed to show that I was anti-Stalin and anti-Bolshevik. Yet I had been approached by the OSS agent, and I knew clearly where my duty lay. Even so, there remained the instincts of everything my stepmother had instilled in me, and for the moment I was silent.

"Frankly, I don't know," I finally said. "I really have to think this through." I paused for a moment.

"Who do you have in mind to lead this revolt?" I asked Alex. "Or who do the Russians have in mind? Just a group of dissident politicians and generals, all presumably with the same beliefs as Stalin? Are there even any left over from those old idealistic revolutionaries who supported Lenin but afterwards were dissatisfied with the dictatorship he installed? They all disappeared in the Terror Trials of the thirties, as far as I know, in Stalin's almost total destruction of the old guard."

"Ah, but that's the point," said Alex. "With Stalin and his close supporters gone, the others would have to offer something new. They couldn't just take over Stalin's slogans. But a country like this" — he swept his arms as if embracing the whole land mass from the Baltic to Vladivostok — "the nationalities will break up, and if they want to appoint their own governments, so be it. Then that is the way the future will lie." He stopped and looked at me again. "Are you with us or not?"

CHAPTER ELEVEN

Father stared at us as though he were confronted afresh with that question, and Mother and I both looked away, unable to face the intensity of his stare. At length Mother said, "I think you should stop, dear. You really have exhausted yourself, and you're really doing yourself absolutely no good going on like this." Father closed his eyes for a moment, as if this were answer enough for the time being, and nodded his head.

We went downstairs exhausted, not having realized how tiring it was merely listening to Father's narrative. I had given up taping his monologue, even for our own use, since I could remember what he was telling us almost word for word — and still can after all these years. I thought briefly that we might as well let the State Department have the tapes of the story we were getting from Father, in a calculated risk that they would show their hand; but I decided that I would do nothing. If they asked for the tapes again, I would simply shake my head and say that we were no longer using the machine.

Since we were exhausted, we decided we would go out to lunch in Washington. I called a restaurant and booked a table, and then called for a taxi. We left as though we were fleeing the house — not fleeing Father, but what seemed to be turning into a hellish morass of intrigue. As we entered the restaurant, the first person we spotted was Emil Segalov, who was sitting at a table by himself and rather glumly eating a lonely meal in this rather expensive restaurant. We approached him, and as he stood up, Mother said, "Do you mind if we join you?"

"Certainly not — please do, dear ladies." He gestured to the waiter, who led the three of us to a larger table and brought over Emil's plate.

"One eats very well here," he said. "That's why I come here alone sometimes . . . when I miss my country and my family."

"I thought you were unmarried," I said impulsively.

"Oh yes, I am." He looked at me with a broad smile. "But you can still miss your family without being married."

"Of course," I replied, sheepish about my impulse.

"And how's your father?" He was asking both of us, though he directed his eyes at me.

"Well, we're looking after him as well as we can at home," I said. "We've been assured that he is as well cared for at home as he would be in the hospital, and we do have nurses as well."

"Ah yes, of course." He looked down at his meal, cooling off at the new table.

"At one point I thought I was going to be transferred back to Moscow, but they have left me in Washington." He stopped, though he seemed to be on the verge of divulging something to us. Then he checked himself and studied his meal once again. Was he all that lonely, or was he trying to get our sympathy? It was hard to tell. It had always been difficult for me to figure Emil out, yet I still felt an attraction to him, and I believe he was attracted to me.

"What happened to Edward?" he asked after we had chosen from the menu. "Does your State Department move people around that quickly and frequently?"

"Do they?" I was somewhat startled by his question.

"Oh yes," he said. "There have been several changes recently. When I call over there, there are always different voices on the phone.

"What a strange idea democracies have," he went on. "You elect the leader of the country, and the leader of the country brings in his own officers. They must be very flexible and loose-jointed at the top, so to speak."

"It may seem strange," said Mother, "but once they are there with their careers, they have the usual powers that go with those of diplomats. I won't say those powers are as great as your diplomats, but they certainly control the country in ways we're accustomed to."

We settled for a time into silence, which Emil broke when he turned to me.

"I will say again, as I mentioned before, that it would be good if you could come and visit our country." He held his glance on me and then looked back at Mother. "It is a beautiful country. We have a great variety of scenery, and we've already discussed how one can go from what you call the 'frozen north' all the way down to the glorious Black Sea, which is like the French Riviera, where so many of your countrymen go each winter."

"As did many of the Russian aristocrats before the Revolution," I added softly.

He smiled at me. "Agreed," he said. "One or two of the grand dukes must have turned it into a little Russian Riviera, so to speak. And Yalta itself, where the Czar had his summer palace, is surrounded on three sides by mountains, with the Black Sea on the fourth side, the sun warming it all the year round . . . it is very much a coastal resort, a playground — I believe is your American expression — of the aristocrats."

There it was again, the reference to Yalta, and I wondered about his returning to it.

"As you know, my father was there years ago, right at the end of the war, at the conference that bears its name, though I believe it was originally intended to be called the Crimea conference."

"Oh yes," he said. "Does he ever speak about it now?"

"From time to time," I replied, and he nodded. "It was a great experience for a young man to attend one of the really significant conferences of the war, when the three leaders of the world's greatest powers were present."

"Yes, yes," he said. "It was a most important conference, and they were very great men. I think that it was . . . perhaps it was the high point of Allied unity."

"What happened afterward, then?" I asked, pushing him toward an answer I knew would not necessarily come from the history books I had read in school.

"Well, the West did not believe us." He spoke slowly and very deliberately, and I noticed that he was crumbling his roll in his hands. "We carried out our part of the bargain, but they thought that we were being dishonest and that Stalin was about to launch an attack on the whole of Europe. And so the Cold War started. But if the mood in Yalta had continued, then it would all be very different now, and we would be living in peace."

"Aren't we now?" I asked. He shrugged.

"Well, I suppose that, with each of us threatening the other with a hydrogen bomb, it is peace, yes. One of the most unusual periods of peace we've ever had." Abruptly Emil asked: "Was your father very involved in the conference?"

Mother took up the conversation. "As much as any young naval officer in his mid-twenties might have been," she said. "I expect the same was true of those of similar age in your services and diplomatic corps."

Emil turned toward me to pursue his point: "I believe your father did interpreting, didn't he?" I was somewhat surprised because at no time in our previous conversations had I mentioned Father's translating activities.

"How do you know?" I asked. He was suddenly caught off guard, realizing that he had perhaps gone too far in revealing the research that was obviously behind his observation.

"Oh," he said, "it's just something I had heard. We naturally have to find out everything we can about people who are assigned to Moscow; and this was particularly true later, when Henry disappeared in Moscow. But he must have been a fluent Russian speaker . . . for your government to trust him the way they did. Interpreting is very important, and he would have met many of our people. I know that our interpreters met a lot of your people. In fact, they worked together in many cases — in arranging and running the conference."

"But there was a lot of routine work to do," I said, "reading documents, studying papers — the sort of thing anyone would be ready to do without actually meeting those speaking Russian."

"I have to confess," Emil went on, "that we have some very mixed memories of your people. So many of them were like your President Roosevelt — friendly, amiable, willing to please us, to make sure that the world was safer for us. But there were some who were not happy with us at all, and I'm afraid they have had more influence on what has happened since. Those people have gotten into power, and the ones who supported us seem to have disappeared."

"It wasn't all black and white," I said, "if you understand that expression." But I wondered for a moment whether, in fact, it had been black and white. Perhaps that was what Father was driving at as he lay in bed trying to remember and express exactly what had happened to him at Yalta.

"One day I would like to meet your father," Emil said. "Perhaps I may visit him sometime, if you will permit me."

The idea seemed astounding and yet at the same time strangely sympathetic, and I wondered whether this was a ploy on Emil's part or was based purely on amiability. Surely he knew Father's background, and the background to the story Father had been trying to tell us. But for the moment I hesitated.

"Yes, perhaps that would be nice," I finally said. "He would like to see you sometime. After all, you were responsible for telling us that he was safe — you and Edward. That was a wonderful moment." I suddenly felt warm toward him again.

He smiled delightedly. "I was glad to be the bearer of good news. Things like that seldom happen in one's lifetime, because so much is taken up not so much with bad news as half news — hidden news. Things you do not know yet pass on, and then you wonder what the consequences are." His plunge into philosophy rather surprised me, but I nodded in agreement.

"Yes," I said, "we must think about you having a meeting with Father one day, though I'm afraid he is very ill right now, and we have to take great care with him."

"Yes, of course." There was a pause, and I had the impression that he was wrestling with what he wanted to say next. Suddenly, rather unexpectedly, he asked, "Has he told you everything?"

"What do you mean?" I said.

"Well, I'm sure that he had a lot to tell you about his past. Being at Yalta must have been one of the highlights of his career, and perhaps it's something we can talk about. I was too young at the time, but I, too, would like to know what happened."

"Oh, he forgets some things and remembers others," countered Mother, rather cleverly, I thought. "There are all sorts of things he has probably forgotten altogether, just as others must stick in his mind."

"I'm sure that what he might be able to tell you about Yalta is in all the books now," I said. "There are certainly books in English, and there were Russian reports as well, I've noticed."

"Yes, obviously," Emil said, not eager to drop the point Mother and I were clearly avoiding. "Anyone who was at the conference would have much to tell us, since so much of the history of the world has turned on it, and there are not many left to tell us what happened. The old leaders are all gone; only a few who were quite young at the time, and a very few who were middle-aged are left. But even they are now out of power, so their influence on those in Washington or Moscow can only continue in a second-hand way." Emil changed his approach: "When did Henry leave the Navy?"

My mother answered him: "Very soon after the war. By that time, he had a wife and a young child — Lorina. You see, before Henry joined the Navy right after Pearl Harbor, we had gotten married and he had already partially completed his degree. There were many in that position."

"Yes, like our own young people," said Emil. "Only with them, of course, in many cases the enemy arrived at the doorstep and swept over the country and the universities rather than merely interrupting their studies. The fascists were beasts!" He spoke with bitter animation and, I knew, from his heart. "Many of my family were lost," he continued, "killed by the Germans, or rather the fascist Germans, the Nazis, in the most terrible circumstances."

Mother and I sat in silence, both contemplating the fact that we represented a country that had never been invaded.

"That's why," he went on, "Stalin placed so much emphasis on Poland at Yalta: he said it was a country through which the Germans had twice invaded our country, and this time he wanted a neighbor that was strong and friendly and able to help us in our defense." This was no time to argue about the subjugation of the peoples of Eastern Europe, so Mother and I held our peace.

"Anyway," he said, standing up, "with your permission, I'm afraid I must leave you now because my duties call. I give you my very best wishes and hopes for your father, and perhaps I may meet him sometime." He stopped for a moment as if he had forgotten something, and then said abruptly, "Was he one of them or one of us?"

The remark caught Mother and me completely off guard; but what he meant was quite clear.

"He was a U.S. Navy officer doing his duty for his country," Mother replied, kindly but formally. Emil Segalov bowed toward us and left the restaurant.

So the conspiracy in 1945, more than fifteen years ago, still worried the Soviets as much as it did Washington, as we already knew. As if in a common impulse to protect Father, we quickly left the restaurant, hailed a cab, and instructed the driver to return us to Georgetown. As we settled back in our seats, Mother said, "I'm surprised that Emil showed his hand so obviously. Are they desperately anxious to know, or is it merely to satisfy an old curiosity?"

"What worries me," I said, "is that the anxiety seems to be coming from our own people as well."

"Perhaps that is where the struggle is now," said Mother. "He mentioned our elections. I suppose there were two sides to everything that was happening at Yalta. After all, most of the American delegation loathed the Soviets then, but Roosevelt went out on a limb in his friendship to Stalin."

McCarthyism, the whole backdrop to our conversation at the moment, shot through my mind. I also remembered the furious debate about how Roosevelt's supporters were supposed to be full-blown members of the communist party, and I wondered just how Father and his story fit into the controversy. We almost ran from the cab into the house and up to his room, where one of the nurses was sitting talking softly to him.

"He's had a wonderful sleep," she said. "I think he is very rested now. Try not to disturb him if you can help it. His recollections seem to put such a strain on him."

It was strange that the nurse seemed to know what Father was talking about; she must have come in from time to time and realized that he had been discussing the past. She left us with him, and we both kissed him. He smiled and said, "So glad to see you're back. Did you have a nice lunch?"

I had not realized how much of the afternoon we had spent with Emil. Father had already had some tea, but he eagerly accepted another cup when the nurse brought in two cups for Mother and me. I could see that he was alert and obviously eager to talk.

"May I go on with my story?" he asked with a bit of mock supplication.

"Only if doesn't tire you out too much," Mother responded.

"Well, someone's got to tell it, and I may be at the end of the line."

My mother grabbed his hand. "Please don't say that, Henry," she said. "You'll get better and all this will be in the past."

He nodded to acknowledge her love and concern, but his voice said: "No . . . no, I won't, you know. But it is what no one knows that I want to get across to you, and I'm sorry that you and Lorina are the only ones hearing it." He seemed calmer somehow, as though he had come to a decision and could relate to us more than he had before.

CHAPTER TWELVE

You may think it strange — possibly disloyal — but when Alex asked me if I was one of them, I answered that I was with them, whoever they were, and that, above all, I wanted to topple Stalin. In my own mind I knew it was at least temporary and a lie, but I still had my stepmother's instincts. I welcomed the possibility of overthrowing Stalin and the Bolsheviks. At the same time, my mind was in utter turmoil: I was an American, a U.S. Navy officer, and my ultimate loyalties had to lie with my country — which was allied with the Soviets.

Alex, I could see, though welcoming my response, was somewhat startled by the immediacy of my reply. He merely shook his head and said, "In that case, you must meet more of us — on both sides — who have one objective in common."

"But exactly how many Russians are there?" I persisted. "That's the important thing, because I can't see any Americans defecting."

"Oh no, I agree — there's nothing like that," he said. "Only secret support and a readiness to back up the dissidents when they take control. We have to see if we can organize your work so that you can meet more of the Russians. At the moment you're largely isolated within your own department dealing with documents. We have to have more face-to-face meetings with them — that is, with the Russians. You'll meet them soon enough, maybe even tonight. There is a big banquet going on, and I expect all of us interpreters will be standing by and mixing with each other, a sort of minor jollity among us, I suppose."

Alex and I left the mess together, and when we separated, I went up to the room I was sharing with Philip. He was sitting at his desk scribbling a note home, which he hoped would go with the next courier. He looked over his shoulder at me as I entered the room.

"You know," he said, "there's something about that fellow I don't like — he's shifty. Always seems to be asking for information that really isn't relevant to what we're doing. Does he strike you like that? Does he know any more about the Russians than we do or you do? Is he up to something?"

"No," I said, "although he does have a strange outlook. I think he was rather lonely this evening and was glad to share a drink. Anyway, he's gone off to bed now, and I'm going, too. It's been an exhausting day, and tomorrow, I gather, will involve not only a full meeting in the afternoon but a dinner hosted by Stalin. No doubt we'll have to stand by as copious notes of their trivial conversations flood out."

"When they're not toasting each other."

"Which can involve some kind of underlying meaning," I said. "The way they make their toasts, the replies to them, the emphasis, you know the sort of thing — bravest man in the world, but a man I can depend on and accept . . . and so forth."

"I know what you mean," said Philip. With that I departed to the one bathroom we shared with many others. Fortunately, I found it empty and was able to use the cold running water, which was all we had for washing purposes.

Were there really all those Russians ready to bring down Stalin? I wondered. They seemed united now in a vast assault across Europe, but I suppose generals quarreled, just like everyone else. I had learned from even my limited Navy experience in Washington that admirals certainly did. But would the Russian generals really quarrel enough to depose their leader? I was supposed to know more about Communist Russia than most of my comrades. I could not avoid thinking to myself that they were ready to hatchet each other if necessary, but it didn't necessarily mean that they would unite and turn on their leader. When I finished washing and returned to the room, Philip was already asleep; and after I turned out the light, I fell asleep almost immediately. Perhaps it was Yalta's climate and air, perhaps it was the secretive conversations — but that day had been enough to exhaust me.

I had made my decision, though it was not a full-blown one: I was at least temporarily on the side of those who believed the most important thing was to destabilize Stalin rather than trying to face him down with the bland words that had been coming from President Roosevelt's lips and from the transcripts of the conference discussions. In short, I was now, to a degree, against what Roosevelt stood for, against my commander-in-chief — but for the sake of my country! I was bewildered. Was this treachery?

I certainly wanted to meet the people I was supposed to be allied with in this subterfuge beneath the surface of the conference itself. That evening we in the U.S. delegation were taken to Corice Palace, the Russian delegation's headquarters and the site of the banquet. We were put on full alert to handle any documents and translate any statements that might be made at the banquet, since it was possible for anything to be said by any of the leaders, even in their toasts. As I've mentioned before, the banquets were pretty incredible affairs of alcohol and apparent good wishes; but there were side conversations as well. During this particular banquet, nothing of any consequence did in fact take place. But I would not have wanted to be the primary interpreter of remarks passed back and forth among the participants. The British and the Russians had come with their diplomats and military staff; but the American servicemen were completely unrepresented. From time to time I had to deal with the Russian translators, and it was one of those who abruptly said to me in Russian, "I gather you have spoken to Alex."

"Yes," I said guardedly, "he's one of our delegation."

"I know that," he said. "He's also one of us, isn't he?" He looked me square in the face. "Of course, it is really up to us Russians to deal with the problem. But it's up to you and your countrymen to support us if there is any weakening in our resolve . . . although we hope that we shall achieve our ends quickly and without any real opposition."

"How?" I asked.

"To begin with, there is so much moving to and fro at this conference, and, you see, the main thing is that Stalin is away from Moscow, away from his routine, away from his standard guards. Just as your President and the British Prime Minister are away from their capitals, so he is away from the fortress that surrounds him. He is away from the standard route from his rooms in the Kremlin to his dacha, and he has to move among the various delegations. It is true that Roosevelt is away from Washington and Churchill away from London, but they travel freely anyway. Not our leader. He is forever surrounded, like some terrifying superman, by all the police that can be gathered together. But do you think that all the NKVD guards are loyal to him? Why do you suppose Beria, the head of secret police, is here? He's here to watch over his men, and they in turn are watching over others. He learned his lesson during the Terror, where most of the NKVD who participated in the slaughter were themselves subsequently shot. So Beria comes to protect Stalin because, frankly, he hopes to be his successor."

It was difficult to imagine that: a mad president running the United States — only a thousand times more savage than anyone could dream up. What a future, what a country! No wonder I was still resolute about the goal of ruining this régime as fast as it could be ruined.

"What exactly is the role of the Americans to be?" I asked the Russian.

"Well, we will know who you are," he said, "and then, when we succeed, we shall call on you to give us your backing in the event that official Washington policy, particularly from the White House, is to continue serving a régime that we hope to have destroyed. We want you to come out with a direct policy that, if not supporting us, at least accepts the events that will have precipitated our claims."

"So you don't want *us* to assassinate Stalin?" I asked, half laughing. He looked at me seriously.

"If you could, we would want you to," he said. "After all, you and the British, on many occasions, get much closer to Stalin physically than we Russians do. He doesn't trust any of us; but he certainly doesn't expect either the President or the Prime Minister to draw a gun on him — or anyone else in your delegation. If we could persuade some American to do it, of course, we would. But I think that would be a very difficult task. No, we want your backing in case someone like Molotov — or Beria, as I've said — takes over the régime before we've had a chance to clear away this mess."

"But you are Communists in your country . . . you're Marxists," I said. "Doesn't that imply a form of government that must continue, whoever is at its head. Stalin succeeded Lenin, and Lenin himself would have understood."

"Ah, but there is Lenin as Lenin and Lenin as Stalin."

I was not prepared to go into the intricacies of Lenin as interpreted by Stalin. All I knew was that Stalin was head of the state, no matter where he had learned his doctrine. He hated us, he hated capitalism, but above all he hated all those who stood in his way, as he had hated Boris all those years ago. If the Russian dissidents saw the role of the U.S. conspirators as standing by and accepting the *fait accompli* of the régime's destruction, well, that was one thing. But was it true that this was all they really wanted of us? How much more were they really hoping we would achieve in our support of them?

The validity of the opposition to Stalin had crossed my mind several times, but the rather shallow remarks that he was relatively unguarded when he went from the villa to the car or moved around during the conference did not really bear the marks of a properly plotted conspiracy, and I wondered whether I might have been merely listening to the griping of discontented men. Yet I knew some of them were obviously intent on demolishing the régime, and they seemed to know some on our side who were willing to help them.

I decided that I really had to seek out Stefansky somehow, much as I disliked the man. He was clearly at the center of things as far as the dissidents were concerned, and his word had triggered my involvement. I didn't know where to begin looking, so one morning, as we were working away at transcripts, I glanced over at Alex, who was across the room from me. I waited for a moment when a number of the translators were taking a coffee break, and went up to him.

"Alex," I said, "do you know where Stefansky is? Or Stevens — or whatever he calls himself now?"

"That's the curious thing," he said, shaking his head. "No one has seen him for a day or two. Admittedly, he is among the higher-ups attached to this delegation, but he seems to have disappeared. Whether he has gone over to the Russians completely, I don't know, but they are hardly likely to welcome him. After all, he is one of what they call their 'former people,' and they must know of his outright hostility to them."

"I need to see him."

"Why?" Alex asked sharply.

"For my own satisfaction," I said. "I've known him for many years, long before you would have come across him. . . ."

"Having second thoughts?" He looked at me curiously.

"No," I said. "I just want to satisfy my own mind. I can only repeat that he's a key figure in this movement, at least on our side." I gestured rather vaguely around the room, inadvertently including many of the loyal Americans and Russians working there. Philip looked up just as I did so, and he thought I was inviting him to join us. So Alex and I broke off our conversation, and the three of us went for coffee together, discussing, if I remember correctly, the latest hockey scores and other news from home. Philip was the first to leave and get back to work.

"Of course, you must know," Alex said, "the dissidents work in cells: no one knows who gives them orders or where they come from, so I can't really look up Stefansky for you. Anyway, it would bring suspicion on me. I'm afraid you'll have to do it yourself. All I can say is, move carefully. He is not really someone I would like to cross swords with — here or anywhere else. But as long as he does his job first and helps us bring down this ghastly régime, I won't question his methods or those of anyone else we are involved with."

Returning to work, I decided that the moment we were to break for lunch, I would see if I could find Stefansky somewhere, even if it meant questioning some senior member of the delegation. I went over in my mind the list of names the Russian had shown me in the garden, determining to approach them one by one if necessary. But I, too, feared drawing attention to myself, since there was always the possibility of double agents among them.

I left the work room unobtrusively at noon and once again headed toward the grand staircase that led up to the mess hall. Suddenly there was no need to look for Stefansky; he was at that very moment walking toward me.

"Just the man I'm looking for," he said. "Can we have a word?"

"Absolutely," I said.

"Come along to my room — it's on this floor. It's quiet, and no one will disturb us."

He led me down one of the corridors and into a room that overlooked the sea. He closed the door, taking care to lock it, and pointed to a chair by a table. I sat down and he sat opposite, and I wondered why he now seemed so determined to talk to me again — since it was I who wanted to ask him the questions. He traced his finger on the surface of the table as if following the lines of an invisible chart.

"As you know from recent Russian history, the opposition to Stalin goes back to the time when he successfully plotted for power during the last years of Lenin, when he drove Trotsky out in 1929, when he drove the older people from the party, and when he tried other Bolsheviks — and eventually had them shot. He then went on to kill millions of his countrymen. Some survived, God knows how, and there were others who prospered under him, became successful. Some of his generals, some of the politicians and the administrators — well, most of those who saw him firsthand — were repelled by him but put up with him. They were ambitious for power, and naturally they lived in fear of their lives. You know how much I loathed Stalin and all his works. Since I had my contacts in the States, I was more than eager to come here and try to see whether we could bring his rule to an end.

"To a certain extent, you have shared my feelings. So now let me tell you what I've discovered here in Yalta, this hell-hole of a place. There's nothing these leaders are going to achieve. They are all pursuing their own ends, and Stalin, merely by being Stalin, plows ahead determinedly and will stay in charge of the nation . . . well, it's not really a nation, what they so grandly call this Union of Soviet Socialist Republics."

He spat out the words and glared at me as if I were a guilty party. Rising from the table, he went to the window and continued speaking with his back to me. I thought that perhaps he felt somewhat ashamed of what he was going to say.

"Can't you see that the man in power, entrenched with his armies sweeping up well into Germany, will be in France before de Gaulle or anyone else can stop him. There is only one country that can possibly bring it to an end, and that is the United States. The British have been terrified of this for ages. Churchill has privately — almost publicly — expressed his fears. Eden and others know that the only way they can exert any influence is to try to stiffen President Roosevelt's backbone. Even his ambassador in Moscow is aware of this now. If there are dissolutionists working with us against Stalin, I can tell you that many more are working against Roosevelt. He has his natural enemies, of course, in the Republicans; but the Democrats themselves are by no means totally united. At least the Republicans believe in a strong foreign policy. I don't think you'll find that those close to Roosevelt are anything more than a chorus of sycophants agreeing with him in a lunatic attempt to set up a worldwide organization: the three policemen who will keep the world at peace, and that means — in Roosevelt's mind and even in some public utterances — placating the U.S.S.R. at almost every turn. You have seen the papers from the conferences, and you have seen some of the material from the dinners. Does it strike you that the United States is being led by a man of iron will?

"Good God," he burst out, turning around to glare at me, "does it?" He was shouting now. "We've got the wrong man! Can't you see that? We've been after the wrong man."

"Shall we get the Russians to help us against Roosevelt?" I asked, somewhat childishly. "That'll be the day. But what is the value of doing that if Stalin can get everything he wants from Roosevelt now."

"That's clear," said Stefansky, coming toward me. "You've seen Roosevelt, haven't you?"

"Not recently," I said.

"Well, I have . . . I have seen him. He's nearly dying, he's dead on his feet. And what happens when he dies? We'd get Truman, and I can tell you Truman hates the Soviets' guts. That's why the dissident Russians want Roosevelt out of the way; they know that is their only hope. If they want to build up the opposition to Stalin, it can only come from a change in the White House — not here or anywhere in this damned country. Otherwise, I'm afraid the free world is lost."

As I listened to him moving from personal vitriolic attack to sweeping generalization, I remembered hearing him talk to my stepmother all those years before, exploding about the Bolsheviks, about Stalin, about Lenin, about any number of them. And I could see that his whole hatred was now trained on this one hapless invalid in the White House. In a way, I knew that he was horribly right, that the United States was not mounting opposition to the relentless thrust of Stalin's armies. This was being reflected in the behavior of the communists at the conference.

I had nothing to say. I had certainly approved — or agreed with — a plan to remove Stalin and destabilize the Soviet empire, if that would mean peace to the world. But I had not gone further than that. I wondered now where Stefansky was going with his diatribe. I had realized a long time ago that he was a man of extreme, even unstable, temperament, that there was no arguing now with what he was saying.

"You may ask what are we going to do now," he said, anticipating my question.

He shrugged his shoulders, and I interrupted him, having decided to bring this conversation to some sense. "You can't just ditch all those Russians who have been plotting against Stalin — as well as some of our own people — just hang them out to dry."

"Oh, most of them will still be with us, because they do have one object in mind, and they will be happy to come over to a better and more likely scheme. You know what we do with the Russians? We shop them to their own people. There are enough of them to shake Stalin's ruling bureaucracy when their numbers and names are revealed. That will weaken them for a while, and then we can turn to Roosevelt."

"Shop them?" I asked, appalled. "Are you nuts? You mean, hand over their identities to the NKVD? They'll be taken out and slaughtered, tortured to death — you know the consequences of any such action."

"Yes, I do," he said. "And I'm sorry. A lot of them are close to being my friends, but basically they are no better than the people we are handing them to. At least it will shake up the Russians for a while — give us a break while we try to hold our own during the rest of this god-awful conference."

If I had been reduced to silence earlier, I now sat absolutely dumbstruck. Stefansky himself seemed overwhelmed by what he had just said. He turned back to the window, looked down at the Black Sea, and then leaned against the window frame, looking half at me and half back in the room. "Well," he said, "that's the plan I propose to put to our fellow American conspirators."

"And you think they'll swallow it?" I asked. "These men who have a sufficient hatred of Stalin to betray their own country? Do you think they'll go so far as to agree to this sort of mass betrayal? Good God, you expect a lot of your fellow men, don't you?"

"Or nothing," Stefansky said. "At least they can see the issues at stake."

Was I treacherous and despicable for even listening to Stefansky's rant? I think that perhaps I was. His suggestion of a betrayal of the Russian dissidents was unbelievable, and it was difficult to guess how much of his further revelation about turning on Roosevelt was a crazy rant and how much was a wild plot he was hatching — with me as a possible accomplice. Did I really think he would betray all those Russians? I didn't know. Was I to become something like a liaison between Stefansky and other Americans just because I had known him all those years. There must be others, I thought, who know Stefansky and know of his plot. I wondered whether he had already notified them of his change of heart.

Stefansky had, I knew, via his money ingratiated himself in Washington circles and had quickly moved up in them. He had then appeared in Yalta in a senior capacity, and he had contacted me there. Now I was getting an astonishing revelation of this man changing his mind. Who was he? I wondered. Who was this man who seemed to be the *éminence grise* behind all the plotting — unless there were others behind him who were pulling the strings? During the time he knew my stepmother, he had certainly been an independent agent, but an agent for whom? I couldn't remember his name being featured in the Washington press, and I never saw him in any reports. I was just over twenty when the war broke out, and of course I was in the Navy right after that. But when I was in Washington on my curious half-assignment with the State Department and involved in Soviet-American matters of a fairly humdrum nature, I didn't remember ever coming across his name there.

I can still see Stefansky, his back to me, suggesting his proposition as part of this grand strategy — and the horror of my reaction. The horrible thing is that what he suggested is exactly what they did do: somehow they shopped the whole lot of Russian dissidents to the Russian delegation, and God only knows what happened to the poor devils. (Remember that Beria, the head of the secret police, was there at Yalta.) I'm sure they went through the whole process of torture and final extinction that the NKVD and the Russian secret service would have meted out to them. And what did it accomplish? It could have done nothing but extend the war, at least from the point of view of the Allies, who wanted to end it as soon as they could. The Russians could have been in Berlin in a few days — probably before the Yalta conference was over. The Russian general who was leading the drive to Berlin wrote that he was absolutely convinced that the capital of Germany was within their grasp, and others supported his contention. He could not understand why they were brought to a halt.

There was, of course, the contrary view: that the Russians had advanced so fast and so far that they were overextended, that they needed to bring up supplies, that their flanks were at risk. But that was rubbish. They could have walked into Berlin and presented us, the Western Allies, with a *fait accompli*. Why did they stop? One view was that Roosevelt had told Stalin, "You can have Berlin" as part of his effort to bring the Soviets over to his great peace-keeping plan. But perhaps the sudden revelation to Stalin of the conspiracy against him and his regime, of the seniority of those involved, and of its possible ramifications brought the army's advance to a halt as he weeded out all those he regarded as disloyal. The regrouping at Berlin was necessary for his own internal security, not for the safety of his armies. It was plain as day to me what had happened: it was Stalin's personal flank that he feared had been turned, and he became aware of it only because some Americans let him know what was happening.

Thank God, I was not included among those who conveyed the information, though I curse myself for being involved in conversations with Stefansky and others. It was a horrible thing. Men we had been working with side by side, day by day, suddenly disappeared. I knew enough to understand what was happening to them, though such was the naiveté of many in the U.S. delegation that they could not even guess what was going on. I'm sure they had a fear and loathing of Communism, but they knew nothing of Bolshevism in its pure evil and savage guise.

Some of the Russian-Americans stayed with us, but some who were thought to be involved in the plot were quietly sent home. They had their protectors in Washington, just as there were possibly a few Russians who had theirs in Moscow, which I guess is what "diplomacy" is all about. It was a most appalling breach of faith; and we Americans, I'm afraid, were responsible. At least the Russian conspirators had their country's future at heart in a curious way: they felt they would be better off without Stalin. But we had taken people into our confidence, and frankly our good name counted for nothing.

CHAPTER THIRTEEN

Mother and I felt that this was enough emotion for one day, another day that had brought its share of unraveling. Father was exhausted; he sank back on his pillow and closed his eyes, murmuring, "I love having you both here, but now I would like to be left alone — perhaps even to sleep."

"Oh, my darling," Mother said, leaning over to kiss him. I kissed him too, and we both left the room silently, slightly numbed by what we had heard. The house seemed haunted now by his memories, by the events of all those years ago, of the treacheries that were being revealed to us, the hatreds, the false loyalties, and the confidences that meant nothing — and by the knowledge that those treacheries still influenced some of those who were currently in the seats of power.

"I wonder whether Henry's name was revealed by the Russians," Mother said once we were downstairs. "He didn't mention it, and I wanted to ask him. Or perhaps he was lucky and escaped disclosure."

"Maybe they wanted to leave him in place, as the spy expression goes," I said.

I stood up and wandered around the room. I was restless and wanted to get out of the house, but I didn't feel I could leave Mother and could think of no reason why both of us should leave Father. We certainly didn't want to go out to dinner, and there was no one I could think of calling up. Mother spotted my restlessness and said, "Why don't you go for a walk, darling?"

"I thought I might, but I didn't want to leave you alone."

"Don't worry about me," she said. "It would do you good to get some air. Why don't you go over to Kate's and see how she is?"

"She's not in town right now," I said, "and I can't think of anyone else. Don't you really mind if I go out?"

"No, no, no — go ahead."

I bounced down the front steps and started walking, with no real destination in mind. I had gone only two or three blocks when I heard a voice: "Lorina, Lorina, I was just coming to see you and your mother."

I stopped and turned around to find myself facing Edward. I felt like flinging myself into his arms. "Edward," I said breathlessly, "what are you doing here?"

"Well, to begin with," he said calmly, "I've come to visit you. . . ."

"But I thought you had been assigned somewhere away from Washington, sent miles away, so we were informed — even overseas."

"I was," he said, "but I've given it all up . . . and that's why I can come here to see you." He smiled warmly. "We can get re-acquainted."

"What do you mean?" I asked. "Have you been assigned back here?"

"No, I resigned from the State Department. There are all kinds of reasons — and you probably are aware of some of them. Anyway, where are you going?"

"Just taking a walk. We've had a rather" — I hesitated — "frightening afternoon reliving Father's traumas with him, and I felt like I needed a change."

"I'll walk with you. Are you going in any particular direction?"

"Not anymore," I said. "And you're very welcome at home." I put my arm through his. "Come right home — Mother will be delighted to see you." We broke into a sprightly walk and within minutes were back at the house. Mother welcomed Edward with the same open pleasure that I felt when I saw him.

"What can we offer you? Coffee, tea, drinks . . . anything?"

"Just whatever you're having," he said.

"I'll be having a rather stiff drink, I'm afraid," said Mother.

"Well, then, that'll be good for me."

"Good," Mother replied, and then without a pause, "You'll stay for dinner, won't you? You won't go away yet . . . you won't leave us yet?" She sounded almost desperate.

"Wouldn't think of it," said Edward. "I've got the evening to myself. Well, I guess you could say I've got the immediate future to myself. Anyway, I've got all the time in the world." Mother shot him a questioning look, and he answered before I could pipe up.

"I've left the Department. I'm a free agent — at least, relatively. I'm still bound by all sorts of official secret restrictions, of course, but I'm no longer a member of the State Department."

"But it's your career," Mother said. "You mean you've thrown it all overboard because of some" — she shrugged — "some events in the past?"

"Oh, it's more than that. The past never ends, you know. It runs into the present and indeed into the future. I'm sure T. S. Eliot had something to say about that. Anyway, I'm out and, as I say, a relatively free man."

Mother asked him where he was living now, and he replied that he'd rented out his Washington apartment when he left and then, just before he returned, had persuaded the tenants to move out.

"So you might say that I'm really back home," he said.

"No girlfriend, no wife-to-be?" Mother asked, almost girlishly.

He shook his head: "Afraid not — not yet anyway."

Mother and I looked across at each other, and we knew that what we had been hearing from Father was going to pour out. But before it did, Edward asked about Father's condition, and how we'd been getting along with him back at home.

"Do you think he'd like to see me?" he asked.

"Oh sure," we said together, though we had no reason to know one way or the other. At least we knew that Edward was not one of Father's contemporaries and therefore not involved in the story he was forcing out, nor was he someone bent on prying information out of him. Then it all started coming out of Mother and me. We jabbered on and on about the information that Father had been divulging for days. Edward listened silently as we took him, step by step, through Father's narration, until we came to the most recent revelation, that he had been confronted by Stefansky's proposal to shop the dissident Russians to their own government.

"Yes, yes, that certainly happened," Edward said. "And there are people now in power in Washington whose hands are stained with the blood of that appalling act. The effect was much more far-reaching than I think even Henry understood at the time: it not only brought the Red Army to a halt — those few miles from Berlin — it almost brought Washington to a standstill. It paralyzed the U.S. delegation at Yalta because they had no clear instructions to counterbalance it from the White House or the State Department — or from anybody else who was aware of what was going on. All they saw was the renewed warmth on Stalin's

face at the plenary sessions, and the warmth among his delegates generally, at the cooperation they believed they were receiving unstintingly
from their American allies. The scenario — if you were to reverse it —
was as if the Soviets had willingly unveiled to us, the Americans, that almost half of our OSS members were traitors. It went as deep as that."

"How much did you know about this when you came to tell us of
Father's sudden reappearance in Moscow?" I asked. "Or how much did
you know before you were sent away from Washington?"

"Nothing, absolutely nothing at all. But I did know that the politicians and the State Department were fighting savagely as the election approached — more viciously than I'd ever seen them before. Yet none of it
was in public. And that's what surprised me the most, and alerted me."

"And you are fully aware now?" asked Mother.

"Not really," he said. "There's not really an end to this story. I heard
a lot about it when I was out of the Department, meeting the odd Russian, even the odd American, who was prepared to talk and sometimes to
hint at it. But I always knew there was more. I knew there was something
that made this a secret battle beyond the reach or the attention of the
media. Something that was being kept secret even between the two antagonists, something that no one else could be party to."

He paused. "But wait a minute — can't I take you two out to dinner?"

We both shook our heads. "No, Edward, please stay here with us,"
Mother replied. "We want someone to warm this house, to help us feel
that we're not alone and rattling around in a haunted domain." She went
to the kitchen, leaving Edward and me to look at each other in comfortable and companionable silence. He sank back onto the couch, and I
curled up in the armchair opposite him. After we'd heard Mother rum-
maging around in the kitchen for a few moments, she returned.

"Well, that's settled," she said. "You're staying for dinner, and there
definitely is enough to eat." She filled our glasses and looked affection-
ately at Edward, who was staring into space, clearly thinking about the
discoveries he had made in and out of the Department, now confirmed
by Father's story.

"Of course, the interesting thing," he continued, "was that it was
Roosevelt who really gave Berlin to Moscow."

"I thought they had come to a standstill," I said, "the Russians, that is."

"They had. But once they got going again, it was in direct response to messages to Stalin from Eisenhower, whose strategy now was to leave Berlin to the Soviet Army. But there were many who believed it was Roosevelt who decided on this, bypassing the combined chiefs of staff and opening the rest of Europe to the Soviets."

Edward rose to his feet and crossed over to look out the window. Then he turned and abruptly said, "But enough of that. Let me give you a break from it all. How about if we play Scrabble or something." Mother and I both laughed. It was the first time we'd felt like this in ages — almost light-hearted.

At dinner we talked about various trivial things. About halfway through, Edward asked, "What about Henry — does he have dinner? Won't he be awake by now? Maybe right after dinner would be a good time to have just a word with him before he goes back to sleep? You know, I was the guy who watched over him when he was in the hospital here, when he arrived in such bad condition. I don't think he can suspect me of anything."

"I'll go and ask him first," said Mother. "He was asleep when we left him some time ago, but he's probably awake now. I'm sure he'll be happy to see you."

Father *was* happy to see Edward, and Mother and I allowed them to have coffee alone together. When he came back down, Edward said, "He seems happier now, but I know there is more — I'm sure of it. There's more I could tell you as well, but I don't think I should burden you with it right now. Anyway, it's nothing compared to whatever he's holding back."

He stood up. "I'm afraid I'll be out of Washington for a few days," he said. "I'm going to see my family." He had never mentioned family before, so when we asked him about it, he told us that his father was a corporate lawyer in New York, divorced from his mother, who had run off with another man. His father, however, appeared to have settled into what Edward described as a comfortable bachelor life. Edward was going to pay him a visit, look up an uncle, settle some of his home affairs, and be back in Washington in a few days. He gave us the phone number of his father's office, and he warned us that, as he had left Father's room that evening, it was quite clear that Father was eager to resume his revelations to Mother and me.

"I know that you are his first listeners," Edward said, "and the only ones he wants. I'm sure he means that. Sometimes he is going over ground that others do know, but at least he knows both sides of the story. There is still some kind of ending that I can't guess at."

"Shall I call a cab?" Mother asked as he went toward the door.

"No, I'm happy to walk," Edward said. "It's a nice feeling to be free. . . . I'm enjoying it."

Mother and I saw him off into the warm, dark night and then returned to the living room, happier and more relaxed than we had felt for a long time. The fact that he was someone we knew and could trust, even if he knew less than we did, was enough to give us considerable relief.

"An awful lot seems to turn on this election coming up," Mother said after Edward was gone. "It's as though they're squaring off with each other and not letting the public know what they're fighting about. Edward talks about men in power with blood on their hands, but maybe they've all got blood on their hands now."

"Damned politicians," I said, echoing the voice of Jerome Harris, whom I had once heard consigning both parties to the garbage can. Mother went up to her room to dash off a short note to someone before bed. She kissed me good-night and told me not to stay up too late, but she could see that I was not immediately ready for sleep. We had all probably drunk too much coffee. I assured her I would not be long, and after she left the room I picked up a newspaper and glanced idly at the front page.

Among the reports of the election campaign was an out-of-town speech by an elderly senator referring to what he called the political assassination of Roosevelt. It seemed irrelevant to the main thread of his address, and I read it with mounting curiosity. His theme was that the men of ill will who stalked the land and were enemies of the New Deal, and of everything that the Democrats stood for, were engaged again in some sort of conspiracy that had to be fought. I remembered Father telling us how Stefansky had begun his speech that fateful day with the words, "We've got the wrong man." For a moment I saw the past linking up with the present. I wondered if this was what Edward had told us we would be discovering — what Father would get around to telling us. All we knew at the moment was that treachery on the U.S. side seemed to have put an end to the initial plotting of a Stalin assassination. As I sat holding the paper, I repeated my father's words: "Yes, we did shop them." I wondered how it had worked out in detail. Who had told whom? Who was involved in this? Father had been very general about what he obviously still remembered with horror. Suddenly I felt I wanted to know more details about it, since there were people alive who were involved in what had happened. I imagined there would be retired politicians, senators, and some journalists who had been involved on one side or the other.

I was much too restless to sleep, so I got up and walked to the front of the house, where I looked down at the street, remembering that night in Moscow, not so long ago, when Father had failed to appear. Rather, I remembered the night before, when I had thought I heard people outside my bedroom. Was the whole thing really as much like a gangster movie as all of this? Was it all a nightmare, or maybe even nonsense? Edward had confirmed that this was all real, and that we would soon learn more, more than he himself knew as a result of his own independent researches. I went downstairs into the kitchen and made myself some hot milk, which helped me get to sleep.

"You know," Mother said the next morning, "this is getting quite absurd — plot, counterplot, and all that. The further we go into it, the more it's like fiction."

"Well, there's certainly no contradiction of what Father has told us in the books I've read," I replied. "Even Father has suggested that the transcripts of those who were at the main conference do exist. But so far in his tale, Father hasn't been an eye witness. He was only able to see Stalin on one occasion, walking out of his villa on the way to Livadia Palace."

"I wonder if he did get into any of the main meetings," Mother said. "Well, he'll let us know, I'm sure. You know, most of the newspapers at the time were really on the side of Roosevelt. They were about as gullible as he was."

"You'd think after nearly thirty years of savagery," I said, "since the beginning of the Bolshevik Revolution, we would have learned more as a country."

"But I was around then," said Mother, "and you have to remember that the Russians were doing all the fighting against the Germans. They took the full onslaught. And we were naturally happy to have Russia on our side. Even Churchill said that, if the devil was going to fight Hitler, he would help him — though he did add that it wouldn't change his own long-held beliefs about the horrors of the communist system."

We lingered for a few moments over our tea, and I pressed the sugar granules against the bottom of my spoon in a kind of distracted concentration. After a short time of musing, we both went up to look in on Father. The nurse had shaved him, the bed looked pristine with its clean sheets, the curtains were well pulled back, and the room itself exuded an atmosphere of freshness and light. It was certainly helping Father's mood, for he smiled at me and said, "You know, I really do feel much better this morning. Do you think perhaps we could go out a little later?"

Mother and I looked at each other and nodded in agreement.

"Of course," she said, "where would you like to go?"

"I'd just like to go have a look at the White House from the outside — get a sense of still being in the world and try to relate all the past events to today. You could even give me a look at the old Executive Office Building, which housed the State Department before 1947 . . . and anything else that comes to your mind. Just wheel me around, treat me like a tourist. I feel like I want to get out of this room for a while."

So, after an early lunch, we set off in a car Mother had hired, with Father eagerly looking out the windows as we passed through the streets of Georgetown and into Washington. His eyes fell on the Capitol and the Washington Memorial with the recognition of someone who had lived among them for a good deal of his working life — but had not been back in a while. He didn't ask us to push him through the streets in his wheelchair, so we stayed in the car, with the heat of the city streets coming in through the windows. At last we reached the State Department, and he asked the driver to stop.

"That's where some of the culprits are still working now," he said, "as they were in 1945. Although, to be fair to them, it wasn't with them but with the White House that the problems arose. But it was to that building, the Old Executive Building, that they were spirited away after our awful hand-over to the Russians of the secrets of the conspiracy." His face darkened again at the thought of it. "It was absolutely terrible. The Americans simply vanished, though we knew they were alive and well; but the Russians vanished, too, and we could scarcely think the same of them. God knows what happened to them — perhaps their ultimate extinction.

"Let's have another look at the White House," said Father, "where the devil himself lived, according to Stefansky."

Mother and I looked at each other, guessing by the increasing extravagance of his language that he was becoming agitated again. We judged that it was best to return home.

"I think we should go back now, Henry," said Mother. "You've had rather a long day, and this has been your first trip out of the house for some time."

"Do you think they'd admit me back to the State Department now?" he asked suddenly. "After all, I'm still on their books. I have a right to go there."

The thought of his returning to the place where Mother and I had feared he would be trapped and possibly would disappear into thin air was too much, and Mother adopted a firmer tone.

"No, Henry, it may be a good idea some other time, but not now." She asked the driver to turn around and drive us back to Georgetown.

Father seemed almost sullen about her decision, and we realized that once he was back in his bed at home, he would probably burst forth with memories that were again beginning to roil in his brain.

"You don't understand . . . you don't understand," he kept repeating.

"Ah, but I think we do, Henry. You need to tell us everything that happened, everything that has been bottled up in you all these years. But we need to keep you well and happy — that's the most important thing."

"Oh, I know . . . I realize that, and you two have taken great care of me," he said, reaching out for her hand. "I'm sorry . . . I'm very sorry, but you will let me continue, won't you?"

"Of course," she said. "We are both desperately interested, and as long as it helps you, you can tell us everything you need to."

The nurse greeted us with the news that Alan Clarke had called and asked for Mother to call him back. After we had settled Father in bed and helped the nurse with tea — which we put in his room to show that we were not deserting him — Mother went down and dialed our lawyer's number. Fortunately, he was not in conference, and Mother asked whether we could come and see him.

"Don't bother," he said. "I'll drop by to see you around lunchtime tomorrow. I have to visit some clients in Georgetown, and I'm sure it would be a more relaxing atmosphere for you to be able to talk to me at home rather than here at our office."

Clarke showed up just before lunch the next day, and we offered to share our tuna sandwiches with him, which he was only too eager to help us with.

"Has there been a further approach from the State Department?" he asked through a mouthful of sandwich. "There shouldn't have been — without my knowledge. I think I am fairly well briefed on whatever steps they might be taking now."

"It's more general than that," Mother said. "We are simply concerned about the things Henry's telling us — the way he is going over his past, his career, his wartime activities. And there is no one else who —" she hesitated "— well, could you explain to us what he is trying to tell us?"

To our surprise, Clarke answered quickly and decisively: "You're talking about Yalta, aren't you?" We nodded in unison. "Well, of course there are others. There were Russians and Americans in what was revealed as a plot to overthrow Stalin. I'm young, but one can't live and work in Washington without knowing about something like that going back all those years, and knowing that something is still afoot today that has the same savagery now as it did then."

"You mean they are still fighting over that damn conference?" asked Mother.

"They are not fighting over the results of the conference, but they *are* fighting over what took place during the conference — and the distrust and hatred they had for each other then. They, or their successors today, bear the same grudges they had against each other then."

"We've *had* McCarthyism," Mother said. "I thought we got over it."

"Oh, it's not that," he said. "Well, it is to a certain extent; but it's much deeper, much longer lasting, much more treacherous than what McCarthy even pretended to uncover."

"Can we do anything about it?" I asked. "We're not politicians, and we're not concerned with that. We're concerned with what happens to Father. He wasn't a politician either; he was a career diplomat. Now, from a common-sense point of view, his career has been cut short and he's dying in office."

"No, there's nothing you can do about it," Clarke replied. "But if your father wants to talk to you, you must listen. It's obviously something he needs to say. If he doesn't want to go on, so much the better. As far as I'm concerned, I'll make sure that we keep a close watch that the State Department does not do anything that may jeopardize him. At least for the moment, they are leaving your father undisturbed in your care."

Mother returned to her previous tack: "Is there no one we can turn to who can give us some explanation of what Henry seems so driven to reveal?"

Clarke looked up with a serious expression. "Well, there are people, but you will only endanger yourself, your daughter, and your husband if you attempt to find them. You'll find yourself taking sides, at the very least; at the most, you'll become involved in something that I can frankly say you would prefer to avoid. I'm sorry that I'm not at liberty to tell you any more than that. All I can do is ask you to rely on me, carry on with life as normally as you can, and of course look after Henry." Then he added, as a premeditated afterthought, "You might also keep an eye on the nurses."

When he left, Mother and I immediately went up to Father's room as if to reassure ourselves that he was still there and that all was well. He greeted us eagerly.

"I'm glad you're back," he said. "Who was that you had to lunch?"

"Oh, a young partner of Anthony," said Mother. "You remember Anthony, my father's attorney. His young man, Alan Clarke, felt he should come here and discuss our affairs, bring us up to date, and we could let him know how we're doing."

"Good idea," Father said, nodding. "I'd definitely keep in touch with him. You never know when you may need him. Anything can happen these days."

After our conversation with Clarke, we realized that his sense of paranoia might be rubbing off on us. We felt as though we were reaching some kind of crisis in the whole affair. Both of us spent hours trying to fall asleep that evening, afraid that the phone would ring in the middle of the night. When we did awaken, it seemed to be halfway through the morning and the doorbell was ringing. We found two men standing at the front door showing identification cards to establish that they were from the State Department — part of its Special Investigation Division. We presumed that they were there to protect us from any feeling that we were now on an FBI or CIA list as objects of suspicion. But when the two men asked whether they could possibly speak to Henry, we stood in front of the door, refusing to grant them entrance.

"He's not well," I said, "surely you know that."

"In fact," Mother said, "he really is dying."

"We do appreciate that," one of them said, "and you have our profound sympathy. But I'm afraid this is really a question of the security of the state. Do you think we could possibly speak to him?"

We relented and let them into the den and offered them coffee; they politely refused. They seemed to be behaving with utmost courtesy, far more courtesy than shown by Dr. Berg and some of the other visitors who had gone so far as to suggest that we change our names and addresses.

"It really is very important," the other State Department man said, and I wondered on what grounds we could refuse.

"We need to call our attorney," I said.

"Please, go ahead," he said. "I think you'll find that he has no power to reject this request."

Alan Clarke was out of his office, indeed out of Washington for the day, and we had no immediate way to contact him. But we were able to speak with one of his assistants, who seemed well briefed on the case. This young man, Dennis, insisted that he come to our house immediately and that we were to hold the two men at bay until his arrival. When he arrived a few minutes later, he spoke to us briefly and then asked us whether we would mind if he spoke to the two State Department men privately. It seemed like a curious request, but Dennis insisted that it was the only way forward and that it would be to our advantage if we both stepped out. When at last he called us back into the den, he said to Mother: "If your husband can receive us, I think I should take them upstairs now. There really is no alternative — unless he is desperately ill. But I can assure you that there is nothing for you to fear right now." He said this openly, in front of the two State Department agents, who nodded in agreement.

"May we come, too?" I asked.

Dennis shook his head. "For the moment, no. I think we should talk with him alone, and then I can report everything to you afterwards."

"Well, at least let us go up first," I said, "and tell Father that he is receiving visitors."

"Of course," one of the men replied, "that would be fairly normal, wouldn't it? I wouldn't think he sees anyone except you and your mother these days."

Upstairs, Father was awake and the nurse was giving him breakfast. I noticed that the coffee she had poured for him was particularly strong, perhaps to counteract the somewhat stronger sleeping pills he was getting since the hospital visit. But he was in full possession of his faculties and greeted us warmly.

"Father," I said, "two men are here from the State Department, and Alan Clarke's assistant is with them. Do you mind talking to them for a while? I'll be downstairs with Mother, so we won't be far away."

"Oh no, that's good." He nodded in agreement. "Show them up. I'll be glad to see some people from the Department." Perhaps the immediate transition from deep sleep to the caffeine stimulation had clarified his mind, and the stronger sleeping pills had dulled the surging recollections of the previous day. We had noticed that he usually awoke without fear or stress, and it was only as the day wore on — and his recollections progressed — that he became more anxious.

Downstairs, Mother and I tried to keep our minds from what was happening. We settled into a perfunctory reading of newspapers and talking in the den. The men were still there after forty minutes, and we could still hear the low murmur of voices above us. We asked the nurse whether anything had happened, whether she had been called into the room, and she said, "They just asked for more coffee for Henry. I checked his pulse and blood pressure, and there was no change. I hope they're not upsetting him."

Not long after that, all three men came down, smiling and seemingly full of gratitude for the opportunity to speak with Father. They all seemed very relaxed and, after thanking us for our hospitality, the two State Department agents left.

"What was that all about?" Mother asked Dennis as soon as they had left.

"There are certain congressional inquiries," he said, "hearings into security by the Department itself. They came here to question your husband about his knowledge of some people he had come across in the past."

This seemed fairly innocuous, but Mother pressed him further: "Are you sure they didn't come for more than that?"

"They did," Dennis said, "but it didn't seem terribly important. It touched on something that Henry apparently had not revealed in his recollections to you — let's put it that way."

"What was that?" I asked.

"The government's research . . . the New Mexico work — Los Alamos." We looked at him in astonishment.

"But that's crazy," I piped up, "that had nothing to do with Father. Nor did it have anything to do with Yalta. I don't see why they would come here and ask him about that."

"It did and it does," he replied. "Perhaps I should tell you that the Russians your father came across in Yalta were very much aware of the progress of our atomic research, though Stalin never gave a hint of this to Roosevelt or Churchill. In fact, the Russians knew far more about this than most members of the State Department did, with the exception of one or two people — the Secretary of State, for instance. But Edward Stettinius had only just been told by Roosevelt of its existence, so even his knowledge was very limited and very restricted. That knowledge definitely did not extend to those at your father's level, or anybody he had regular contact with. Try as they might, those two agents could not get any information from him, simply because he was totally unaware of what they were driving at."

"You mean the Russians knew about our atomic bomb preparations, and our people didn't?" I asked incredulously.

"I'm afraid that's the case," Dennis said. "Apparently, much of the reason the Russian dissidents angled for your father's support in their talk of disestablishing Stalin was a cover to obtain any information he and his colleagues might have about the atom bomb. Oh, there were genuine dissidents against Stalin, and there was a plot to remove him. But there was also — to use the current jargon — this 'double-agent' aspect. Some of the Russians were not really opposed to Stalin; on the contrary, they were privy to Stalin's spying throughout the whole of our research program. Your father's noted antagonism toward Stalin and the Bolshevik régime was an obvious asset to them, and that's why they approached him for his support in toppling the régime. But it was more than that: some of them were asking for — or rather hoping for — something entirely different."

"So there were Russians and then there were Russians," I said.

"Exactly, and now there are calls from Congress for the State Department to be cleaned out of all those who could have taken part in this spying conspiracy — the kind of cleanup that led to such things as the execution of the Rosenbergs."

"But why is Henry so terribly agitated, if he knew nothing about the atomic secrets?" Mother asked. "As he goes on talking to us, he seems to get more and more disturbed, as though he is approaching something that is almost more than he can bear."

"Well, he knew there was something in the offing, but he didn't know what it was. I think perhaps he was suspicious of some of the Russians, but obviously it had nothing to do with the bomb. It was probably about their approach to their own social problems. And, of course, as you said, there were Russians and then there were Russians: some of them had a far greater hatred for Stalin than even your father could possibly guess — based on the terror they had seen inflicted on family members and friends, which had gone on throughout Stalin's whole régime."

Although it was a great relief to Mother and me to learn that one apparent hurdle — even if we had been unaware of it — had been removed, we were quite sure it was not the real hurdle, that there was still some fearful secret he had to tell us. Mother was certain of it and repeated her observation:

"But there's something more — I'm sure there is. Standing by and watching those Russians, whose language he could speak and who were, don't forget, our allies, preparing to dispose of their leader in some way — that must have been bad enough. But there seems to be something even deeper — some charge or task, say — that was imposed on him and that he has not yet been able to tell us about. So far we've heard his description of the conference, laced with his own dubious and slightly sketchy liaisons with certain members of the Soviet delegation. But something specific seems to be disturbing Henry, and we'll have to allow him to tell us as it comes to him."

"I think perhaps there is, too," Dennis said. "As we approached the question of the bomb, which the Department investigators asked about in an indirect way, Henry became agitated that a new line of questioning was to follow, and that it was about something he had not yet managed to divulge to you two — because you are really his first line of defense. I think, once he has gotten whatever it is off his chest with you two, he will be able to face it." He shook his head sadly. "Whatever future he has left he can face with great composure."

He stood up and picked up his briefcase. "Now, I'm afraid, I must go. I'll report everything to Alan, but for the moment I think I can assure you that you don't have anything to fear from the Department — or the CIA or FBI. Please, as we've always said, be in immediate touch with us if anything else happens, and we will remain on the alert."

Mother and I stood looking at each other after Dennis left. The issue of the atom bomb seemed to be entirely unexpected to Father; and we were confident, since we had been listening to him all this time, that this was not the secret he was still harboring. We went upstairs to have a word with him now that all his visitors had left, and we asked him whether he had found his visitors interesting.

"Oh yes," he said. "I learned quite a lot that I wouldn't have known — either then or now. I hadn't realized how much the Russians were ahead of us, at least in their discussions — not in their research. But that they suspected we would be able to update them does surprise me. Whereas, on our side, we were in the dark — with the exception of one or two men at the top. Anyway, that's over. Shall we have lunch?" He showed an unexpected turn toward gaiety, and we asked the nurse to bring all of our lunches upstairs.

"Do you feel like going out for a ride again?" I asked him. "It's a very nice day out, and it would give you a change of pace."

He shook his head. "No, I don't really need a change of pace like the one we had yesterday. But going into Washington, I must say, was quite an experience for me. It brought back an awful lot, and the reality of what happened in those days in the Crimea stabbed through my heart again. It wasn't the State Department itself that instigated the plot against Stalin, or rather indicated the assistance they were prepared to offer the Russian dissidents. It was instead a cross section of those who hated the man and the régime: some in his armed services, some in our own, the émigrés, and some of those, like me, who had enough knowledge of the past and the present to understand what we were faced with.

"There's still a lot I want to get off my chest," he continued, "and I don't really need to go through the streets of Georgetown to jump-start it. This morning was rather frightening in a certain respect: I thought those men were going to pull something out of me that you were not yet aware of."

"Yes, that's what Clarke's man told us," Mother said.

"Oh, they were tactful enough," he said, "but I obviously didn't know what they were driving at. When they revealed the true nature of the subject, it was an utter relief."

"So we understand," I said.

CHAPTER FOURTEEN

Three days after Stefansky's remark about "shopping" the Russian dissidents, the atmosphere in our translation room was subdued, and one or two faces were missing. I wondered what reasons I could muster to get into the big conference and sit behind our main interpreter and his staff. At last I decided to make a direct appeal to the head of our group, who was fortunately not a Russian speaker — or he himself would have taken the role. When I approached him, I felt that I was entitled to put myself forward as the next in line.

"What's your problem?" he said. "We've got Bohlen there — he's a first-class interpreter. We've got Freeman, and Page . . . what's your problem?"

"Well," I said lamely, "there do seem to be some idiomatic phrases that really do need more sensitive readings." I was laying it on a little thick, trying to think of some way to justify my presence at the meeting. "It seems to me," I added, "that they've reached another impasse, and it will only get worse if they are misinterpreting each other." My superior nodded sagely.

"Okay, I'll have a word with Ed," he said, meaning the Secretary of State. "He doesn't know a word of Russian, so maybe I'll be able to convince him. Anyway, leave it to me and I'll see what I can do."

Fortunately, the foreign ministers were lunching that day at Livadia Palace, the American headquarters, and he had an opportunity to speak to Secretary Stettinius as soon as they came out of their meeting. As I was finishing my lunch in the mess, my boss came up to me.

"I worked it out," he said. "You're on this afternoon. Here's the agenda. You'd better brief yourself as fully as you can, so you'll at least know what they're talking about before they start arguing in more than one language."

If there was a problem, it wasn't what our interpreters were doing, as I had intimated, but what Stalin's interpreters were making of Roosevelt's remarks. I wanted to check their work; but mainly I wanted to be present to see the three leaders in action. As four o'clock approached — the time of that day's full-scale meeting — I waited in our translation room, knowing that the principals were filing into the great ballroom of the Czar's palace, which was being used as the conference hall, with President Roosevelt's private quarters in the adjoining room. I knew that they would sit at a huge round table, each leader flanked by his advisors: Roosevelt with Ambassador Harriman and, if necessary, the chiefs of staff of the military services on each side of him; Stalin with his cabinet and his own military advisors; and Churchill accompanied by members of the British cabinet, the foreign office, and Clarke Carr, the British ambassador to Moscow, a man whom I had seen frequently in the Moscow embassy because he and Harriman worked together closely.

At last I was summoned and quietly shown the entrance to the conference hall, where the door was open but guarded on either side by Soviet officers and a sprinkling of U.S. military men. After showing my identification, I slid quietly into the room and sat behind the President. I looked around me: the windows that I knew looked down to the sea were tightly curtained, and there was a fire blazing in the open fireplace behind me and the President. I looked from one to the other: opposite Roosevelt sat Churchill, and Stalin was to his right. I could not see President Roosevelt straight on, of course, but I could tell from the sound of his voice, the droop of his shoulders, and his posture that his physical condition was indeed poor.

I had been told that Stalin spoke in a soft, level voice, scarcely gesturing; but I also knew that, in politburo conferences during the 1930s, he prowled the room terrorizing his underlings. Presumably, he felt that he could achieve little in this setting with that approach. Churchill's body English was typically British: his glasses slid down the bridge of his nose from time to time, and he periodically pushed them back up again, never bothering to pause in his speaking. He spoke eloquently, in perfect Victorian English. Once he had begun speaking, though, I could sense Roosevelt's impatience. On one occasion, the latter exchanged notes with Bohlen to the effect that they were now in for another half hour of this. Stalin, however, sat quietly and gave the impression — borne out by everything I came to know later — of listening to and absorbing every word.

On this occasion, however, since the main subject was still Poland, Stalin behaved differently. I could see Churchill bristling as Stalin occasionally stood up to address the room from behind his chair, pointing out yet again that on at least two occasions Russia had suffered invasions through the Polish corridor and that his country could not protect herself unless she had a friendly and stalwart neighbor. Molotov also did a good deal of talking; but Roosevelt, I thought, seemed locked into a programmed approach that had probably been prepared for him by his Secretary of State. He did not seem personally involved, and he did not appear to be the man I had hoped to see — disturbed and animated about what was happening to millions in the European states that were occupied by the Red Army and a puppet Soviet administration. His only concern seemed to be what impact any success or failure to reach a Polish solution might have on the Polish-born voters in the United States. He had said as much at the earlier conference in Tehran, where he declared that Polish descendants in America were innumerable and scattered throughout the country.

It was clear that Stalin, even when he was opposing Roosevelt on the make-up of a new government for Poland, had set out to endear himself to Roosevelt, whereas he never hesitated to collide head-on with Churchill. We had seen this in earlier transcripts on other subjects that had come through the translation room: Roosevelt had fallen in with Stalin more than once in disputes between the Soviet leader and the British leader. Churchill remained unflappable and resolute throughout, very much the British bulldog Roosevelt had once caricatured him as at an earlier conference. It was clear to me that there was an impasse on Poland, a complete disagreement by Churchill and Roosevelt, particularly Churchill, on the Russian proposals. They were firmly opposed to a Polish government made up of communist stooges backed by the Red Army, which was now murdering the underground Polish forces who had fought valiantly against the Germans during the occupation and were led and represented by the legitimate government-in-exile in London.

Roosevelt's resistance, however, was weak, and I was galled at the almost obsequious way he addressed his remarks to Stalin. The latter, on the other hand, merely stuck to his position like the rock of Gibraltar, and Churchill to his — both of them resolutely trying to control the conference table. At one point Roosevelt turned and questioned one of his State Department advisers, who was behind him and slightly to his left, and I was appalled to see the marks of fatigue, of downright exhaustion and illness, on his face. My own feelings were an ambivalent mix of anger at his apparent weakness and a surging pity for this man who had probably saved the country from revolution during the Depression, but who now was reduced to such an exhausted shadow of his former self. As he turned back to the table, I could see that he was flagging, and I shared his obvious relief that this particular discussion was ending. The discussion switched to another subject, which was hastily disposed of, and, after a fairly short session, I was dismissed with the other auxiliary translators before the main participants left the ballroom.

To my disgust, Stefansky was waiting for me in the hallway, and I wondered whether he had engineered this occasion for me to get into the conference so that I could see for myself what he had been trying to tell me. He fell into step beside me as I headed back to my room. I wanted to shower and change my shirt, but he sat on Philip's bed and started talking before I could even get my coat off.

"Now you can see the problem," he said. "Now you see what I've been driving at — what we are all driving at, at least those of us who have decided. As I said before, we have chosen the wrong man. But it's not too late — this time we've just got to be quicker."

"What do you mean," I said, "we've got to be quicker?"

"Well, as long as Stalin wins in Poland with his whole politburo or communist organization, or whatever you want to call it, it isn't really a question of tomorrow but of today. I mean, if the United States caves in now — that is, in the course of this conference — it will probably all be too late."

"But can't you see what's apparent to everyone?" I replied. "The Red Army is in Poland, it is already halfway across Europe, and we can't start a war and drive them out. They are already there — or rather, they are here. What do you expect us to do, turn around and start fighting them?"

"No, we've got to stop Roosevelt in his tracks and fast, and all the others who follow what he is doing without question."

"Oh, for God's sake, shut up!" I was tired and hot and didn't want to hear his ranting voice go on any further.

"Just listen to me," he shouted back. "How many on the White House staff do you think there are who agree with us? And how many in the State Department? How many of the service people agree with us?

There's a line forming right now, and it isn't even according to party loyalties. The few Republicans here are on board, it's true, because they're always opposed to the Democrats; but there are Democrats on our side as well. It's a mixture of politicians, servicemen, fellow travelers — call them what you will. But I'll come back when you're in a more receptive mood."

It was an odd thing to quarrel with Stefansky because, whether I disagreed with him or not, he had been close to my family for such a long time. I didn't watch him go out the door, but he slammed it with some emphasis, and I knew he was in a flaming hot mood. At that moment I longed for an American bathroom with a good hot shower and a clean pile of towels. But what would have to suffice would be to change my shirt, find the bathroom we shared with numerous others, splash some cold water in my face, and go up to the mess for a good long drink.

On my way to the mess hall, I thought, *If only there were some third person I could share my thoughts with.* For one mad moment it even crossed my mind to try someone from the British delegation. Churchill had struck me as a rock sitting at the meeting — frankly, the only sound person there because he knew his own mind. But I dismissed the thought of a British connection from my mind, which was soon becoming numbed by the Scotch I was having little trouble getting down. Philip came in carrying his own drink and sat down next to me.

"How did you do?" he asked. I described the course of the session objectively. "They want us again on duty tonight," Philip said. "I believe the foreign ministers are going across to the Russian headquarters to thrash out the statement on Poland. Anyway, we might as well get as much rest as we can; at least it'll give us a chance to compose our thoughts, if we indeed have any. After all, we're only really messenger boys in this."

Unexpectedly, General George Marshall came into the mess hall, and the few of us who were in the room stood up to attention respectfully, even though some of us were in other services. He waved us to sit down. As I looked at his stern, craggy face, I reflected that though he was perhaps the most moralistic and yet the most dangerous strategist of the war, he might be the American voice of sanity. At least he was a good man; but I wondered whether he had even the slightest idea of what was going on behind the scenes among the turbulent politicians whom he, as chief of the services, protected. He glanced around the room as if looking for someone and then left, and we carried on our conversation.

I was trying a cautious approach with Philip: "What do you think of things so far? You've seen the way the discussions are going, pretty well headlong at times — headlong into each other, I mean."

"Well it's to be expected, I guess," he said. "After all, Churchill has a history of anti-Communism, Roosevelt comes from an utterly liberal background, and Stalin is basically an Asiatic monster. They aren't very likely to agree, are they?"

"Each one thinks he's got to have a strategy in accordance with his own views," I replied. "Churchill needs to protect the Empire; he also remembers 1919 and his initial revulsion toward Bolshevism. Stalin probably doesn't trust Churchill an inch, and he wants as much of Europe as he can grab. As for Roosevelt, I don't think he knows exactly what he's letting us in for."

I paused, waiting to see what Philip's reaction would be. When he looked up at me, I could see that I had rung some bell in his mind.

"You mean that he's giving away too much?" he asked tentatively.

"I suppose you could call it that at best. At worst, seems to me, it's like a wholesale retreat. But he wants a world organization at all costs, which he thinks will hold the peace indefinitely, and will work where the League of Nations utterly failed. Don't forget, Roosevelt is an old Wilsonian: he was in Woodrow Wilson's cabinet during World War I. But what's the value of a world organization where one of the three policemen, as they keep referring to themselves, is frankly out to smash the others, if possible?"

"Do you think it's as bad as that?" Philip asked.

"Well, it's the theory of Communism that a struggle with capitalism is inevitable, and Stalin himself, in any of his previous behavior, has never indicated the least democratic or liberal approach. I frankly don't think Roosevelt has a clue what he's up against. That frightens me, and I think it should frighten anyone who is willing to acknowledge what's happening."

"Maybe you're right," said Philip.

"Oh, it's more than maybe," I responded. "It's more than maybe — it's happening right now, right under our very noses. It's what we've been hearing and reading daily, twice daily. If we listened to Molotov at the foreign ministers' conferences, the Soviets are on their way against us, and they know they've got us by the throat. We can't dislodge them from almost the whole of Eastern Europe. And Western Europe, once it is cleared of the Germans, will be an absolute wasteland into which they can march."

"The Allies had better stop the Soviets," said Philip, somewhat lamely.

"What, stop the Soviet Army once it's on the move? We won't know what hit us, we'll be so completely outnumbered. His armies are twice the size of ours and the British armies combined. We know about the forces they've disposed of — artillery scattered over the ground like confetti. They employ an Oriental type of strategy, which means that they'd throw men at us left and right, regardless of casualties. We wouldn't stand a chance."

Philip seemed completely taken aback by my cataclysmic address. "That bad?" he muttered.

"Well, you're here with me, damn it, we're sharing the same room and basically the same duties. It's true that I had a glimpse of them today, but look around you, Phil! The saddest thing, really, is that, judging by Roosevelt's appearance, it is quite beyond him to put up any resistance, except in support of a United Nations concept, which he believes will lead us all to the happy heartland of permanent tranquillity. But do you think it will? Stalin, of course, is happy to join any international organization as long as he has veto power over anyone else who might interfere with him. Do you think a world body has a snowball's chance in hell of existing as long as the devil himself is stalking abroad? And Poland is now trapped in the Soviet mesh — not only for the present but for the future. Has Roosevelt ever seen a free election in a Communist country? Has he ever read Lenin? Does he know anything about the failure of the Constituent Assembly's attempt to bring democracy to Russia after the 1917 Revolution? Does he know anything about Europe other than listening to what he wants to believe? He's showing no signs of it!"

I had lowered my voice and was looking Philip straight in the eye. I could see that he was grappling with what I had said, and then he, too, lowered his voice and looked me in the eye.

"Well, we obviously can't do anything about Stalin, and for the life of me, I don't know what we could do to slow Roosevelt from falling in line with him." He flinched at his own words. "Look here," he continued, "I think you're leading us both down a path of madness. Is it that damned Russian friend you've known since childhood who's been talking to you like this? I saw him prowling the halls this afternoon, waiting for you to come out of the conference. What god-awful plots is he cooking up now? I always knew he was a conspiratorial and shifty type. Can't say I ever liked what I saw of him. By the way, what the hell is he doing here anyway? I'd be curious to know who invited him to the conference and how he got here. Wonder where I could find out about him."

"Yes, I think we should try to find out something ourselves," I said. "I'm becoming less inclined to ask him, but let's have a look and see if you can do some sort of checking."

"I will," said Philip, standing up. "Let me get you another drink. You need it, and after this conversation, frankly, so do I." Philip returned with our drinks, and we sat quietly for a while. But since we were due at the foreign ministers' conference together, we soon went up to our room, put on our coats, and went to where the limousines were waiting to take us to the Russian headquarters, where that evening's conference of foreign ministers — without the Big Three — was convening.

The Russian villa was a pleasant building that had a beautiful view of the sheer mountains of the peninsula, as well as lovely gardens, pools, and statuary, plants and luxurious vegetation, shrubs that had obviously been brought in from all over the world by its wealthy pre-Revolutionary inhabitants. Molotov was, as ever, the genial host, plying the Americans and British again with caviar and vodka. He was, I could see, one person who actually made his views known without continually checking with Stalin first, and he conducted business adroitly. He could negotiate, though he was blunt at times and lacked almost anything in the way of tact; there were occasions when he would give way and smile when it suited him, and he could retreat so gracefully that it was difficult to believe one had previously disagreed with him. Anthony Eden was courteous, if perhaps slightly chilly. He knew how to stand his ground with courtesy, to make his point, and also to give way when it suited him. Like Molotov, he knew where he stood. Edward Stettinius, the U.S. Secretary of State, though he had been a successful businessman, was a complete amateur and new to the game. He was originally the head of U.S. Steel, and had not been in the State Department long. But his administrative talents had been greatly appreciated when he administered the Lend-Lease program.

With Harriman, our ambassador in Moscow and my boss, sitting in on most of the meetings, I knew where I stood. His formal and dignified — yet determined — opposition to the more overwhelming and inconsiderate Soviet demands, and his insistent request that Roosevelt draw the line somewhere, made it clear that he viewed the proceedings with considerable anxiety. I was glad that he was my boss.

Occasionally we could hear voices inside the assembly room, though they were never raised. I wished that I could somehow get into that room, but at the moment it was clearly impossible: security was very tight — the NKVD guards were everywhere — and the list of attendees was very limited. The presence of Stalin in the building had turned Corice Palace into a miniature Kremlin. I doubted whether we could have coughed louder than a normal clearing of the throat without a guard rushing up to make sure that it was not some kind of assault on their leader.

The room grew warmer as we worked late into the evening on the points of discussion. But at last the conference ended and the main participants, the foreign ministers — other than Molotov — left the building. Those of us on the American translation team went down to the black limousines that had driven us there, and we rode back to Livadia Palace. We were quiet and tired, but, above all, we were apprehensive. I looked across at Philip: he sat with his head sunk in his shoulders, his face lined with fatigue and closed tight to the bright features he usually presented to the world. We climbed out of the limousines numbly and went upstairs to our rooms. Neither of us felt like having a drink; neither of us felt like doing anything but going to bed. Philip and I sat on our beds silently facing each other for a few moments, until he at length broke the silence.

"Do we always have to capitulate to the demands?" he asked, then put up his hand to stop me, as I was about to reply. "Don't answer that. I already know what your answer is going to be, and I've got to think this out for myself. All I know is that it gets more troubling every hour. What can we do — is there anything at all? It just seems to me that we're absolutely against the wall, and even that wall seems to be slowly moving backward, so that we're forever being faced with demands that we never even expected in the first place." He took off his tie, which was already loose, and flung it across the room. "Oh God, what an ungodly mess!"

"Come on," he said, "let's see if the bathroom is free. We'll splash some cold water in our faces and see if that brings us to our senses."

We were fortunate to find the bathroom available, and we quickly showered under the water — cold as it was. We put on a few clothes and returned to the room, where we both lay on our beds smoking. I had not taken Philip into my confidence before, and I was not inclined to do so now. But it struck me that he, too, was at least beginning to face up to the developing situation, and so I decided to give him at least a short outline of the clandestine conversations I'd been having. I pinned it on Stefansky, which was indeed correct — though I had not turned him in — and at least I placed the charge of plotting and counter-plotting at one remove from those I had been talking to. He listened in silence, and when I was finished, said:

"I can understand the Russians wanting to kill Stalin. But I'm amazed to hear that some of our people were involved. Are you sure that's correct?"

"Absolutely," I said. "Haven't you seen how many of them have disappeared? A few of the Russian-Americans have gone back to Washington safely. As for their opposite numbers in Russia, well, one can only guess at their fate."

"And now you say that some in the U.S. delegation are involved in a plot against Roosevelt? This is inconceivable — beyond belief! I know Americans have a history of assassinating their Presidents, but this would be the first time someone tries it abroad — though that's the appropriate place, of course. It's where the Europeans usually manage to kill their royalty. How are they going to do it? Shoot him, poison him . . . or simply smother him?"

He had crossed over into his bizarre humor. But he stopped himself abruptly, got up from his bed, and flicked his cigarette butt violently out the open window toward the blackness of the Black Sea.

"How are you involved?" he asked. "For God's sake, Henry, do you really know what you are doing with that bastard Stefansky? Let him carry the can, let him take whoever he wants with him. But stay clear of him yourself. There are a few CIA and security people here. Why not seek out one of them and report what's happening? At least keep yourself clear. Unless you're already complicit with his plans?"

"I'm not sure there's anything we really can do," I said, pacing the room. "Stefansky has said that what happens in the next few days is crucial to the outcome. I think we can agree that he's probably right about that."

"Well, the man behind it all seems to be crucial, and he seems to be your friend," Philip said with his little half-smile. "Stefansky! Can't we track him down and really find out when and how he proposes to strike? That way we'll have our finger on the trigger, so to speak — or at least we'll be close to it. I wonder where that spooky guy is in this great shambling building. I suggest we go and find him now. Let's take a cue from Churchill and settle things right here, right now."

We quickly put our clothes back on and left the room. I remembered that Stefansky's room was on the first floor, where we knew the State Department was housed with the President, but I didn't remember which hallway of the first-floor maze it was on. The American MPs and a couple of CIA men looked at us curiously, but no one interfered with us as we descended the stairway and moved along the corridors as if on a mission. We saw Secretary Stettinius come out of a room and walk down the hallway, and we guessed that he was probably going to a late-night conference with Roosevelt to discuss the outcome of that evening's meeting of the foreign ministers.

When we came to a right-angle turn in the corridor, something looked familiar to me — though the room doors were all identical and did not have numbers on them. So Philip and I each walked a side of the corridor, hesitating at doors and listening for whatever internal noises we could hear. At the third door, Philip held his finger to his lips.

"There's a lot of noise going on in here," he whispered. "American voices obviously — they all seem to be talking at once. Maybe he's got a meeting going in there." I pressed my ear to the door as Philip knelt down and tried to look through the keyhole. Unfortunately, it was blocked by the key on the other side. I listened at the door for some time, until I could hear, as silence fell on the room, what was clearly Stefansky's voice. He seemed to be addressing the room.

"There's nothing to do but go straight in," I said. "He'll either take us for fellow conspirators or a couple of bumbling drunks. Well, he'll recognize me right away, so I'll go in first." I knocked urgently on the locked door, as if demanding a reply.

Stefansky stopped speaking, and there was silence in the room, followed by one or two voices asking who it could be. We could hear Stefansky say, "I'll go see who it is."

It seemed curiously brave of him to identify himself right off, but it was in character: he was brash and impulsive, and he was certainly Russian. Of course, he recognized me as soon as he opened the door.

"Henry, come in!" he said immediately. "I could almost say we've been expecting you — though you might feel a bit out of place here. Who's this?" He turned toward Philip.

"My roommate," I said. "We share a room, perhaps the same views, and we are both coming in."

He swept down in a low, mocking bow to us, and we entered his room to find ourselves confronted by faces we knew from every department and unit of the delegation. Philip and I concealed our surprise as we identified those faces in that room. I didn't know whether Philip would turn away and leave the room, but I think he instinctively felt, as I did, that we should stay and play out our roles long enough to find out exactly what was going on — if only to protect ourselves. There were certainly no senior service personnel there — only a sprinkling of young Navy lieutenants and ensigns, young presidential aides, and, admittedly, a few from the State Department.

CHAPTER FIFTEEN

"So that's why we've been getting such a strange collection of visitors," Mother said. "This attempt to have you taken back to the hospital, the switching of doctors, and even suggestions that we change our identities and disappear — which we didn't bring up to you before."

I knew Mother must have immediately regretted revealing this, but Father took it in stride. "I'm not surprised," he said. "It's all part of a pattern for those who feel that someone has to be silenced."

We were chilled when he used that expression, but in a way I was glad that beneath his illness, beneath his exhaustion, the resilient Father I remembered — and presumably the man Mother had married — was still holding on and his spirit was shining through it.

"But why now?" I asked. "And why have they turned their attention on you?"

"Oh, I think it's pretty easy to explain," said Father. "They could all have gone on, happily assuming that this event was buried in the past. There was nothing to show for it. But it was my disappearance in Moscow — and the seeming complicity of the Soviets — that's what disturbed them. You see, it would bring to light the whole tortured and splintered nature of U.S. politics. Don't forget that Emil Segalov insisted on joining Edward when he came to tell you that I had been found in that hospital in Moscow. Don't forget that the State Department encouraged you to attend the reception at the Soviet embassy, a highly improbable decision when you think about it, that is, in light of the Cold War. And now they are scared once again that perhaps I'll reveal to the Russians everything I know from that period. Just as the Russians would not be eager to have that plot against Stalin revealed — though that would probably count for less now that he has been discredited so drastically by Khrushchev.

"Can you imagine senators and congressmen pointing the finger at each other as to who had taken part in this incredible conspiracy? Can you imagine the chaos in the State Department? Can you imagine the White House itself not knowing which way to turn? And, most of all, can you imagine the voters facing the knowledge that some of their leaders had been ready to go after their own President in a time of war? Previous mudslinging at elections would be child's play compared to what could take place as a result of this."

Father sank back on his pillow, clearly exhausted by having to explain his long narrative. Naturally, I was very curious to know how his confrontation with Stefansky had gone, but I could see that Father had come to the end of his energy, at least for the time being. The sudden summoning up of some of his old strength had finished him for the day. Mother rose first and, straightening his pillow, said, "You'd like to rest now, wouldn't you, dear?" He nodded and closed his eyes.

I had searched the room in an amateurish way, and I felt reasonably confident that it was not bugged. We certainly did not want the FBI, the CIA, the State Department, or anybody else listening in on us as we sat with Father. As we left his room and sank back into armchairs in the living room, I had a growing apprehension of any knock on the door, any phone call, the arrival of any messenger. It was somewhat unnerving to realize that the more Father told us, the more we became trapped in the intrigue of the past, and the more the outside influences of the present could be brought on us. We again wished there was someone we could turn to, just as Father had when he turned to Philip.

"I wonder what ever happened to Philip," I said to Mother. "Surely the same pressures that are being put on Father could be put on him. They might have ignored him until Father's disappearance. But now both of them must be coming in for" — I used my father's words — "reluctant silencing."

"You're right," said Mother. "As soon as Henry told us he had gotten Philip involved, I wondered what happened to him. Did he get married later, did he disappear in Mexico or somewhere else — what happened to him? And I really wanted to know what followed his confrontation with Stefansky, because that must be the key to the whole story. It would have been cruel, but I desperately wanted Henry to keep going this afternoon."

I agreed. No doubt we were coming to the ultimate truth that lay behind the web his story had entangled us in.

And then the phone did ring, and we both jumped. But relief surged through me when I heard Kate's voice. "I know it's rather late in the day," she said, "but we wondered whether you and your mother would like to come over for dinner. We've got one or two other people coming, but they'll be leaving early, and I'm sure you have lots you want to tell us."

I accepted without even asking Mother. "It couldn't be a better time for a break, and we'll be happy to come," I told Kate. Mother nodded with relief, and said, "As long as we're sure Henry is all right, it's definitely time we had a break. And Jerome and Kate Harris are certainly a party to our story."

When we arrived at their home, Mr. Harris's greeting was so warm that I thought it was almost a deliberate exaggeration, his welcoming arms outstretched as if to convince us that he was there to support us. The other two guests were both doctors and, I assumed, professionally connected with him. After martinis, which I noticed were served with a liberal hand, we went in to dinner. The conversation was general, and we only referred specifically to Father in answering early questions about the state of his health, which we did in an objective, noncommittal way. The two doctors had clearly been forewarned about the state of affairs, and they did not pursue it.

After dinner, as we sat with our cups of coffee, Mother and I were feeling very relaxed. The conversation stayed on subjects such as foreign politics, Europe and the prospect of its possible integration, and a great deal about the U.S. elections. Who could escape talking about the quality of the candidates and the political news in general? After all, we lived in Washington, though both doctors had only recently moved their practices here from New York. I was lost in reverie for a short while, only half listening to the conversation, when I heard the name Philip Goldsworthy mentioned, and I immediately became alert. Mother, who was following the conversation more closely, was now looking pointedly at one of the doctors, and I snapped to and paid attention to what he was saying.

"I was asked to help because I was an American doctor in the hotel," Dr. Fisher was saying, "and I visited Mr. Goldsworthy in the hospital. It was in northwestern France . . . Brittany perhaps. I gathered that he had suffered some kind of fall, and he was badly injured: his face and head were severely bruised, his right arm and leg both fractured, and his lung punctured by one of his ribs. Even so, I felt he could probably pull through. It was a good hospital, and after I talked with the French doctors, we were reasonably optimistic. His wife, who was French but not from that region, was off visiting some relatives before the accident happened. And because Philip was going in and out of consciousness, we could not get a number where we could contact her before her scheduled return. Well, the long and short of it was that he died during the night, something we did not expect at all. It was almost as though he had given up his will to live. There was no real reason for his death that we could see. Chances of recovering from injuries such as his, even though they were multiple, are normally high. But there it was. When Mrs. Goldsworthy returned the following day, she was, of course, distraught. It's true that where they lived was a hilly part of the country, but she said that Philip wasn't much of a walker, certainly not a hill climber or adventurous hiker. She thought it was a mystery that he would have fallen at all. And how sad it was . . . very, very sad. My wife and I felt upset enough by it to cut short our vacation and return home."

"When was this?" I asked as casually as I could.

"Not more than a year ago," he said, calculating when he had taken his vacation. "The memory is very fresh to me."

There was a pause, and then the conversation returned to its previous level, until the doctors stood up and said they had to go. Mr. Harris saw them out, leaving Kate with us.

"Are you two all right?" she asked, noticing that something had rattled us.

"Sure, we're okay," I assured her, but I could see that she was unconvinced. Mother and I had previously agreed that, though we would report generally on Father's condition, we would not relate to them the contents of his narrative. But when Mr. Harris came back into the room, we knew that we had no alternative but to take them both into our confidence. It was too much to carry alone, and this report of Philip Goldsworthy's mysterious death made it clear that there was some threat to Father.

Mother said that what had really shaken us was hearing Philip's name from the doctor.

"Unless there's another person by that name, he was Henry's roommate at Yalta, and we didn't expect to hear about him at all outside of that context, especially in the mysterious circumstance of his death."

She hesitated, but then she took the plunge and told them both in detail what we had just recently been hearing in Father's room. I looked over at Kate as if to apologize for involving her in this intrigue; but she came over and sat on the side of my chair with her arm around my shoulders.

"Thank God, you told us about it," she said. "But it won't go beyond this room, I assure you, will it, Daddy?"

"Of course not." He stood up and went over to get the brandy decanter.

"Nothing good would even come of saying anything," he said. "It would only make the situation worse. The Soviets quite clearly have watched Henry's case carefully, and it would only emphasize the danger from our end by repeating what you've just told us. We're all casualties of the Cold War, but at least we know now why the pressures on Henry have been so intense. So you say you don't know any real details of who was in Stefansky's room when Philip and Henry walked in?"

"No," Mother said. "I dread to hear it, and yet I want to know. But we need to let him tell it in his own time. I think it's been destroying his health to bottle it up inside him."

Kate's father fixed a somber gaze on the Oriental rug and said again, "Well, there's nothing we can do now." He looked over at his daughter: "As Kate said, it won't go beyond this room. But when you do hear, whatever you do, you know that we are with you. And if it comes to any practical steps that we can help with, come back to us immediately."

Kate stayed on the arm of my chair, right beside me, and when I broke into tears she held me close. I pulled myself together quickly and was about to get up, but she pressed me back into the chair and said, "Why don't you stay here for the night. I'm sure your mother won't mind, will she? Perhaps you would like to stay as well, Mrs. Winthrop?"

"No," Mother said, shaking her head. "Thanks for the invitation, but I need to get back to Henry. But Lorina can stay with you. Wouldn't you like that, Lorina?" I merely nodded, and within a few minutes Mother was gone and I was sitting on the sofa next to Kate, quietly holding her hand. Both of us were silent until Kate anticipated my thoughts.

"Don't feel guilty about letting her go home alone. You'll just tie each other in nervous knots if you're together. Stay here till morning, and then we'll see if your father is up to telling more of his story."

I could see that by now Kate — and particularly her father — were not only as concerned as we were but equally curious about what Father was about to reveal. Mr. Harris looked at his watch. "Well, I think we should all go to bed" — he looked at me — "and I'm going to give you something that will help you get a good night's rest." Whether he was a trained physician or not, I was grateful to him for his suggestion of something that came by way of prescription, confident that he knew it to be safe. I had not joined Mother and him in their brandies, but once I was in bed after swallowing the sleeping pill with a glass of warm milk, I sank into what seemed like the deepest sleep of my life. In fact, I was still drowsy in the morning when Kate brought me breakfast, which I enjoyed even though I only half noticed what I was consuming.

Kate's father came into the room as I lay back with my head against the pillow, still somewhat drowsy.

"I'm afraid you are going to have to stay with us for a little while," he said. "There was a bit of a crisis during the night, and your father is back in the hospital. Nothing serious, mind you — well, no worse than he has previously been. But your mother and the nurse had no choice but to call an ambulance, and he's now back in a hospital bed."

"Ready for the vultures to gather," I said, smiling grimly.

Mr. Harris shook his head. "I don't think they'll do that at the moment. He's well guarded by the doctors looking after him. You've got your own man there, Dr. Johnson, and I can assure you that there won't be any interruptions — on medical grounds alone. I'll go down to see them on the way to the office, and I'll call to let you know of any other developments. In the meantime, of course, your mother sends you her love."

It was halfway through the morning by the time I was up and dressed, and Kate and I decided on a short expedition to the university area. We'd heard nothing further from her father by early afternoon, and we stayed out for lunch at a bright little café that had recently opened not far from the university. It was full of students who seemed young and silly — though they were our age or a little older — but they were at least diverting, and I realized that we had become somewhat serious for our age. Two young men joined us at our table, and we enjoyed their conversation; we even laughed out loud when they began lampooning the politicians currently running for office. They invited us to a dress rehearsal that evening of a satirical review they were putting on at the Georgetown

University Theater. Kate was quick to nod her assent, and they peeled off two tickets from wads they had in their pockets.

When we got back to Kate's, I called the hospital and spoke to Mother.

"They've sedated him," she said. "They think they can do that safely, and in fact he's sleeping well now. But there's nothing we can do except wait for him to pull out of this, I'm afraid. It's not just the strain of talking to us. His condition has deteriorated — that seems to be the consensus of the doctors examining him. Maybe we weren't good at noticing that while we were listening to him the last couple days. You just stay where you are, and I'll let you know when you can come down and see him."

Then, forcing a brighter tone into her voice, she added, "I'm perfectly all right. Please don't feel you let me down by staying at Kate's last night."

Fortunately, I didn't have much time to worry about whether Mother was really okay, because Kate and I were soon off to the dress rehearsal of the student review, and the evening passed cheerfully. We were even able to laugh uproariously at some of the character portrayals. Afterward, we drank beer with several of the student actors and joined in their conversations as they continued to satirize politicians.

Kate had been valiantly trying to get my mind off Father's return to the hospital, but when we returned to her house, I said, "Thank you very much, you're a great friend. But it's no good. I've got to get to the hospital and see Father again. I can't leave Mother alone."

So as soon as I was dressed the next morning — and had made it clear that I had not changed my mind about going to the hospital — Mr. Harris offered to drive me there on his way to the office. Kate rode along, but I didn't want her to come to Father's room with me. When we reached the hospital, there seemed to be a policeman hanging around every entrance. I was used to seeing holsters on MP's at embassies and the State Department, but somehow these side arms seemed more prominent in the hospital setting. Was this entirely a figment of my imagination?

I was escorted by one of these policemen, rather than by a hospital orderly, to a small office where Mother was in conversation with a young cardiologist.

"I'm afraid I'll have to ask you to decide whether your husband should stay in the hospital or go home," he was saying. "I know it's not an easy decision, and I'll more than understand if you decide to take him home. In some ways it may be better for him: it may relax him in the sense that it could increase his peace of mind. But please don't let me influence you. If you want to ask me anything else, just give me a call, or call any of my colleagues." He patted Mother's shoulder, and she grasped his hand and smiled, tears glistening in her eyes.

Neither of us moved after he left the small office. We just looked at each other in anguish, and Mother said, "I think we'll delay any thought of a decision for at least the next few days. We'll just leave Henry here. It'll be better for him, and I don't think I can make any decision myself at the moment — except to get him home at all costs sometime in the future so he can . . ." She paused as if ashamed to mention the story whose telling was such a compulsion and seemed to accompany Father's decline. "He may want to talk, and he may not. Let's give him a chance to be properly nursed, get his strength back, and we'll see what comes to his mind. If it somehow eases his mind to tell his story, I need to know that he can do so. I think there's a chance that if he stays here, they may restrain him and leave him in a more tense frame of mind. . . . Oh God, I just don't know."

She burst into tears, and I put my arm around her.

"It's hideous," she said, "absolutely hideous. Why did he ever disappear that awful night in Moscow? And spend all that time in that dreadful Russian apartment house. . . ."

I reminded her gently that Father's heart condition was such that it could have occurred at any time, and he could have been anywhere. It was only the grotesque circumstances of when it did happen that had brought about this chain of events. We sat down for more indecision and the agony of wondering what to do. As husband and father to us, indeed as a human being, he deserved to be at home, which we both preferred. We couldn't guess what his impulse would be when he awoke — whether to talk further or to lie back and rest and inexorably decline. But opposed to our longing to have him home was our faith in the safety of the hospital setting, and we both clung to that as we clung to our indecision.

When Father had finally finished his breakfast, an orderly allowed us into his room. Another orderly was just removing his breakfast tray; he had obviously slept longer than they anticipated and had had his breakfast much later than was usual. But I could see that he was alert, and he welcomed me warmly.

"Hello, darling," he said, and turned to Mother. "Now I've got both of you here. Are you having a nice time, Lorina? It's so good of the Harrises to put you up."

"Very much so," I said. I described the satiric dress rehearsal that Kate and I had seen the night before. While talking, I was glancing furtively around the room, looking for anything that might be a bugging device. But then I realized that, if Father wanted to talk, there was nothing we could do about it anyway. We certainly weren't going to silence him.

"What have they been doing for you?" I asked, in an attempt to divert what I thought was really on his mind.

"Oh, the usual drill — tests I've had before, and they're always the same: listening, looking, taking blood, and so forth. They're very kind here. I must say, I like our doctor very much. He came in real early this morning, when I was asleep, and I understand that the results of the blood tests were mostly available by the time I woke up for breakfast. I hope I'll be able to come home in a few days, even though I'm told the rest won't harm me — and it will certainly do both of you some good."

"We want you home," Mother said, "but not before you're ready to be home. We miss you. It's no rest when you're away."

"I'd like to get on with what I was telling you — just before I was brought back here," Father said abruptly.

"Do you need to continue now?" Mother asked. "You'd be much more comfortable at home talking to us alone. Here, we don't know who is going to come in and out of the room."

"I realize that," he said, "but I need to get it off my chest. I'm afraid I don't have much time left."

"Of course you do, darling," Mother said.

"I don't know," he said, shaking his head. "Anyway, do you want to hear more about the conspiracy?"

My eyes met Mother's as though we were silently beseeching each other to stop him, but she seemed resigned to the inevitable and offered only token resistance:

"It can always wait, darling, you know that."

"It can't," he said, "it simply can't. . . . . I need to go on."

CHAPTER SIXTEEN

In Stefansky's room, surrounded as we were by his recruits, Philip and I played along as fellow conspirators. All of those in the room, I'm ashamed to say, were fellow Americans, bonded together in a common hatred of their own President. I recognized most of the men in that room; one or two had even been at Yale with me. But how were they going to accomplish their goal, I asked, looking from face to face around the room. Stefansky answered me immediately:

"We need to silence Roosevelt before the final communiqué, before all these agreements have been put into writing, before they've been published and issued to the rest of the world. Most of the documents have been carefully worded — at least most of the decisions have been — so that they reflect merely the opinions of the heads of government. Roosevelt, at least, cannot commit his government without congressional approval; Stalin, of course, can do whatever he likes. I'm not sure what the British constitution allows, but I assume that Churchill, as Prime Minister, can speak for the cabinet — and probably did so anyway."

"But how on earth do you plan to silence him?" I asked, becoming more agitated.

"It turns on the banquets that are being given every night," someone in the room volunteered.

"You don't mean you're going to poison him!" I said.

"Well, no, but it won't take much to weaken him now," Stefansky countered. "I've seen some of the medical reports. As you know, he really is in appalling physical condition, and it wouldn't take much to tip him over the edge."

"And what's our role?" asked Philip, catching on to the trend of the conversation.

"Well, to begin with, it will need some planning. There's the trip between here and the Russian villa — their elaborate cavalcades of cars. Then there's the meal itself, and God knows what Stalin will choose to serve them. Presumably, the U.S. State Department has some say in the choice of food. I don't think it's going to be too difficult, really."

The proposition seemed to have the same haziness that character-ized Stefansky's earlier "plot" to kill or destabilize Stalin. But this time there were more Americans involved, and I could see their determina-tion. There was also the fact that so many of them already surrounded the President, which made it much more likely that an attempt would be successful. What Stefansky and this group seemed to be planning went beyond the bounds of anything we had anticipated: this was treachery on a monumental scale.

"Now that you know what we're planning," said a voice from the back of the room, "by God, we'll kill both of you if you spill it to anyone else!"

I chose to ignore the threat. "What about you, Vlad?" I asked. "What's your role?"

"I'm the one who can move between the Russians and ourselves. They don't necessarily trust me, since I am one of what they call their 'former people.' But they accept me now as an American who is Russian speaking, and I can play a significant role when we have decided exactly what to do. In fact, I hope to make whatever arrangements are necessary when Churchill hosts us at his villa. And you, of course, the whole bunch of you, will probably be transported there to translate and fine-tune whatever they talk about. You can witness for yourselves the complacent way that Roosevelt is letting Stalin walk all over him. It's a good lesson in political naiveté. But you must also look for lapses in security, anything we can use to slip inside the President's security."

I shuddered. Although the building was supposedly heated, it was basically cavernous, and I could almost feel the cold from the walls creep-ing in on me.

"Well, Philip and I are off to bed," I said, making as if to leave. But the man who had threatened us from the back of the room now stood in front of the door, blocking our departure.

"Let me repeat," he hissed, his black eyes smoldering. "I swear to God, we'll kill both of you if one word of this leaks out. So don't go sneaking off to the FBI or anyone else, because we will be following you.

You will always have someone's eyes on you. From now on, you are not going to be left alone."

To emphasize his words, he opened the door and preceded us into the hallway; we were followed out of the room by another of Stefansky's conspirators. And the four of us, in single file, retraced our steps down the corridor and back to our room. A State Department patrol looked at us curiously, but one of our escorts smiled and waved at him, and soon they left us at our room.

I decided to test the security of this and left the room to go to the bathroom. But as I walked down the corridor, I realized that a fresh-faced State Department official named Williams was lurking just behind me; indeed, he followed me into the bathroom and back down the corridor again afterwards, until I rejoined Philip in the room.

Once we were alone — and neither Philip nor I felt that the room could have been bugged by our own people, or anyone else for that matter — we felt safe to discuss in low voices how best to proceed from now on. We decided that the safest way was to feign utter complicity with the plotters, hoping that they would not subject us to continuous surveillance. We figured that that might give us freedom to decide on a course of action. The first thing I believed to be essential was to seek out Stefansky again. I needed to know whether he was playing, as he had suggested, a key role in the assassination plans. It would be just like him to have others doing the dirty work for him. I wanted to find out whether plans had proceeded too far for him to either change or stop them. I lay in bed considering how I could best deal with this. I saw no point in involving Philip in my conjectures until I had some firm plan of my own. It had been a tiring and nerve-wracking day, and soon I heard the deep breathing of sleep, just shy of a snore, coming from him, and then I fell asleep myself.

The following morning, however, the problem was on my mind as soon as I woke up. In the lowest voice possible, I said to Philip, "I think I've got a solution, but I'll tell you at another time and place so we won't be overheard. The crucial thing in shaking these people off is to play along with them. But leave that to me — for right now anyway."

After we had dressed and gone up to the second-floor mess for breakfast, we went down to join the other members of our unit in the translation room. Scattered among the crew were a few of those who had been in Stefansky's room the night before; but it was refreshing to me to see that they were still in a considerable minority. Suddenly I stood up and announced to the whole room that I wanted to see Stefansky. I quickly explained that he had been a friend of my father and stepmother, and that I had met him frequently while I was growing up. I announced that there was a particular problem of translation, of an idiomatic meaning that I was sure that he would understand — because it dealt with a situation that arose during the Revolution. This was a transparent bit of rubbish, but the conspirators could not stop a couple other members of the translation team from coming forward and saying, "Oh, I think we know where he is — we saw him this morning. Anyway, we know where his room is. Why don't you come there with us?"

"We will," I said, nodding toward Philip. "I wouldn't mind if you two came with us, so we can find it all right."

Four of us left the room together, trailed by one of the conspirators, who was clearly taken aback by this development. We retraced the steps we had taken with such incredible consequences the night before. I knocked on Stefansky's door, and, before he could invite us in, we had stepped inside. He was obviously surprised and confused by the group now standing in his room, but he greeted me warmly nonetheless. He recognized our follower lurking in the hallway, as well as Philip and me, of course; but he was wondering what the other two members of the team were doing there. I started in with some elaborateness about the problem, which had to do with the liberation — if I'm remembering accurately — of the Baltic states after the Revolution. I had my facts pretty straight because I was talking about borders my stepmother had crossed back in 1918. Stefansky listened with interest, and I could see that he was genuinely aware of why I had come to him — and flattered by it as well. He called me over to his desk, where he pulled out a piece of paper and rather ostentatiously traced the boundaries of the three Baltic states as they had existed before the 1917 Revolution, and then as they were finally settled by the Soviets. I pulled the paper toward my side of the desk and sketched out a few details of my own; but my details were bogus, just a visual cover for me to scribble the words, "I must meet you — it's important. I think I can help you." When I pushed the paper back to Stefansky, he looked at it closely for a moment, and then said: "No, you've got Estonia wrong here and here. . . ." His hand made flourishes on the paper. But when the paper came back to me, Estonia had not changed, but Stefansky's own scribbling said, "Wait here — I'll dismiss the others." He then retrieved the "map," crumpled it, and threw it into the fire burning in his open fireplace.

He stood up and addressed the others in the room: "Henry and I really do have a problem here. He's right to think so, and there's probably no one else in the delegation who can help him. It's going to take a bit of time, so why don't you fellows go back to your workroom. I'll sort this out with Henry, and he can catch up with you there later."

The two translators who had accompanied me and Philip to Stefansky's room rose to go. I was happy to see that the conspirator obviously had no alternative but to follow them. As he moved toward the door, he gave me a look I knew was meant to renew the threat; but I was pointedly looking the other way. When they all had left — with the exception of Philip — Stefansky gestured for him to leave as well, and I nodded.

Alone with Stefansky, I decided to play the straight role of a co-conspirator; there didn't seem to be any point now in arguing the virtues or vices of the treachery. In any event, I had come to the conclusion that Stefansky was probably mentally unbalanced, that his obsession with halting Bolshevism, Stalinism, Communism — call it what you will — in fact, of everything that had happened in Russia since 1917, had so taken over his mind that he was beyond being rational.

"You are really looking for a concrete way of getting rid of Roosevelt," I asked, "of stopping him before he signs off on everything he has supposedly agreed to?"

"That's what you heard last night, didn't you?"

"I know. I just want to make sure I've got it straight. And you think that will really achieve your purpose?"

"Absolutely," he said without hesitation. "We know what stuff Truman is made of, and once Roosevelt is gone, all the New Dealers and his supporters will be left without any leader. It won't be much different from the plot to kill Hitler last July, except that that plot failed and, in doing so, merely reinforced his position. So we've got to make sure that there are no mistakes this time."

"Okay," I said, "to begin with, I don't think we can do anything here in Livadia Palace: they are all our own people, and none of them would attack or do anything to the President here, even the conspirators. They would probably be lynched. I think the answer lies in the trip he is taking tomorrow to Churchill's banquet at the British villa. Between here and there are steep mountain roads, and it should be possible, if we can get the right people driving Jeeps, to somehow force Roosevelt's car off the road. Either along the road or at the British headquarters itself, there won't be the guards and close security he has here at Livadia. Tip him over the edge. That's what I suggest you get your people to look into — at least those who accompany him to the British banquet. There will only be a few of the top people invited to the banquet itself. But there will be the usual horde of advisors and translators in the complete migration from here to there. So that's what I suggest. Obviously I don't control the deployment of your people. But you should at least be in a position to know who does, and to get hold of the right people."

"That's no precise solution," Stefansky said angrily. "I thought you had a definitive plan, a genuine blade between the shoulder blades — you know, 'Et tu, Brute.'"

"Well, it's far better than your original hazy idea of getting to Stalin, who is more or less physically invulnerable because of his guards. At least here you've got a chance: you have a bunch of people, some of whom are utterly disloyal, traveling with Roosevelt across perhaps the most mountainous part of southern Russia. If they can't get it done there, frankly, they don't deserve to succeed."

"I get your point," he said. He could be a man of swift opinion changes when he had a mind to be. He stood up quickly and went to the door. "Come on, I'll take you back to your unit. The longer you are away from them, the sooner they will start suspecting that you and I have some sort of plot between us."

As I reached the door, I couldn't resist saying, "Do you really mean all this?"

"My God," he said, almost knocking me over. "You must be mad. Didn't you hear anything last night?"

"Yes, I did, but . . ." I shook my head. "It's just that it's all rather extreme, isn't it?"

Stefansky would not acknowledge that he had any doubts about his course. When I got back to the translation workroom, I could see Philip carefully avert his eyes until I was seated for a moment and the eyes of the others had gone back to their documents. Then he looked over at me, raised his eyebrows, and I raised mine with a slight nod. It was at that point that I knew he and I would somehow have to be responsible for stopping the conspirators' plan.

At least one consequence of my meeting with Stefansky that morning appeared to be that the tail the conspirators had put on us was removed: when Philip and I went up to the mess for lunch, we saw that we were walking unaccompanied. I said nothing of any consequence to Philip then, merely giving him monosyllabic answers to questions he had carefully phrased to be meaningless in any context of conspiracy. After we filled up our trays in the food line, we carefully chose a table where there were two other members of the translation team who, we knew, had not been present at the meeting the night before. This made it easy to act normal and without restraint, and we conversed in such a way that even the most sharp-eared and sharp-minded person overhearing us would find nothing to object to.

Our two colleagues rose from the table when we did, and the four of us left the room together. When Philip and I reached our own room, we went in for a moment for our usual postprandial cigarette. Between drags, I told Philip about my conversation with Stefansky, how I had concocted for him a plan to force Roosevelt's car off the treacherous road between the palaces. But then I admitted to Philip that it was really the plan I had for Stefansky himself — because I knew it was he who needed to be eliminated. I was convinced that, with him out of the way, what there was of a plot would collapse. I said it wouldn't be too difficult to get him on one of those terrifying mountain roads, the one that twisted its way to the British villa, for example. A driver had to hug the wall of the mountain on one side, while on the other side of the road was a sheer drop to the Black Sea below. If you could somehow isolate a car or Jeep, and force it over that edge, it would be all over.

Philip gasped softly, but the look in his blue eyes told me that he was behind my idea and wouldn't simply sit on his hands.

"And how are you going to achieve that?" he asked. "Stefansky may not be attending the banquet at all, for all we know."

"It's not the banquet I'm thinking of. He's included among the delegates to the foreign ministers' meeting and luncheon that is being held beforehand. Even though it'll be light out, there won't be so many of us then, and we'll just have to handle him as best we can. Somehow we've got to get into the car nearest his, or perhaps in the same car. Maybe we can get him into a Jeep. We have to get him isolated in some way — either ahead of or behind the rest of the convoy. The difficult thing is going to be doing this without the other Americans or Russians seeing us do it."

"What about the FBI?" asked Philip. "Can't they help?"

"Phil, I don't believe they do assassinations. And it's really too late for that. Besides, with all of Stefansky's money connections with heavyweight Democrats, plus with half the White House staffers laughing them to scorn, you think they'd believe us? They'd probably put us in handcuffs — or whatever they do — and fly us back to Washington as conspirators ourselves. I'm not saying we'd be summarily shot, but we wouldn't stand much of a chance with them."

"God," Philip exclaimed, "what a situation we're in!"

"I'm afraid we're really on our own. And we've got to kill him quickly, before he can execute his appalling plan — before he can accomplish whatever he's got planned for Churchill's banquet tomorrow evening. That means we've got to strike tomorrow afternoon, when the foreign ministers go to the British villa for their afternoon conference."

Philip was silent for a moment. "He's really crazy, I guess, isn't he?" he finally said.

"Oh yes," I said. "But there's a certain fierce logic to his madness. As unbalanced as he is, he has a quite justifiable grudge against the Bolsheviks. He told me once something about his past: the estate his family owned, the peasants suddenly turning on them, burning down the barns and wreaking their hatred on the manor houses, putting what they called the aristocrats through harvesting machines. He has every reason to hate what happened, and he doesn't want it repeated in his adopted country. You know, most of his family did not survive; some were even forced to dig their own graves before they were shot into them. I could tell you a lot more. He has long sought his chance for revenge, and now Roosevelt, the leader of his adopted country, of all things, stands in the way."

"You obviously heard a lot of those stories yourself from your stepmother," Philip said.

"Yes, though she wasn't from Stefansky's social level. I think his status in Russia made it possible for him to win many Russian-Americans over to his original plot against Stalin. The real mystery is how he wormed his way into the position he had in Washington, and how he managed to convince opponents of Roosevelt to follow him and frankly believe the promise that he would be successful. I'm horrified to think of everything that implies."

I stared into space for a moment, then returned my gaze on Philip.

"With Stefansky out of the way," I said, "and us seemingly not involved, that should be the end of it."

"They might go ahead without him," Philip said.

"They might, but I doubt it. What would be their justification, without Stefansky to back them up. No, we've got to do it — secretly and quickly — and we've got to do it successfully. Now, I've taken the risk of telling Vlad that I thought this plan could work with Roosevelt as the target. I'm hoping to get him to come to lunch with us tomorrow. I'll say something about how we need to pinpoint the location and go over the ground as a preparation for the strike itself. And that's when we do it ourselves. It's probably our last, best opportunity."

Philip and I went down to prepare ourselves for the plenary meeting that was to take place that afternoon. We anxiously watched the details of what was being discussed, looking for any context that would be persuasive in getting Stefansky to join us on that road the next day. Roosevelt had given a small luncheon party for Churchill, who then took a nap in the palace so that he would be fresh for the evening meeting. He lived by his naps and his ability to sleep, which kept him at the top of his strength. The formal discussion, when it did take place, was mainly devoted to the wording to be used in the communiqué on the future of the Polish government.

In general, this was all rather mundane stuff, as far as we were concerned, except for the exceptionally long discussion about Poland, which led to proposals that the foreign secretaries again meet at the Russian villa later that afternoon to discuss the final wording of the Poland statement. The emphasis on Poland throughout the conference had been consistent and insistent, and it clearly showed the split between the West and the Soviets in general, and between Churchill and Stalin specifically. It certainly gave us further ammunition with which to persuade Stefansky to accompany us to that meeting, concerned as he was with the way Stalin would use his powers in an occupied country.

*   *   *

It was a relatively short drive to Vorontzov Palace, the British villa, half an hour — just over twelve miles. Philip and I would ordinarily travel that road by Jeep, unless it was particularly cold, when the Russians provided limousines for the delegation. I had told Stefansky that we would be going by Jeep to scout a location on the road for a strike, and even though he no doubt always expected to travel in the grander manner of the senior diplomats, he agreed to the Jeep ride with us. The bright sun made my plan realistic. He met us in front of the palace and, claiming that he knew the road well, he dismissed the driver. Indeed, he had traversed this road earlier in the conference, and he went on to tell us that he had taken it many times before the Revolution. Feeling the crispness in the air, he excused himself briefly to put on a thicker jacket. Meanwhile, the small convoy of Jeeps and limousines, spaced well apart and moving slowly, set off on the short journey to Vorontzov.

Stefansky returned and took control in the driver's seat, and for once I was glad for this predictable characteristic of his personality. We went south from Livadia and soon were traveling along the coastal road up the mountain. Although it had been cleared of snow, the road was always dangerous, one side flanked by sheer mountainside, the other falling straight down to the Black Sea below. Philip and I sat in the back seat of the Jeep, and we both observed that Stefansky was driving somewhat too fast for the conditions. Perhaps he wanted to show us how well he knew the road, perhaps he wanted to catch up to the convoy; but perhaps his driving was a reflection of the emotions raging inside him. Philip and I had to sit and listen to him expound on his hatred of everything the Soviets stood for. And even though we did not feel inclined to argue with him, his fury seemed to mount as he drove. I was tuning it out for the most part, noting that the convoy was still not in sight, when he said something with such venom that I pricked up my ears.

"Did you know I helped get Roosevelt into power?"

"What do you mean?" I asked.

"Yes, I did — and how did I do it?"

"What do you mean?" I repeated.

"With Stalin's money!" he shouted over his shoulder at us. We listened in astonishment. "It was easy enough. The Soviets wanted to be admitted into the so-called community of nations after they had become established. The Americans had outlawed them, and Stalin thought the best thing to do during the Depression would be to help elect Roosevelt, who he knew was sympathetic. I still had my contacts in Russia — even though by that time it was from the safety of the United States — and I got word that funds would be made available to me to feed the Democrats' campaign if Roosevelt would support the recognition of the Soviet Union."

I was amazed. "So it was Stalin's money that helped you get so far in Washington circles!"

"Wait a minute! I'm a very good businessman," he shouted, "and, of course, that's why Roosevelt owes me so much. That's why I'm in the position I'm in now. You think he'd do it for nothing? He was definitely helped into the White House by Stalin, and now he is prepared to accept the usual payback Stalin offers all his victims: he walks over them . . . tramples them . . . wipes them out. That's why Roosevelt has got to be stopped! Because he vainly thinks that he will prove to be the exception. He's got to be silenced. He's way too weak, and he'll give everything away to that monster!"

"But perhaps you, too, are to be silenced," I shouted.

Stefansky whirled his whole head around to glare at me in his rage. As he did so, he took his eyes off the road and his foot off the gas pedal, and he raised his hand from the steering wheel for an instant. We had come to a dangerous curve in the road, and no vehicles were visible ahead of us or behind us. The Jeep suddenly swerved halfway across the road and toward the cliff edge. I yelled at Philip to jump out. On impulse, I jumped forward and pulled on the emergency brake. The Jeep skidded and stopped just a few feet from the cliff side of the road. Then, with a rush of adrenaline and the whole weight of my body behind it, I smashed Stefansky's head against the steering wheel with all the force I could muster. His body went limp. I released the handbrake and leaped out of the Jeep myself. Philip was picking himself up off the road, and I shouted for him to help me.

We pushed the Jeep with all the strength we had left in our trembling arms and chests. Slowly it moved forward, ever so slowly, until its momentum picked up. We fell back as the momentum carried it over the edge. Crawling on all fours to the edge of the cliff, we could see the Jeep bouncing off rocks with muffled crashes on the way down. Then it hit the blue of the Black Sea far below us with a small splash, and within seconds it had disappeared into its frigid water. By this time Philip and I were on our bellies shuddering, both with the cold and with the narrowness of our escape.

"What the hell was he doing!" Philip said finally.

"God knows," I said, trembling all over. "His fury was pushing him over the edge, and he saw we weren't on his side. So we had to help him over the edge."

By this time we had pulled ourselves up and moved to the other side of the road, where we stood huddled and shivering. Yet there was also an overwhelming feeling of relief: we had just escaped certain death, and the person who had become most threatening to us had not escaped. And I did not regret my impulse for a moment. I had shared Stefansky's views on Stalin and the Soviet Union for many years, but not the murderous plot he had in mind. When he revealed that he had set the stage for it with his behind-the-scenes fundraising activities in the 1930s, I no longer had any conscientious objection to eliminating him.

We stood on the mountain side of that road for some time, not talking and not knowing what to do next. Presently we heard the sound of a Jeep coming toward us from the direction of Vorontzov Palace, re-turning to Livadia Palace. I stepped into the road and waved it to a stand-still. The driver got out and ran toward us, and I quickly told him what I had already decided to say, which was truthful and correct up to the point where I had smashed Stefansky's face against the steering wheel and re-leased the emergency brake. I left that out, and Philip jumped in to say that Stefansky, inexplicably, had gesticulated wildly, lifted his hand off the wheel, and the Jeep swerved toward the cliff — and we instinctively jumped out the back.

The driver ran back to his Jeep and radioed a message down to Livadia Palace. We packed ourselves into the back of the Jeep, and he pulled it in as close as he could to the wall of the mountain, proceeding as fast as he dared — given the circumstances — back to Livadia. When we arrived, we were met by a group of senior delegates, who were ac-companied by the naval medical officer attached to the delegation, as well as some Secret Service agents. We were taken into a room and given a quick medical check-up, then a couple of stiff whiskeys. A debriefing followed, first of Philip and me separately, then the two of us together. We stuck to my original story (the truncated version of the truth, stop-ping before I knocked Stefansky unconscious), and I had no sense that anyone in that briefing room had any reason to believe it was not the complete truth. As we were being questioned, we received a short note of commiseration from President Roosevelt himself, who must have been informed of what had happened, and that also seemed to blunt the questioning.

In our condition, the effect of the whiskey soon wore off, and I began to feel myself trembling and weak — almost incapable of knowing what to say next. Fortunately, the debriefing was over, and Philip and I were released to go up to our room. While we lay on our beds, trying to get control of our emotions, the medical officer came in and asked if we wanted a sedative. We both shook our heads. I, in particular, was negative about it because I had heard that a sedative could in certain circumstances act as a truth drug, and I had no desire to make a full confession of everything that had happened on that mountain road. I still felt a chill under my blankets, almost as though the experience had given me a fever. But we were both able to drift off into uneasy sleep, and eventually noises in the hallway of our colleagues going to the mess hall awakened us. Philip and I had had no lunch with our whiskey, and suddenly our hunger was intense. So we hurried up to the mess and quickly wolfed down a couple of hamburgers each, along with black coffee, while other members of our translation team crowded around us asking for details and congratulating us on our escape. No one seemed to talk much about Stefansky, other than to mention his name as a casualty. It was almost as if it was a dark secret, and only the two of us had ever heard of him.

I wondered whether President Roosevelt would send a message of condolence to Washington, to members of Stefansky's family — if there were any. Philip and I, of course, were apprehensive that we would be approached by one or more of Stefansky's supporters. But none of those we had seen in his room that night came forward to suggest that we had any knowledge of his plot or that we were either complicit ourselves or aware of their complicity with him in his outspoken attack on the President and his White House advisors. And no one stealthily approached us to say they were entertaining the thought of going forward with his plot.

Immediately after that dramatic afternoon on the Black Sea road, there was little else for us to do. In fact, we were relieved of our duties, because Churchill's banquet that evening at Vorontzov Palace officially marked the end of the Yalta conference. The following day was merely taken up with settling the press announcements and the protocols, and there was a final lunch hosted by Roosevelt. I was not scheduled to return to the embassy in Moscow, so Philip and I joined the rest of the delegation driving back to the airfield in Saki, where the majority of the U.S. delegation had landed when they came from Malta. From there we flew back to Washington, where we parted ways, each going on home leave, and where I was permanently assigned to the State Department for the rest of the war.

I had really hoped to go to sea now that the war in the Pacific was heating up, but my wartime service had been all too limited to land assignments, with not much naval training at all before I was assigned to the State Department. Philip returned to the office of the Lend-Lease Administration, where his physical unfitness for military service had not ruled out his ability to act as an economist on the basis of his early work at Harvard. It had been as Lend-Lease administrator that Edward Stettinius first took on his own major role in the war; when he was named to his new position as Secretary of State, he called on some of his Lend-Lease staff to join him and thus included Philip on his trip to Yalta. Philip and I never met again; whether that was by accident or design, I don't know. All I know is that he went into banking and achieved a fair measure of success.

After the war, as you know, I returned to do graduate studies at Yale. My appetite had been whetted by my State Department experience, particularly in Moscow, and that led me to apply to work in the foreign service, where I was accepted. I often wondered whether there was ever any question about me, any objection on the basis that my stepmother was a resident alien and had formed a substantial part of my upbringing. The point was never raised, though I felt they possibly wanted to keep an eye on me. In any event, it did not seem to have upset my career, such as it was.

Somehow, I suppose, there must have been some leakage of what happened that day in Yalta, probably from one of the dissident Russians whom the Americans had overlooked and who has now survived Stalin. Some opponents of Roosevelt who were part of the second plot are also still living, of course; in fact, a few linger on in positions of power and authority. It must have been my disappearance in Moscow that somehow brought the Americans and the Russians into the picture together — on our side the CIA, and on the Soviet side the KGB. They were both eager to know more about what happened behind the scenes at Yalta, and they thought that perhaps I was the key to the enigma.

CHAPTER SEVENTEEN

"So now you know all there is to know," Father said, looking over at us wearily.

I rose quietly from my chair as he lay back on his pillow, and I whispered to Mother that I would go for the nurse so that she could check that all was well. As I stepped into the corridor, the senior cardiologist was walking up. He said that he had come to examine Father, and he asked us not to leave the room as he pulled back the bed sheets and put his stethoscope to Father's chest. When he pulled the sheets forward again, he beckoned to us to follow him into the corridor. He made sure we were sitting down before he sat across from us.

"I'm afraid he hasn't got very long now," he said. "Something seems to have kept him going — his mind ahead of his body — and now something seems to have gone out of him, as though he can relax and assume the normal physical state for someone suffering from his condition. Do you have any idea what it was — what was keeping him going?" His face, as he scrutinized ours, was utterly guileless; he seemed only to be curious. We shook our heads.

"I think you both should go home now and get some rest," he said to Mother. "It's been a long ordeal for you, Mrs. Winthop, and I'm sure you could do with a long sleep in your own bed."

Mother shook her head. "No, I'll stay here," she said, "at least for the next few days." Then she added that I should go back to Kate's house, instinctively knowing that the more youthful were not up for the long vigil she foresaw. I did not object.

As I rode in the cab to the Harrises' house, I resolved that Mother and I had an unspoken but obvious agreement not to tell anyone the concluding information that Father had given us that afternoon. It was not fair to burden Kate and her father with those details, and it would only make us feel uneasy for the rest of our lives. I had no problem with keeping the secret to ourselves. I knew I wouldn't even tell Edward; I would say something to the effect that Stefansky's plot had ultimately fizzled.

Within a few minutes I was back with Kate. Her father was not yet back from the office, and we recalled earlier days — how long ago they seemed now! — when Father was still missing and we were attempting to retrace his steps in Moscow. When Mr. Harris came home, he told us that he had looked in at the hospital and found not only Father sleeping but Mother as well. The nursing staff had insisted that she lie down on the extra bed in his room.

Mother and I were now enclosed in our cocoon of secrecy, I knew, alone together in that and in our eventual grief. But now I had to respond to the question both Kate and her father had, the one Mother and I had avoided when the cardiologist brought it up: what was it that had kept Father's adrenaline and anxiety level up so high that he desperately needed to tell us about it, and what was it that had now given him some kind of release? Kate and her father knew what Father had revealed right up to this last day, and I decided that I could only satisfy them by concocting some reasonable explanation for his continued agitation.

I told them that there had eventually been a confrontation at Yalta involving Father and Philip on one side and Stefansky on the other. They managed to confront Stefansky in his room, where they more or less threatened him not only with ultimate exposure but even with death, if necessary, unless he gave up on the ludicrous plot he seemed to be spearheading. He left them muttering that he could get on with things by himself; but shortly thereafter, to the amazement of the whole delegation, he seemed to vanish altogether. No one knew whether he had returned to Washington or where he had gone, and that was the reason there was no record of his attendance at the conference. I said that some suspicion had fallen on Henry and Philip simply because of their angry confrontation with Stefansky; they were not suspected of any violence toward him, but of somehow being complicit in his disappearance. But they were eventually cleared, attested by the fact that Father was subsequently accepted into the foreign service. When I finished my story, I had almost convinced myself, and I believed I'd convinced them. I was now warming to my theme.

"Obviously," I continued, "with both political parties interested in the plot and counterplot, it may even be that the anxiety has preyed even more on his mind as his medical condition has deteriorated. Anyway, the cardiologist warned us that now, having gotten this all off his chest — even though he has relaxed — he may have lost that edge of his will to go on living."

And then the only natural thing that probably could have happened to my emotions during my hastily concocted story, happened: I burst into tears. But even as I was sobbing my heart out, I knew I had to inform Mother of the story I had made up so that we would remain consistent in what we told anyone else. Kate came to console me, and when my sobbing had subsided, I asked her to have the hospital leave a message for Mother to call me the minute she woke up. Mother did call me shortly after that, not so much at my request but of her own volition. It was to tell me that, with considerable hesitation and some careful consideration, she had consented to a visit from a Secret Service agent. He was accompanied, I was glad to hear, by the senior cardiologist, who protested the intrusion all the while. The recognition that Father might die soon had apparently alerted the authorities — and the politicians behind them — to move the Secret Service into action. The agent wanted to know whether Father had revealed anything further in his conversations with us. Clearly, though, he regarded his job with some distaste; in fact, Mother told me she couldn't help but feel some sympathy for him. She was quick to assure him that Father really had been eager to talk to them about his past life, along with the various events that seemed to reach crisis level in his weakened state. The cardiologist supported this contention, though perhaps by now even he had begun to suspect that there was more to Father's anxiety than anyone else knew about.

The agent whispered to Mother, "I wish that perhaps we could have a word with Mr. Winthrop."

But the cardiologist shook his head with some impatience: "No, he's sleeping soundly, and I forbid waking him up because it's a risk to my patient."

It was only after both men left the room that Mother spoke to me in confidence, and it was then that I told her how I had reported the final episode of Father's story in my conversation with Kate and her father. She agreed to concur in my version of the story; but she went on to say that there seemed to be not so much any suspicion of Father in the sudden disappearance of Stefansky as there were obvious behind-the-scenes accusations and counter-accusations that some Americans — other than Philip and Father — had somehow been involved in it. She hazarded a guess that the Soviets, too, were aware of this position and may well have instigated the American inquiries to clear themselves of suspicion.

The next morning Father greeted me happily, and Kate as well, and he asked her to stay so that all three of us could enjoy talking to him as he ate his breakfast. It seemed clear that, as far as he was concerned, there were no more secrets he was prepared to reveal to us. He even spoke somewhat wistfully of recovering and returning to the State Department, and we quickly nodded in agreement. The cardiologist came in to say that he hoped there was nothing more Father had to tell us because of the great stress it seemed to inflict on him. I felt that he was still curious himself about Father's revelations, but we quickly assured him that there was nothing that could come up among the four of us that could upset him in any way.

When Kate and I returned to the hospital that afternoon, Father was relaxed and telling Mother about his childhood. In fact, he was relaxed enough that he volunteered to see anyone from the State Department, if anyone there wanted to come and discuss current affairs or even get further details about his stay in Moscow during those lost months that may have just come back to him. I felt secure now in the thought that they could hardly ask him any direct questions, such as who was involved in attempting to assassinate Roosevelt. The one point of information they might ask him about would be the disappearance of Stefansky; but that inquiry had been closed years ago. I suppose it was Father's evident relief that had spread a mood of relaxation through Mother and me. Kate must have sensed that herself, because, when she offered to depart, we both insisted that she stay, demonstrating that she, too, was a welcome visitor.

Later that day, when Kate and I were about to settle down for the evening at her house, a call came through for me. It was Edward Wilson. He had called Mother at the hospital, and she had suggested that I might like to hear from him. I asked Edward what he was going to do now that he had left the Department and, as it were, shaken himself free from the infighting in Washington.

"Well, I have had several talks with my father," he said, "and I think now, elderly as I am, I may become a law student at Yale." We both laughed. Edward's age had always been hard for me to guess; he was certainly a good deal older than Kate and I were, but was not, I felt, as old as Mother or Mr. Harris — though he did fall into the category of the older generation, if I thought about it at all.

"I may get a law degree," he went on, "and join my father in his practice. We get along very well together, and in due course he'll have to retire; then I'll have his practice to take over. He has an outstanding reputation, and I'm hoping that his clients will take me on as his son. They will be able to assume that we can always discuss their affairs with each other, and some may even be pleased that I've had some government experience. If I can't make it in law," he added with a laugh, "there's always government work, as you know."

He said that, after closing his affairs in Washington — mainly disposing of his apartment — he would return to New York, probably in the next couple of days. He wanted to assure me that Mother and I could always contact him there.

*   *   *

It seemed as though I had been asleep for a scant few minutes that night — though it was probably a couple of hours — when I felt Kate gently shaking my shoulder. I looked up at her and was instantly awake when I saw her expression.

"There's a call from the hospital," she said. "I think you'd better get there as soon as possible."

As I quickly got dressed, I guessed that this was the call I had been dreading as inevitable all along. Kate's father drove fast through the deserted streets, and every time I looked over at him for some look of reassurance, he seemed to be concentrating on his driving. Kate was equally silent in the back seat. It was the time of night that made us all fear the inevitable. By the time we arrived at the hospital, Mother met us in the lobby, and I could see immediately that it was all over. She had obviously tried to stay strong and restrain her grief, but she was in shambles. When she saw me, her emotions gave way to a flood of tears.

"You know," she whispered hoarsely in my ear, "it was as if that wretched Yalta conference really killed him. . . ."

I took her hand as we walked down the corridor to Father's hospital room, where he still looked as though he were sleeping peacefully. I lingered only long enough to lean down and kiss his forehead, knowing that it was no good for Mother to spend any more time in that room. When we got back to the nurses' station, Kate and her father were there waiting to express their sorrow. Mr. Harris took Mother's hand and offered to take over all the necessary formalities, which we dreaded but knew were bound to follow. Dr. Ben Johnson, the cardiologist appointed to our case by Mr. Harris, came down the hall in almost a run to tell us that Father had died before he or any other doctor could reach him. It had been sudden but not, of course, unexpected, and at least it was in his sleep.

Despite Kate's invitation that Mother join me and stay at their house, we looked forlornly at each other and decided to return to our own home. After speaking briefly with Dr. Johnson, Mr. Harris drove us straight home. As empty as we were with bereavement, the house seemed emptier still: the on-duty nurse had left, of course, when Father was readmitted to the hospital, and the house was dark and cold. Kate's father quickly turned on the heat and switched on the lights in the rooms he thought we were likely to use. We offered coffee and tea and whatever we had available to dull the pain of the moment, but they both declined, and we knew we couldn't keep them with us. There was no alternative but to face this moment alone — and as soon as possible.

When they left, and Mother and I were alone together, we knew that we wouldn't be going to sleep anytime soon. I couldn't help reminding Mother of the hereditary nature of Father's heart condition: the early death of his father was part of his story, and, indeed, he himself had collapsed in Moscow. Whether the revelation of what he had done at Yalta, which he had finally succeeded in telling us, had hastened his death — it was very difficult to tell. It might have even prolonged his life; there was simply no way of telling. But I knew that we were going to be plunged into the terrible "if onlys" that his death would evoke.

At length we went up to our bedrooms. No doubt there were sleeping pills somewhere in the house, left by previous physicians or even by the nurses who had been caring for Father. But neither of us wanted them: we didn't feel the need to be artificially induced into sleep. Whether we stayed awake or not would not alter what had happened or the immediate bleak outlook for our future. Eventually we both must have drifted off a little, because we were awakened by early phone calls from some of Father's colleagues who had heard of his passing and wished to convey their condolences. There was no way of avoiding these calls, or the messages that came by telegram and special delivery throughout the day. Nor did we want to avoid them; hearing and reading them was a distraction we almost welcomed to fill the void we felt that day. Mr. Harris took over the hospital and funeral arrangements, and Kate was a gem as she threw herself into helping us.

The funeral service, two days later, was attended by more people than could have known Father personally: many people were there whom we didn't recognize, including politicians whose names had been making headlines in the newspapers in recent weeks. Mother and I told the funeral director that we wanted a list of those who attended, partly out of sheer curiosity and partly to give to our lawyer in case anything should come up. The funeral director had, through his representatives in Chicago, published the death notice and details of the memorial service in that city because I had mentioned to him that Father had some distant relatives there. But no one appeared at the service that we could recognize as a relative, nor did anyone introduce himself to us as such. Father had been an only child, the son of an only child, and his stepmother's family had all perished in the Russian Revolution. Just as he had described his own father's funeral to us, no family members seemed to exist. It was as if they, like Stefansky, had disappeared from the face of the earth.

Emil Segalov came to the funeral service with a handful of others from the Russian embassy, and I greeted him with genuine warmth. Mother thanked him sincerely, not only for attending but for all that he had done in the past. A sprinkling of men we knew to be Secret Service agents, as well as members of the State Department, appeared in an official capacity. Two of them approached us after the service and asked whether they could provide alternative accommodations for us; they wanted us to be able to get away from Washington after everything that had happened. It crossed my mind that, with us out of the way, they would perhaps search our house for material they had failed to uncover while Father was alive. But I'll never know, because we thanked them and said no, we preferred to stay at home. We certainly would have welcomed the presence of Edward, but, through the worst of misfortunes, he had had to leave for New York earlier than he expected to help his father with a very important case, and he could not return to Washington in time for the funeral. It was clear that this was unavoidable, and he expressed his deepest regret more than once over the phone.

We had arranged for a caterer to provide a formal luncheon after the service, to which we had invited a few close friends, plus members of the State Department and colleagues who had worked with Father. After our guests had left, Mother and I were alone again and went into Father's study to start sorting out his papers and books. He was a meticulous man and had left everything in complete order when he had been assigned to Moscow; of course, little if anything had been disturbed after his return. He had never asked for any particular book or paper, and it was only the occasions when I had looked for a map of the Black Sea area or for the Chicago telephone directory that we had had any reason to go into the study. As far as we knew, he had not kept a diary; but just because we weren't aware of one did not mean that he had not kept any records or even weekly notes.

In our hearts, I guess, we were both searching for any papers or reminiscences he might have had relating to Maria; unfortunately, there were none. We came across press clippings of obituaries that had been published at the time of her death, and longer ones on the occasion of Grandpa Harry's death — mainly from local New York newspapers. There was an English-Russian dictionary, and we flicked through it quickly to see whether any particular pages had been dog-eared or whether it contained any documents; but, though it was reasonably well thumbed, there appeared to be no secrets inside. Father had learned good idiomatic Russian at his stepmother's knee, and he probably would have later used the dictionary, after he was assigned to the State Department, only for words and phrases of a specifically military or diplomatic nature — words he might not have learned as a child. When I saw the photograph of Maria that was on Father's desk, I reminded Mother that she had once suggested that he might like it down in the living room, where the photograph of his father was displayed. But he had shaken his head and said that it was probably more appropriate to be upstairs in his study, since Maria had been his tutor as well as his mother.

We knew that there were more papers, largely dealing with his professional life, sitting in a safety deposit box at his bank, as well as some other documents in his safe at the State Department. But as far as we could tell, there was nothing in his study that was of any great interest to us or would be to any investigator from a government or political source. Later that afternoon, hospital employees came to the house to pick up the medical equipment they had lent us during Father's stay at home. After they had gone and his bedroom had been cleared out, it almost felt as though he had never been there. As we looked into that room, it was a moment in which we knew with stark clarity that we both had to face the future without him — Mother without her husband and I without my father. During his last illness and his telling of the story that had been inside him for so long, he had seemed so close to me that it was as if I, too, had lost someone much closer than a father. I shared with Mother all her own emptiness and lack of direction.

My thoughts eventually turned to Radcliffe, which I had originally planned to attend. But I was determined not to do so before I had discussed Mother's immediate future with her. She did not wish to travel abroad, even though she'd been the wife of a diplomat. She had no immediate family: her parents were both dead, and her only brother had been killed fighting in Normandy shortly after the D-day landing.

"Oh, I'll have plenty to do around the house," she said when I asked her about her plans. "And I know enough people in Washington to keep me company. There'll be plenty to do — look at all this." She shrugged her shoulders and pointed generally around the whole house. If she was trying to convince herself of how well-occupied she would be, she was not doing a very good job. Finally she said: "Well, you're right, I don't want to end up rattling around this big house with nothing to do."

"I'll come home often," I said.

"Of course you will, dear. But the main point now is, you don't want to stay in Washington, do you?"

"No, not a minute longer than I have to," I replied. "I don't feel like I can breathe here a second longer."

"That's how I feel, too," she said. "We seem to agree on that."

"Why don't you go to New York?" I said. "It's busy, and there are diversions galore."

"It can also be a very lonely place to live."

"Yes, but you know Edward and his father — what about them?" I suggested.

She laughed. "I'm now a widow, and I can hardly impose myself on an elderly lawyer and his son. I gather that they're living together now — at least until Edward figures out where he's going to live."

"Well, it's a thought," I said, and we let the matter drop.

A few days later, we received a call from a soft-spoken member of the State Department, asking — almost begging — whether he could come and visit us to discuss Henry's death. I guessed that what preceded the death was really more important to him. It crossed our minds that we should have our lawyer present, but Mother decided that we were now calm enough to deal with him; if necessary, we could make a tape of the conversation for our lawyer to consult later. After all, we had nothing left that we had to hide — nothing except for Father's final confession that he was not only involved in but responsible for Stefansky's death, and then, of course, the latter's extraordinary remark that he had financed Roosevelt's presidential campaign with money from Stalin. We knew that we could keep the circumstances of Stefansky's death to ourselves, since the Department seemed to have satisfied itself long before that it was an accident, and that Father had merely been involved by chance.

It was an afternoon visit that did not oblige us to offer lunch, drinks, or any other tangible form of hospitality. Lindsey Smith proved to be an engaging and indeed rather pleasant man of indeterminate middle years. We offered him coffee, which he enthusiastically accepted, and he opened by apologizing for the visit in the first place. He said that Henry's death was, of course, a great loss to the Department and, from a diplomatic point of view, it had obviously been a great disaster when he disappeared in Moscow and was discovered later in such bad health. He was clearly aware of the great strain Father had been under, and we told him openly about his long narration of the problems he had faced earlier in his career, particularly during the war. We even described the pressures that had been brought to bear on him during the Yalta conference, as if to anticipate any questions Mr. Smith might have on that score — though we did not refer to the plotting and counter-plotting of Stefansky and his group. We could not tell whether he had any inkling of the accusations going back and forth between the politicians, or whether there had even been any plotting at all; but he did not question us on the subject.

Smith seemed much more interested in Father's stay in the Moscow apartment, and whether we knew anything about what he may have learned then or earlier that could have led to his disappearance. We assured him that that had been entirely a matter of his health and his collapse on the street; there was nothing about it that we were aware of that could have been affected by politics, even if it was during the Cold War. Smith appeared to accept that the disappearance in Moscow was by chance, as we did. (We had been assured by all the doctors that Father's heart condition and its first onset at the entrance to the apartment complex was not an atypical symptom of the disease.) Leaving his card, he expressed the hope that this would be the last imposition on our time by the State Department, and he spoke of its unfaltering support of my mother and me.

When he had gone, we felt perhaps 90 percent relieved; the remaining 10 percent of our suspicion that further intrusion might come was not focused on the State Department but on preparing ourselves to deal with those politicians who would, we felt, almost certainly be inquisitive about Father. In fact, it was only a few days later that we did receive a call from a Republican party official, who said he was interested in Father's career and would like to discuss it with us. He asked whether we would like to have dinner with him. We consented to see him, but we certainly were not going to be seen publicly dining with him. So we invited him to the house, once again at the awkward time of around 2:00 p.m., so that he could not expect either lunch or any other form of hospitality.

When he arrived, he oozed what we agreed could only be described as an oily kind of charm, which slid off us as we escorted him into the living room, where Mother had arranged for him to sit with the sun in his eyes. His suspicious questions, we came to see, were all about Yalta, Father's wartime career, his membership in the delegation, whom he had met there, who his working colleagues were, and what he knew about the great leaders who had convened the conference. It was easy for us to give him straightforward but noncommittal answers, but we could see that he was becoming increasingly irritated. At length he burst out, "Was your husband aware of any plot in Yalta against one or more of the great leaders? Were they plotting against each other? What about the British, who were trying to save their empire? And what about the Soviets, who were trying to extend theirs? What about us, fighting for freedom?"

Mother decided that, since this man had said he was interested in discussing Father's career with us, she too could show her annoyance at his antagonistic manner. She rose to her feet and pointed to the photograph of Father on the mantel.

"That," she said, "is my husband. He has just died, and I am, in the words of the press, 'the bereaved widow.' I have no idea of what you're trying to slur Henry with, and I don't intend to carry on this conversation unless it is done in a civilized manner and I am convinced that you are genuinely interested in him. The same is true of my daughter: she has just lost her father after giving up a year of college to help nurse him, and you come here with your — " she hesitated for a moment " — cheap, third-rate, speculative questioning . . ."

I could see that Mother's anger was about to boil over, and I interrupted her before she could go further.

"I agree with my mother," I said in a measured voice, though I soon felt myself rising to her level of indignation. "You haven't come here to console us or express your sympathy. You're just another . . . another cheap politician, and as such you are not worthy of our country, which my father served and died in the service of."

Both Mother and I remained standing, and he had no alternative but to rise from his chair. We both moved toward the door and I opened it; it was obvious that he could think of no way to delay his exit.

"I'm sorry," he said, "very sorry. I did indeed come here with sympathy for you both. I understand your feelings, but I think you misinterpret me and the nature of my questions."

"Whether we have or haven't," said Mother, "they were ill-expressed and ill-informed. I suggest that you go to the State Department and get the official information on the Yalta conference. You can then judge whether there is something missing, or whether we hold a secret that has been kept from you."

He paused for a moment as he was stepping out the door, and turned to face us, searching for words. He formally thanked us for our hospitality, and then he disappeared back into the Washington that we so much loathed at this moment.

"Well," said Mother, "I guess he's the first of them, but I have the feeling he will spread the word among those who might have been involved at Yalta — at least those in his own party."

There was nothing they could pry out of us; they would either have to adopt a different approach or give up altogether. In fact, I felt quite proud of the fierce front Mother and I had presented to him, and I doubted that we would hear from his party again. We knew that at some point we would probably have to deal with a Democrat, and we wondered aloud how he would behave.

We didn't have long to wait. Initially, his approach was the same: a phone call, an invitation to dinner, our declining it, a request to visit us at home, met again by our insistence on the awkward 2:00 timing. This time, however, a courteous young man appeared, and I thought that perhaps he had been selected for his ability to deal with awkward situations, a sort of public relations man. He certainly couldn't have been old enough to have been at the Yalta conference, but I assumed that he'd been primed by his party with the sort of questions that they hoped he could expand at his visit.

He went through the usual expressions of sympathy and commiseration that we anticipated; he even offered any help he or his party might be able to provide. Mother said that we would call on him, of course, if we had to, but at the moment we felt that we were managing quite well by ourselves. He, too, asked about Father's career, but he didn't immediately focus on Yalta. In fact, his series of questions covered Father's early years and Yalta in passing, his various diplomatic assignments, his disappearance in Moscow, and his sad return to Washington. The difference that really struck us between him and the Republican who visited us was that, whereas the latter had asked whether Father had met one or all of the Big Three at Yalta, this young man immediately focused on Stalin. Had Father met him? Had he formed any opinion of him, and had he been able to judge Stalin's standing in the Soviet Union? This was, we realized later, an initial defensive move: whereas the Republican had been eager to find out what we knew about the Roosevelt plot in order to discredit the Democrats, this Democrat was first of all eager to find out, self-defensively, what exactly had been the level of plotting by members of his party against Stalin. We assumed that he would then go on and try to pry out of us anything else the Democrats could use to attack the Republicans.

"No," Mother replied, "my husband saw him only once or twice. You must realize that Stalin was heavily guarded and moved with an escort wherever he went. Henry did not take part in the actual diplomatic meetings, though he did once take on the role of a back-up interpreter for the U.S. delegation during one of the meetings. So he did hear Stalin's voice, and his own knowledge of Russian meant that he could understand the nuances of what Stalin said.

"He told us," she went on, "that Stalin was a most level-headed, wide-ranging, and fully informed man — perhaps the most single-minded of the world leaders. He was bent on spreading his power wherever he could, whenever he could, and however he could. Roosevelt was still living in a totally impractical world of Wilsonian idealism: he was prepared to sacrifice almost everything for his dream of world peace, the triumph of anticolonialism and righteous self-determination, which would also carry with it the economic domination of the United States. Churchill, who had assumed power fighting for his country's existence — indeed for that of the free world — was, in his own way, doing exactly the same thing. You could say, I suppose, that they all had their specific aims and ambitions. But it was Stalin who clearly saw how to approach his object: he had Poland, he had the Balkans, and he had Roosevelt eating out of his hand. And there lay the tragic forecast of what could ultimately have been world disaster. That, I'm afraid, was my husband's view."

The young Democrat listened without comment, and I felt that he had real sympathy for both of us. On an impulse I stood up and said, "Would you like a drink?"

"I'd love one," he replied.

I brought out the whiskey and a glass and set them on the table so that he could pour his own portion. Mother shook her head when I looked over at her, and I got a bottle of soda for myself. I didn't want him to feel like he was drinking alone. I could sense that he was emboldened by this relaxation on our part and was wondering how far he could press his own points. When Mother was finished with her say, however, he addressed his points in measured tones.

"Was your husband aware of the plots going on at Yalta?" he asked. "Rumors have come down through the years. There were profound differences, of course, and the rumors suggested these might have extended" — he hesitated for a moment — "to active measures against one or the other of the leaders themselves."

It was not a trap, and even if it were, Mother would not have fallen into it. She answered, in equally measured tones, and it was a response that could lead him no further in his questioning.

"He was aware," she said, "that there were those at Yalta who would have liked to destabilize Stalin. Don't forget, there were many émigré Russians in our delegation because of their facility with the language. There may even have been some, I would say, among the British. Remember, these men would have almost certainly been refugees — or children of refugees — from the civil war that came after the Revolution of 1917. And I presume there was even the odd Russian on the Soviet side who was not entirely satisfied with the Soviet régime. Now, as a Democrat, you must realize that from the New Deal onward there were those who thought the leader of your party was the worst person since Pontius

Pilate. So I can only assume that, in the mixed group that made up the U.S. delegation, there were those who would have been opposed to Stalin . . . and some who would have been opposed to Roosevelt — for what they saw as his appeasement of Stalin. But I do not think they would have set out to destabilize him at Yalta."

Short of asking whether anyone had in fact set out to assassinate either Stalin or Roosevelt, there was little or nothing that our young Democrat could pursue from Mother's response. For the moment he remained silent, nodding his head; it was difficult to determine whether it was in agreement or merely to acknowledge that that was pretty much that. He decided not to press the point, but he did raise one that had been lurking behind it.

"Wasn't there a mystery man at Yalta?" he asked. "A Vladimir Stefansky, I believe. His name never appears in the reports." He paused and then, gripping his moral courage with both hands, said, "Weren't your husband and a friend in a Jeep with Stefansky when it skidded off the road and he fell to his death?"

"Oh yes," said Mother. "I think everyone knows about him, at least you and the Republicans, all those who were present, and those who have inherited the stories and reminiscences from those who were there." She paused for a moment, as if anticipating the next point he might raise. "Stefansky was someone Henry knew from when he was a child: he was a friend of Henry's stepmother — they were both Russian émigrés. But whereas Henry's stepmother, though herself violently opposed to the Communists, was not prepared to do more than campaign with other Americans against the régime of terror that followed Lenin's rise to power, my husband always understood that Stefansky was far more active in drumming up support and raising funds for active intervention insofar as was possible."

Our young Democrat was silent, and Mother went on: "My husband, Henry, had met Stefansky on a few occasions in his youth, but he was astonished to find him among those assigned to the U.S. delegation at Yalta. Now that brings up a question I have for you: What was he doing there? No one ever seems to have answered, or even asked, that question. Both sides in this case — I mean both U.S. political parties — agreed on the deletion of his name from the list of those attending."

I could see that Mother was debating with herself whether to bring up Stefansky's final charge: that he had supplied funds to Roosevelt directly or indirectly from Stalin himself. As she paused on that point, our visitor asked if he could pour himself another drink, to which she readily assented. He did not seem put out by the question she posed; in fact, he seemed about to give us an answer to something that had puzzled both of us.

"We — or rather my predecessors in the party," he said, "were really mystified, even horrified, by Stefansky's presence. Roosevelt had handed out various appointments and rewards to those who had contributed to election campaign coffers, and Stefansky's presence in the delegation seemed to be a very substantial reward."

We listened, entranced, as he spoke of the past and with such open contempt for those in the party he now represented.

"They couldn't understand what Stefansky — or Stevens, as he chose to call himself — was doing there. Roosevelt had always had his close confidants and supporters; but what was Stefansky doing there? He did not appear so surprisingly wealthy that his funds would have given him the right to a particular position anywhere. The papers are vague on that point, though they do indicate that he was a frequent visitor to the White House. We can only assume that he had somehow convinced Roosevelt that he knew how to handle Stalin, or at least that he could advise Roosevelt on how to do so. This was something for which my predecessors could not forgive him. Stefansky had established his sugar-trading business in the United States before the Revolution, but he seemed to have no credentials whatsoever that would have placed him at the core of the party and close to its leader, the President of the country. We will probably never know how he did it, but he must have had some hold on Roosevelt. That's why there were those in the White House who were happy to see his name removed from the record. The State Department, of course, never trusted him."

He finished off his drink and looked up. "I think you will find that nowhere is there a mention of his name. I guess we all hoped that somehow Henry, in a final statement, could clear this up for us. Even the Soviets must have felt the same, and I assume their renewed questions were all triggered by your husband's mysterious disappearance in Moscow. It was clear from their willingness to join us in searching for Henry and their cooperating with us in bringing him back here to Washington."

There was really no more to be said, and he turned toward me: "I have overstayed my welcome, and with your kind permission, now I think I should go." He rose to his feet, placed his glass carefully on the coffee table, and we rose with him. "I can only thank you," he said, "for allowing me to talk with you so frankly and freely. And I hope you will not be troubled again."

He smiled in an open and friendly way and was gone. Mother and I looked at each other and felt for perhaps the first time that the burden of hedging about Father and protecting his name was about to be lifted. They could quarrel among themselves, these politicians, and threaten each other with charges and counter-charges; but we believed that they couldn't probe into our lives any further. They had all the evidence there was, and we could not — nor could Father's memory — add anything more. I wouldn't say that peace descended on us like a dove, but at least we felt a good deal more relieved than we had for months.

The only loose end that never seemed to have been pursued was Stefansky's claim that he had provided funds for Roosevelt's election campaign directly or indirectly from Stalin. But he had made that outburst, we knew, on his final, fateful Jeep ride in the presence of only Father and Philip. All the participants in that encounter were now dead, and we assumed that it wouldn't cause any disturbance from the politicians in the future, totally unaware as they were of that claim.

The Republicans and Democrats never troubled us again, and the State Department visitors merely required formal information or came to see how we were getting along. We realized that the mystery of what Stefansky was doing at Yalta would probably never be solved as far as they were concerned. As for ourselves, we were determined not to share our secret knowledge with anyone.

*   *   *

Years later, when I visited Yalta and the mountainous countryside around the palaces where the conference took place, I realized what a stark contrast Father had mentally faced when his memories of that conference came flooding back to him on his white-sheeted bed in Washington. As I drove along the very mountain road where the dramatic events he described had unfolded, I realized the truth of the trivial phrase "it was another world." It did seem to be worlds away from the orderly urban life of Washington, notwithstanding the political furor taking place in the capital as a background to Father's story. The towering mountainside and the sudden drop to the Black Sea below threw into sharp relief the savagery that I knew had accompanied Soviet rule. It was as though the scenery itself had been painted to reflect the régime in place then. But I knew from my reading of history that there had long been savage fighting between the original Russian nation and the Caucasus kingdoms and tribesmen, before they were ultimately conquered in the wars of 1877-1878, a conflict in which Maria's first father-in-law, the general, had played a conspicuous part.

As I drove along the coast of the Black Sea, I was able to grasp the inner conflict Father must have gone through at Yalta: from his initial welcome, to the possibility of getting rid of Stalin and destabilizing his régime, to his subsequent revulsion at the thought of such a campaign now being launched against the President of his own country — and by his own people. By the time I toured Yalta, Livadia Palace had become a showplace of the Soviet government, particularly the conference hall where the plenary meetings had been held. There was a museum on the site that showed photographs of the delegates and of the meetings as they progressed. And, I learned, it was quite common knowledge among the locals that, on those icy roads connecting the delegation headquarters, more than one Jeep or other vehicle had gone over the side onto the rocks and into the sea below. Such incidents had occurred both before the conference and occasionally afterward, and from time to time bodies would float ashore further along the coast — well beyond Yalta.

*   *   *

During my first year at Radcliffe, Mother sold the house in Washington and moved to New York, where she soon found herself engaged in activities involving museums and historical research. She became very well acquainted with Edward's father, but more intimately with Edward himself. And after a couple of years, to my surprise and delight, they were married. Occasionally I would stay with them and we would discuss old times; but Edward seemed content to leave undisturbed all that my mother and I had related to him up to the final days of my father's life. He seemed unaware of my father's ultimate confession, which I'm sure Mother never shared with him. I think it was a wise decision we made to keep that secret to ourselves; it might have caused a slightly jarring note to their otherwise very harmonious marriage. The disparity in their ages was not all that great, and Edward somehow seemed to grow old with my mother. She died rather suddenly of a stroke, though at a reasonably advanced age, and Edward was left to linger on for a few more years. When he did die, he seemed to be a rather elderly man.

As for Kate, she had begun her studies at Wellesley, so we were not in college together. Occasionally, I would stay with her and her father, but I never divulged our secret to them. Whether it would have made for a certain uneasiness between us, I cannot say. Perhaps it would have suggested that we had withheld our complete confidence at a time when they were seeing us through our worst times. When I finally decided to write these memoirs, I knew that I would have to confess to Kate what my father had told us just before his death. When I did, she accepted it almost as if it were a piece of current news; she may have been surprised by it, but I'm sure she wasn't shocked. Her father had died by that time, and we could both live comfortably with the knowledge that only those who were very young at the time of the conference — perhaps some of the service personnel, possibly those in the lower ranks of the diplomatic delegations — are now in on the secret. But it is very much in the past.

Kate married a fellow student who was engaged in literary research. After they both completed their doctoral work — he in literature and she in political science — they were appointed to academic posts in the University of California at Berkeley. I frequently visited them and am proud to say that happiness reigned among them in the political hothouse where they worked. Kate eventually gave up her position for a time to devote herself to bringing up a family, and I am the godmother of her daughter Elizabeth (my mother's name). Kate always was — and still remains — my closest friend.

I remained single. On a couple of occasions I came close to marriage, and I have entertained more than one proposal; but somehow it was never something I could add to my curriculum vitae, as it were. After several trips to volatile locations in the world, I decided to try my hand at journalism — with the active encouragement of Kate and her husband. I have lived by my pen (that is, typewriter and now computer) in a variety of ways, and though I may appear to be one of the world's drones, I have always been fully occupied. In addition, modest inheritances from Father, Mother, and Edward will ensure that I will not be penniless.

For my mother and me, the Yalta narrative was vivid beyond belief.

But Father was reliving his life, up to that critical moment when he grasped the unavoidable conclusion to which his upbringing had led him and took the only step that was left to complete the impressionable childhood he had experienced. One could say that he was one of the millions whose lives were altered forever, swept up as they were by the Revolution and the coming of Bolshevism. The Cold War has now come and gone, and many will regard it as but a footnote to the historic relationship between the United States and Russia. But that cannot erase those terrible years from 1917 onward that very nearly presaged the end of Western civilization as we know it.